THE BALANCE OF GODS

JAY MICHAEL NIGHT

CONTENTS

1. Chapter 1   1

2. Chapter 2   8

3. Chapter 3   18

4. Chapter 4   21

5. Chapter 5   38

6. Chapter 6   42

7. Chapter 7   47

8. Chapter 8   57

9. Chapter 9   75

10. Chapter 10   84

11. Chapter 11   94

12. Chapter 12   100

13. Chapter 13   104

14. Chapter 14   115

15. Chapter 15   121

16. Chapter 16   125

17.	Chapter 17	135
18.	Chapter 18	149
19.	Chapter 19	153
20.	Chapter 20	159
21.	Chapter 21	165
22.	Chapter 22	175
23.	Chapter 23	178
24.	Chapter 24	181
25.	Chapter 25	184
26.	Chapter 26	197
27.	Chapter 27	203
28.	Chapter 28	207
29.	Chapter 29	211
30.	Chapter 30	222
31.	Chapter 31	229
32.	Chapter 32	236
33.	Chapter 33	259
34.	Chapter 34	265
35.	To Everyone	266

CHAPTER I

Mikey's jaw set as he imagined the Devouring unleashed upon the world—on his family, the people he loved sitting beside him, the innocent. Their only hope was for all of Otherside to band together and fight. Mikey pressed his lips in determination and looked up at his friends. They were exhausted and afraid, just as he was. But in their eyes, he saw the same resolve.

"We have to warn everyone," Mikey said.

They nodded, a contemplative silence overtaking the group after what they'd just survived. The misty air and roaring whoosh of water from the large falls beside them filled it. Mikey sat, his head resting against the ancient dwarven door, Marcus unconscious beside him. Laken was sitting on his shoulder. Sabrina, Viki, and Thomas sat across from him.

Within the walls behind them was a horde of creatures made of void and darkness, whose only desire was to consume Source, the energy of creation. Mikey and his friends had managed to seal them back within the lost dwarven city, barely escaping with their lives.

Inside the mountain was a shard of Avalon, the goddess of life. It was a crystal of pure Source, which powered the barrier currently separating the Devourers from the rest of the world. A shield, born from the shard itself, kept the energy from their clutches. But it was cracking. And Mikey knew that if the void creatures got ahold of it, that would be the end. Source made the void monsters bigger and more powerful. With a piece of a goddess, they'd be unstoppable.

The mountain rumbled, making the group collectively wince. Mikey looked down at the rune-carved relics covering his hands. The power he'd wielded had been amazing. With some practice, Mikey knew he'd be able to do more. Much more.

But it won't be enough, he thought, curling his left hand into a fist.

Mikey was grateful for the metal glove sealing the Edax—a name Mikey had given the same darkness within left part of his body that let him drain the nearby Source. Viki had told him the word was what the vampires called their hunger. It literally meant *devourer.* Unfortunately, his Edax had been the only thing capable of killing one.

Along with everything else, he sighed.

The memory of it taking control in an attempt to kill his friends made him shudder. Mikey's heart raced as he pondered their next move. He knew they couldn't sit around and wait for the Devouring to break through the barrier to Avalon's shard. He didn't think Earth had a chance as it was.

And if those creatures got a hold of that energy...no one will.

The ground rumbled again, and Mikey sat up. They needed to act fast. He looked at his friends, the only people he had left in this world, save for the few he'd made during his journey and those on the other side of the country in New York.

His eyes met Viki's, and the vampire pursed her lips. The expression on her face was how he felt, too.

"We're screwed," it said.

"Can we get away from this mountain?" Thomas asked. The Mover turned his head toward the volcano, leaning away like it was the plague, and its touch would spell his doom.

"Yeah. Let's get somewhere safe and figure out what to do next," Mikey agreed. "I can carry Marcus."

A sudden crunch of rocks near the cave entrance drew his attention. He glanced back at the others to see that only Viki had noticed from her stiffened posture. Though not to the level of the Verdaat, Mikey's senses were still heightened beyond human means, allowing him to hear through the roar of the falls. Laken was looking in the direction of the sound, too.

Several people that Mikey didn't recognize stepped into view. He counted six men and women of various ages dressed in Jaecar battle gear. The one in front had a gold stripe on his armor, marking him as an Elder. The rest were blue.

He was a large man with finger-length, dirty blonde hair that was slicked back with gel. The man froze when he saw them. Then his eyes narrowed, and he drew a sword covered in runes. Mikey had never seen him before, but something about the man's face made him want to punch it.

"It's the vampire mutt and the traitors!" the Elder called over his shoulder. "What did you do to the other Jaecar?!"

Sabrina stepped forward. "It's not what you think."

Deep red Source burst forth from the Elder's sword, covering the blade like a second skin.

Damn. That's pretty awesome. Though wider, it reminded Mikey of another energy sword from a particular galaxy, far, far away.

But he didn't have time to admire it, despite the appropriate red color given their situation.

"Do not move another step," the man said. The Source around his blade flared in warning. He tilted his head toward a Jaecar on his left. "Tell the others to prepare to transport five prisoners."

The Jaecar nodded, disappearing as they dashed back along the narrow cliff path along the falls.

"Everyone else," the man said, "be on your guard. If they move, then you are free to attack."

Mikey tapped into his vampiric powers and started bringing energy to his right hand. A white-blue spike of ice rose from his palm, hovering over it, ready to be shot.

"I'm getting sick and tired of being a prisoner," he said in an icy tone. "Don't make me hurt you."

The Elder's mouth fell open slightly. Then he tightened his grip on the sword.

Whispers broke out amongst the remaining Jaecar. Mikey caught the words "elemental" and "two vampires." He snorted. This was getting old. If they wouldn't listen to reason, he would make them. The fate of the world depended on it.

A dozen more Jaecar filled the space, and the sword-wielding Elder grinned wickedly, saying, "Take them. Alive if possible."

I guess we're not talking this out.

The man lunged forward surprisingly fast for his size.

Mikey launched his readied icicle, but the Elder's sword sliced it in half, both pieces falling to either side of him.

In the next moment, a wire appeared at the man's throat, his eyes widening in surprise. A drop of blood slid down his neck from where it dug in.

"You move, your head goes flying," Viki whispered. Her fangs were inches from the man's throat.

Damn, she's good.

"STOP!" a voice boomed near the waterfall.

Surprisingly, everyone froze.

A woman came into view, a dozen more Jaecar trailing behind her. She had an intimidating air, and a stripe of gold adorned her armor.

Mikey's brow raised. There was something familiar about her. She was beautiful. Tall and lithe, with ebony skin. Her long black hair was tied up in a braided bun.

Viki gave Mikey a questioning look, and he nodded. The wire disappeared, and she retreated to protectively stand in front of Marcus.

"That's enough, Elder Dalton." The woman put a hand on the sword-wielding Elder's arm.

Mikey saw a flash of purple near the woman's wrists and two golden bracelets engraved with Celtic symbols around them.

Dalton straightened, a vein bulging on the side of his head. He hesitated, clenching the pommel of his sword, but ultimately took a deep breath and said, "Forgive me, Sect Leader." The Source around his blade extinguished instantly.

"Who are you?" Mikey asked, trying to place her face and why it felt so familiar.

"You may call me Zuri," the woman said. "And you are Mikey Black." Her eyes, a rich hazel, darted to the fairy on his shoulder and then to Viki and the others.

"Hello, Sabrina. The last time I saw you, you were this high," Zuri said, bringing her hand to the middle of her stomach. She smiled.

The genuineness in it made Mikey relax a little.

Maybe they can be reasoned with after all?

"Hello, Elder." Sabrina walked to Mikey's side and held out a hand as if to signal that everything was all right. "How is Omari?"

"He's well," Zuri answered. "And hopes to take the Tribunal next year."

Sabrina turned to Mikey and motioned toward the woman. "Elder Zuri is the Sect Leader for SHOP. She was in my mother's Omada. I used to spar with her son when they had meetings back in the day. Elder Ryan is her younger brother."

Zuri smirked as the realization hit Mikey. "Ryan has said good things about you."

Hope brewed in Mikey's chest.

With her help, maybe we can bring everyone together.

He thought back to what Neema had told him about SHOP. He felt a twinge of pain thinking of the old healer. That time in his life seemed so long ago. Neema had said the Sect Headquarters of Portum—the old name for Haven—was located on the other side of the country.

"He's waking up!" Viki's voice came from behind, and Mikey saw Marcus stir.

He blurred, appearing at his friend's side in the next second. Laken had flown beside him, eliciting more murmurs from the Jaecar.

Marcus was shaking his head back and forth, repeatedly muttering incomprehensible words.

Mikey gently laid a hand on his forearm.

"NO!" Marcus shouted. His body jerked, and his eyes flew open.

"It's okay. It's okay," Mikey cooed as the Shielder crawled backward until he was against the dwarven door. His breathing was panicked and irregular.

After a few seconds, Marcus's vision seemed to clear, and he took in his surroundings.

"We got out?" he asked, looking at Mikey.

"Thanks to you." Mikey gave a halfhearted chuckle.

Thomas walked over to his brother and reached out a hand. "Can you stand?"

"I—I think so." Marcus took it, and Thomas hauled him up, holding out an arm to help keep him steady.

Mikey watched as Marcus swayed on his feet, clearly still disoriented. He turned his attention back to Elder Zuri, who regarded him with a mixture of curiosity and something else he couldn't quite place.

"We're wasting our time here!" Dalton spat. "We have orders from the high council. Look at the trail of death that led us here! My cousin—"

"I lead the Sect and am on the council," Zuri interrupted. "Elder Tem has no say here."

Oooh, Mikey began piecing the puzzle together. *That's why his face is so punchable.*

Dalton was Tem's cousin.

The man's jaw clenched, and his nostrils flared. "For now," he muttered. It was just loud enough for Mikey to hear him. But he was sure no one else save for Viki could have. He met her eyes, and she shrugged.

A tremor shook the ground beneath them, and everyone tensed until it passed.

The high councilor signaled to the others, and they began putting their weapons away.

"Now"—the woman looked at the massive door behind them, then motioned toward the path leading out of the cave—"let's go somewhere more private. It seems you have a story to tell."

CHAPTER 2

"Preposterous!" Dalton exclaimed after Mikey had given the Cliff's Notes version of events. "You're saying the recent volcanic activity is because of giant alien shadows that killed all of the dwarves? No one has been able to get into that mountain for hundreds of years. You expect us to believe such nonsense?"

They were outside, near the base of the falls. Mikey omitted certain details from his explanation: the prophecy, the key to getting into the mountain, Nevra, Laken, and Avalon—in the wrong hands, that information would do more harm than good.

"It's true," Sabrina said. "How else do you think we were able to acquire these relics?" The Mover pointed to her legs and Mikey's hands.

"Then give us the key." Dalton stepped forward, hand outstretched.

"What key?" Mikey jerked his head back, feigning ignorance.

Dalton rolled his eyes. "Our order has kept this area safe for centuries. There is a keyhole in the door. How else would you have gotten in? Now, hand it over." The man took a step toward Sabrina.

Mikey flared his Source claws, eyes flashing a mystical blue. "Not a chance. You'll kill us all." The earth shook as if in response.

Zuri put an arm out in front of Dalton, shooting him a warning look.

"What?" he said, shaking his head in disbelief. "Surely you don't believe them. They obviously found the key by some chance, took out our warriors, looted what treasure they could, and spun a tale using the earthquakes to keep us from acquiring it. Mostly likely to give it to the enemy. With that kind of power and wealth, the Verdaat won't stand a chance against us."

"I hate Magnus more than you, trust me," Mikey said with a snort. "But this is bigger than that. The Clara and Tenefae, Haven, and the rest of Otherside need to come together if we have any chance to stop the Devouring before they reach the shard of Source inside. Because once they do, I don't think anyone will be able to."

"Right, these creatures of pure darkness inside the mountain that there is no proof of. Which you have the key for but we can't open." Dalton gave an incredulous look and then turned to Elder Zuri. "He's lying, and the others are covering for him. We've been informed of his powers. He can drain the Source with his left hand. What other evidence do we need?"

The Sect Leader stayed silent, seeming to mull over what Mikey and Sabrina had told them. Her chin was in her palm, index finger tapping on her cheek. Mikey had to hope the woman would believe them. The idea that they had attacked and killed fellow Jaecar sent to investigate strange occurrences and disappearances around the mountain was absurd.

She looked at Laken, who had perched again on Mikey's shoulder.

"You," Zuri said to the tiny fairy. "I've never seen a fae like you before. Who are you?"

"She's just a friend—" Mikey started, ready to defend Laken's secrets.

But the tiny fairy tapped on his nose, shaking her head.

"What?" he asked.

She nodded, pointing to Zuri before patting his cheek.

"You want me to tell her the truth?"

Laken nodded.

Well, she is an angel and older than time...

"This is The Treasurer. You may have heard of her."

It took everything in Mikey not to smirk at the stunned expression on Dalton's face.

Zuri's eyes widened in recognition. "The Treasurer? I thought you were just a myth."

Laken gave a small curtsy.

"Apparently not," Mikey said, relieved that the fairy was willing to divulge her identity. Maybe Zuri would be more likely to believe them now.

The Sect Leader took a deep breath. "It appears we need to hold a Conventus."

"Yes...I believe that's a good idea," Dalton nodded, not taking his eyes off the fairy.

Mikey searched through his picture-perfect memory until he came upon the word Conventus. The passage was from one of the texts he had to study for the Tribunal called *Portum Politics and Procedures*.

It read:

Should a situation arise that has the potential to endanger the world, a Conventus shall be held.

That was it? Haven sure keeps everyone in the dark.

Clearly, it was some sort of meeting, which was exactly what they wanted.

"Mikey, would you please come with us? If what you all are saying is true. Then the Clarafae and high council need to know about it. Maybe we can stop this war before it goes too far."

Mikey nodded, grateful that at least one person would listen to them. He glanced over at Sabrina and the others, who nodded in agreement. It was a relief to have some support, even if it was just a small group of Jaecar.

"Viki, can you report what happened to the Verdaat? We need to convince the Tenefae as well. Though I'm sure after my talk with Helena, her people won't be a problem."

"I can try?" The vampire shrugged. "You know how my dad is."

"Unfortunately, I do." Mikey nodded. "But we need to get both sides on this. You saw what we're up against."

Viki pursed her lips and gave a solemn nod. "All right. I'll see you soon." She stepped forward, her beautiful yellow eyes locked with Mikey's, an unsure expression on her flawless face.

Viki reached out, and he took her hand.

"Be careful," she said, glancing toward Sabrina and then letting go.

"You too," Mikey said. There was a pit in his stomach at the thought of her leaving. Its presence was as horrible as it was confusing.

"Wait," Sabrina called out, and the vampire turned.

"Yeah?" Viki asked.

"Here." Sabrina reached into her pack and pulled out the dwarven king's letter. "Use this to help convince Magnus. Maybe he'll be able to translate it, too."

"Thanks." Viki took it, appearing slightly stunned by the gesture.

They stood there awkwardly until Viki inclined her head and left.

"You're just gonna let a vampire go?" Dalton scoffed. "That's probably a letter telling the vampires about all the treasure they've found."

The Sect leader gave the elder a deadpan stare before her mouth fell open, and she turned to Mikey.

"You've spoken with Helena?"

"Yes. She doesn't want this war either; she and Izildora know about the Devouring," Mikey said. Something in his gut said that Zuri was someone he could trust. Elder Ryan had a certain code of honor. It was clear to Mikey that his older sister did as well.

Zuri nodded, a determined glint in her eye. "Then we must act quickly. We'll make arrangements for the Conventus as soon as possible. In the meantime, you and your companions can stay with us. We can portal to our Sect."

Mikey felt a weight lift off his shoulders. It was a relief to have a safe place to stay in a world that was becoming increasingly dangerous. "Thank you, Elder Zuri. We appreciate it."

As they began their trek to the portal zone, Mikey couldn't help but feel a sense of unease. He knew they were still in danger despite the Sect Leader's assurance. The Devouring was getting stronger, and with each passing day, they were getting closer to the shard of Source inside the mountain. He couldn't shake off the feeling that they were running out of time.

Dalton's suspicious gaze lingered on Mikey, and he knew that the elder still didn't trust him. But Mikey had bigger things to worry about than Dalton's mistrust. He looked over at Sabrina, who gave him a small smile, her emerald-green eyes filled with determination. They were in this together, no matter what.

A few minutes later, they reached a clearing. Zuri pressed a button on her porter watch, and a shimmering, swirling vortex appeared before her.

"After you," the woman offered, stepping to the side.

Mikey took a deep breath and entered the Sect's headquarters.

When they arrived, Mikey couldn't help but be taken aback. He had heard a few stories about the SHOP, but he was still in awe of its grandeur. The portal room was much larger and more luxurious than the one in Buffalo, with triple the number of platforms. It was made of white marble, with tall golden pillars that seemed to reach for the sky. Mikey and his group followed the Jaecar down brightly lit hallways lined with intricate paintings and sculptures crisscrossed through the center of the building. Mikey also noticed a few tech upgrades: video screens embedded in walls, along with various other forms of technology he hadn't seen before.

"Welcome to SHOP," Zuri smiled.

She led them through a giant training center with what looked like digital 3D training simulators.

Sabrina leaned in to whisper, "Mom has been trying to get them to approve funds to upgrade our Sect. But Elder Tem, who runs the budget, has been thwarting her at every turn with other more pressing expenses."

It was just another reason for Mikey to despise the man.

As they continued down the hall, he couldn't help but notice the strange looks they were getting from the Jaecar passing by. They all seemed to be staring at Laken, and Mikey wondered if they had ever seen a fairy before. Other than a Brownie, he hadn't during his time training to become a Jaecar.

Finally, they arrived at a large door guarded by two burly men. Zuri nodded at them, and they stepped aside, allowing the group to enter.

Inside was a room with several doors. It looked like the living area Mikey and his Omada had been given at the Buffalo Sect, only bigger.

Zuri opened one of the doors to show a bedroom with a queen-sized bed, desk, and dresser.

"These five are bedrooms," Zuri pointed. "The two in the middle are bathrooms, and the one on the right is a training area."

"So we're prisoners," Thomas said. The Sante brothers had been silent most of their discussion, which was especially unusual for

Marcus. But when Mikey glanced back at his friend, the utter exhaustion on his face was evident. The Shielder had saved their lives numerous times in the mountain, using much of his Source.

Marcus met his eyes, and Mikey gave a small nod, smiling.

"You are free to go about the building," Zuri said, her voice kind but firm. "But you will have to be accompanied by a guard at all times. You cannot leave until the Conventus has convened."

Mikey's heart sank slightly at the reminder that he and his friends were prisoners of sorts. However, Zuri seemed to sense his distress and added kindly, "I'm sure you understand why this is necessary for everyone's safety. It will take a few days for everyone to gather. I promise we will make your stay here as comfortable as possible."

Mikey nodded in understanding, appreciating her efforts to make them feel welcome despite their situation. He glanced around at his Omada before turning back to Zuri with a smile and a nod of gratitude. It was a better alternative than bloodshed.

But time was of the essence. Every second they wasted was another opportunity for the Devouring to get to the shard.

Mikey knew they needed to act fast. As much as he appreciated the Sect's hospitality, he couldn't afford to waste time. He turned to Zuri, "Is there any way we can contact Elder Cassandra or my foster father, Arthur Cafferty?"

"Please. I want to let our parents know we're safe," Marcus seconded.

Zuri nodded. "I will arrange for a communication device to be brought to you that works within the Sect. You may contact them, but please remember that we cannot risk word of your presence here getting out to the wrong people."

They all nodded in agreement, understanding the importance of secrecy in their situation.

"Great. If you need anything, ask the guards outside," she said. "For now, get some rest. From your story, it sounds like you all need it."

The four of them each picked a room, agreeing to talk once they rested. Laken had transformed into a Brownie and disappeared to do who knows what. She was an angel with the secrets of the Universe. He couldn't even comprehend her mind.

Shortly after, he'd realized Laken had taken the key to the Dwarven Kingdom. There was an initial panic, but she had been the one to give it to him in the first place.

It's probably better off with her anyway.

Mikey sat on the edge of his bed, feeling the exhaustion of the past few days finally catching up. He couldn't shake the feeling that they were running out of time, that the Devouring was getting closer to the shard with each passing moment. It was doing a number of his anxiety. But for now, they were safe, which was something to be grateful for.

As he closed his eyes, he couldn't help but think of Viki. He wondered if she was safe and on her way back to New York. The thought of her leaving had left a strange ache in his chest, a feeling he couldn't quite place. Sabrina came to mind, and Mikey felt equally lost on that front. Something had changed between them.

Mikey sighed and rolled onto his back, trying to make sense of his feelings. As much as he wanted to talk to her about it, he wasn't sure how she would react. Mikey wondered if she still felt the same way about him or if he really had become so different that her feelings had, too.

Uncertainty clouded his mind as he drifted off to sleep. He dreamt of Viki, Sabrina, and the Devouring, all swirling around in a chaotic mess. But then, amid the chaos, a dark, inhuman voice whispered to him.

"Let me out...LET ME OUT!"

Mikey woke up with a start, his heart pounding in his chest. His eyes darted to his left hand, and he sighed in relief. The Edax was still trapped. Fearing it would try to come out when he least expected it, Mikey always wore the relic gloves.

He shook his head, trying to clear his mind. The situation with the Devouring was already complicated enough without adding his own darkness to the equation.

Mikey got up from his bed with a sigh, his exhaustion weighing heavily on him as he made his way to the door. When he opened it, a guard outside greeted him with a nod. "Elder Zuri arranged for a communication device to be brought to you. Here."

The man put a small black cell phone into Mikey's palm.

"Thank you," Mikey said, taking the device and closing the door behind him.

He immediately started dialing numbers, growing more excited after each digit at the prospect of talking with Arthur. He'd missed his foster father deeply.

"Hello?" the man answered.

"Hey," Mikey said. Relief and a slew of other emotions flooded him.

"Mikey?! Is that you? Oh, thank God."

He heard the old man audibly sigh.

"What happened?" Arthur asked.

"Boy, do I have a lot to tell you. Speaking of God..."

CHAPTER 3

VIKI

"Dammit, that hurts," Viki muttered under her breath as she dashed between the trees, trying to hide from the sun's rays as best she could. It was just her luck that today was cloudless, and the burning ball had free reign to shine.

I need to find a phone.

She had the number for Mogrin's desk.

The goblin was a loyal friend to Viki since she was little. She hoped their escape from the estate hadn't gotten him in trouble.

Finally, after hours, she found a gas station and someone nice enough to lend her their phone. She sighed in relief when Mogrin answered.

"We need help," she said gravely. "The key led to a mountain filled with Devourers. Somehow, we managed to seal them in, barely escaping with our lives. But a shard of Source is inside it, of a goddess called Avalon. Right now, it's blocked by a shield. But if the Devourers get it..."

"Then all is lost," Mogrin muttered before going quiet for a few moments. Then he said, "It's good you called me. Is Mikey all right?"

"Yes. He and the others are at the Sect headquarters in Washington, where something called a Conventus will be held to discuss what we uncovered."

"I see," Mogrin said. "Do you have any evidence in case your father needs more—convincing? He has been in quite a rage after discovering your...departures."

"Yes. I have a letter written by the Dwarf King himself about what happened. But I can only make out a few words. It's in Dwarvish."

"Good. Magnus no doubt knows their language."

Viki let out a sigh of relief. "Thank you, Mogrin. I don't know what we would do without you."

"Anything for you, my dear," he replied warmly. "Give me just a minute, and I'll give you the details for a flight."

Viki nodded, feeling grateful for the goblin's unwavering support. She waited patiently as he gave her the flight details and promised to meet her at the airport.

As she handed back the phone with a "thanks," Viki couldn't help but feel a sense of dread wash over her. The Devourers were unlike any creature she'd ever encountered. Unfortunately, she hadn't been conscious when Mikey fought it. Even now, it was hard for her to imagine anything defeating one.

Killing one changed Wonderboy even more.

Viki had been helpless against it, which was an entirely new feeling. Granted, she wasn't as strong as the ancients like Brittania or her father. Still, there weren't many beings in Otherside that she couldn't handle.

Mikey was scared. Despite him trying to hide it, she could tell. He was scared about becoming a Devourer. But Viki knew in her heart that Mikey would pull through from whatever he faced.

And we're meant to be together.

But their relationship issues were another problem altogether.

Viki took a deep breath and pushed her worries aside. She needed to focus on the task at hand and trust Mikey and the others were doing the same.

Viki made her way to the airport, her heart pounding with fear at the monumental task. Convince the leader of the Verdaat to join forces with his enemies. All to fight monsters no one else has seen but her and a few humans.

As she boarded the plane, Viki couldn't help but think about the consequences of failure. The Devouring would consume everything, and the world as they knew it would be gone forever. It was up to her, Mikey, and the others to stop it, no matter the cost.

No pressure.

CHAPTER 4

MIKEY

"A Conventus?" Arthur repeated after Mikey had gotten the retired Shielder up to speed on his journey. "It's been over a hundred years since one has been called. The last time was when the Accords were signed with Magnus and the Tenefae. But after everything you told me, that makes sense."

"You know about the Tenefae?" Mikey asked.

"Yes. Only those on the high council, the Sect Leaders, and a few Elders know about them. Haven and the fae take their knowledge seriously. But it sounds like you're smack dab in the middle of it," Arthur said.

Mikey nodded, his mind racing with the implications of what he'd just heard. "Yeah, it seems that way. So what is a Conventus exactly?"

"It is a meeting of all the Sect Leaders from around the world as well as the highest members of the Clarafae court."

"And what exactly happens at this meeting?" Mikey asked, his curiosity piqued.

"Well, it's for all the leaders to come together and discuss important matters that affect Otherside as a whole. It's kind of like a UN meeting, but for the supernatural community," Arthur explained. Mikey nodded, taking it all in. "So they will discuss what to do about the Devouring."

Mikey's heart sank at the mention of the creatures. He couldn't shake the feeling of dread that had been following him since the Edax had taken over.

"More like whether your story is true in the first place. That letter you found in the mountain could have come in handy," Arthur tsked.

Mikey thought back to the scene. Sabrina's actions had surprised him. She'd given a historical artifact to someone he knew she disliked.

But why?

The only explanation he could think of was that Sabrina thought the Verdaat would need more convincing than Haven and the Clarafae.

Mikey hoped that was true.

"Our plan is a long shot," he said. "Viki needs to convince the Verdaat to join forces with us against the Devouring. And we need to convince the Jaecar and fae of the same."

Arthur let out a low whistle. "Well, that's quite the task. But I have faith in you, Mikey. You've always been resourceful. Just be careful, okay? This Devouring business sounds dangerous. And when you all are ready to fight them. I'll be there."

Mikey smiled, grateful for the vote of confidence and glad to have the man there for him.

"Thanks, Arthur."

"No problem. I'll also make a few phone calls to some on the high council who I still consider friends. It might help."

"Appreciate it. Talk soon."

Mikey hung up the phone and let out a weighted breath. He knew that the journey ahead of them was going to be treacherous, but he was determined to see it through to the end. There was no other choice.

Sabrina was sitting alone at one of the tables in the common area, staring off into space. He hesitated for a moment before walking over to her.

"Hey," he said softly. "Mind if I sit?"

She looked up at him, surprised. "Mikey. Uh, sure. Go ahead."

Mikey sat across from her and asked, "Talk to Elder Cassandra?"

"Yeah," she said with a nod. "Filled her in on what happened. She'll be here for the Conventus..."

Mikey paused, waiting to hear more, but nothing ever came.

"Gotcha," Mikey said, unsure if the odd tension was because of him or Sabrina's conversation with her mother.

Until she said, "You know, it was the strangest thing...I thought my mom wouldn't believe me. But she did. Immediately." Sabrina snorted. "Even weirder, I could've sworn it sounded like she'd missed me."

Mikey closed the distance between them, intending to comfort Sabrina, but he regretted the act immediately when she flinched back.

"Sorry," he said, scratching the side of his head. "Habit."

She stared at him with a frustratingly difficult, unreadable expression.

"What's happened between us?" he asked, unable to hold the question in any longer.

Sabrina's eyes flickered with a hint of sadness before she looked away. Mikey could tell the question had hit a nerve, but he needed to know.

"I've been thinking," she said, her voice barely above a whisper. "It's been...complicated since we've been apart, and I've been exposed to—*things*."

The way she said the last word gave him a twinge.

"Thomas...things?"

"No, not at all—" Sabrina blurted defensively then tilted her head, "Okay, maybe a little, but much later."

"What are you saying?" Mikey asked, shaking his head.

"I'm saying you're an immortal," Sabrina sighed. "And..."

"And what?"

Sabrina pursed her lips, then threw her hands up in frustration.

"You're talking with fairy queens and sparring with the leader of the Verdaat. There's an ancient prophecy about you. I've been in a mountain that no one has been in for thousands of years!"

"So?" Mikey asked, his face crinkling. "What does that have to do with us?"

"Everything." Sabrina shook her head. "I'm just a human. You're like...something out of a fairy tale. Which is saying a lot, given our jobs. It feels as if we live in entirely different worlds. I'm going to get old, and you...you're going to look like that forever. Your parents were the only instance of Verdaat and humans together that I've ever heard of. And look how that turned out."

Mikey winced, a knot forming in his throat. It began to grow, becoming so large that he feared choking on the sadness.

"Look, that came out wrong." Sabrina reached for Mikey, but he stood up.

"I thought you knew all of that before we got together?" There was a part of him that understood where she was coming from, but Mikey shoved it aside. The reality of what Sabrina was saying meant only one thing. And he refused that thought.

"I did. But then you were kidnapped, and you spent all that time with Viki and—"

"Viki?" Mikey interrupted. "She's got nothing to do with this."

"Doesn't she?" Sabrina snapped.

Mikey's eyes narrowed. "What's that supposed to mean?"

Sabrina folded her arms. "I'm just saying, she's a Verdaat, too. And she's clearly important to you."

"Viki is my—our friend," Mikey said, his voice firm.

"She loves you," Sabrina replied.

Mikey froze, feeling like the wind had been knocked out of him. He hadn't thought of Viki in that way. But deep down, again, he knew that wasn't entirely true.

Stubbornly, he said, "I don't know what you're talking about."

"Mikey," Sabrina said softly, her eyes searching his. "I'm not blind. I can see the way she looks at you. And I know that you care about her, too. She literally said she'll wait until I'm old and dead to have you."

Mikey didn't know what to say to that. But he loved Sabrina, truly.

"And Thomas?" he asked.

"That's...also complicated. It would be a lie if I said I didn't have feelings for him still."

Mikey's heart sank even further. This conversation was not going at all the way he had hoped it would. She spoke as if they couldn't work things out, but he had to try.

"But what about us, Sabrina?" Mikey asked. "We've been through so much together. Something like this...it's nothing, right?"

Sabrina shook her head, tears glistening in her eyes. "Mikey, I don't know. I just need some time to think. To figure things out."

He nodded, feeling defeated. Mikey knew he couldn't force Sabrina to feel the same way. But he couldn't just give up on them, either. Not after everything they had been through.

"I understand," he said quietly. "But I hope that you'll come back to me. When you're ready."

Sabrina looked up at him, her eyes filled with a mix of sadness and regret. "I hope so, too."

Mikey felt nauseous, like his body physically felt his world turn upside down. Now, he didn't know what the future held for him and Sabrina. But he'd always be there for her as a friend and member of their Omada.

"So what do we do now?"

"I don't know," Sabrina admitted, her voice as soft as his. "I wish I had a clear answer, but I don't."

Mikey nodded, feeling the weight of the words like a corporeal burden.

Sabrina looked up at him, her eyes full of tears. "I really do love you."

His heart ached at the sight of her tears and struggled to fight back his own from falling. Mikey knew that Sabrina loved him, but he also knew love wasn't always enough to make a relationship work. Still, he wouldn't give up.

"I love you too," he said, his voice almost breaking. "I always will."

She stood up, wiping her face, and gave him a small smile.

There was an uncomfortable silence until Sabrina clapped her hands together, taking a deep breath. "Unfortunately, we have bigger fish to fry. None of this will matter if the Devouring gets that shard," she said.

Mikey nodded in agreement, grateful for the change of subject.

"Marcus still needs to rest, and Thomas is already up trying to unlock his relic. I was hoping to get some breakfast and then try and do the same. Care to join me?" Sabrina asked.

Mikey hesitated for a moment, unsure if he was ready to face the reality of their relationship being in limbo. But they had bigger issues. World-ending ones.

Guards escorted them to the cafeteria, one behind and in front. The two teens silently walked, preoccupied with the weight of their conversation. Mikey grabbed a package of Pop-Tarts. He hadn't felt that hungry after their talk. Sabrina grabbed a muffin, and they sat down to eat.

She asked, "Do you know anything about the Conventus?"

"Yeah." Mikey nodded, then shared his conversation with Arthur.

"Wow. The elven queen..." Sabrina trailed off, then said, "They have to believe us, right? We're still technically Jaecar. And with Laken here—" She paused, looking around as if the tiny angel was hiding somewhere. "Where is she, by the way?"

"Who knows? Turned into a Brownie and disappeared." Mikey shrugged, taking a bite of the delicious pastry. He wished it tasted like ash, then it would fit with how he felt inside.

If Sabrina noticed his change in demeanor, she didn't show it. "Well, hopefully, she'll be back before tomorrow."

Mikey nodded in agreement. He finished his Pop-Tarts in silence while thoughts of their relationship and the impending danger of the Devouring raced in his mind.

After breakfast, they headed back.

As they entered the room, Thomas looked up from his work. "Hey," he said, wiping sweat from his forehead. The Mover looked exhausted.

"How's it going?" Sabrina asked, motioning to the weapons.

"Slowly," Thomas admitted. "I've tried every trick I can think of and still can't make any headway."

Sabrina hummed thoughtfully, eyeing Mikey. "If only there were someone who recently unlocked one nearby."

Thomas snorted, rolling his eyes, then asked, "Have any ideas, Mikey?"

Did he just nicely ask me a question?

Mikey blinked in stunned silence.

"Uh..." he stammered. "What is it like when you try to push your Source into it?"

"It disappears," he answered.

Mikey tilted his head. "What do you mean 'disappears'?"

Thomas clicked as if annoyed.

There's the Thomas I know.

Then he said, "I mean, when I push my Source through, it disappears into the relic."

"Like it's absorbing it?" Sabrina asked.

"Yeah." Thomas nodded. "Though hearing it out loud makes me think of the thing inside Mikey and it gives me the creeps."

Mikey flinched at the mention of the Edax, but he tried not to let it show.

"How much have you given to it?" he asked, trying to change the subject.

"Quite a bit. I've been slowly giving some since I put them on."

"Interesting." Sabrina brought a hand to her chin. "Have you tried giving it a lot?"

"Yep. Before you got here, I poured in half my Source."

"And it just took it?" Mikey asked, amazed at the relic's behavior.

"Yeah." Thomas nodded. "Weird, right?"

"Fascinating," Sabrina said, gazing at the rune-carved metal covering his fingers below the knuckle. Each ended in a blade, appearing as if the wielder was clenching a dagger if they made a fist.

Mikey tried to think of his relic and what it had been like to unlock it. His was a test of finite control. The gloves needed the exact amount of Source put into it at different intervals. Miraculously, he unlocked it while carrying Thomas as they ran from the dark horde of Devourers. The process had felt like brush strokes or drawing with his Source.

And Marcus said unlocking his was like going through a maze in a game.

While lost in thought, Mikey heard Sabrina snap her fingers in front of his face. "Earth to Mikey, you still with us?"

He blinked rapidly and shook his head. "Sorry, I was just thinking about my relic. It unlocked differently than Thomas's, and Marcus's wasn't the same either."

Sabrina leaned in, intrigued. "So what are you thinking?"

Mikey took a deep breath and tried to articulate his thoughts. "Well, Thomas is kind of a bulldozer. No offense." He turned to the Mover, who shrugged. "And from my experience and what Marcus told me about his, each relic's test is geared toward the user. So what if you have to overload it with Source?"

Thomas raised an eyebrow. "What do you mean overload it?"

"I mean," Mikey said, "maybe the relic is absorbing the Source, but it's not enough. What if you have to give it more than it can handle?"

Mikey didn't tell them the idea came from the time he met Avalon, the goddess of creation, and she had overwhelmed the dark thing inside him with her Source.

Sabrina nodded thoughtfully. "Or maybe it has to reach a certain threshold."

"It's worth a try." Thomas shrugged. The Mover took a deep breath, and Mikey felt Source gather near his relic.

"Just don't overdo it," Sabrina added, an edge of concern in her voice.

Mikey did his best to ignore the pang of jealousy her comment brought. But her worry was valid. Thomas said he'd already given half his Source today. That meant he could only give about thirty-five percent more. If you counted the Source inside of someone as one hundred percent, they needed ten of it to run their bodily functions and stay alive. Once a Jaecar got below ten, their organs began to shut down. It was the reason most never went below fifteen percent.

How fast people could regenerate the energy varied. Each person was born with a finite amount of Source that would increase slightly as they age. That limitation was why Mikey was so unique. He didn't have it. His left hand could drain the Source around him, and his right could harness that energy like a Jaecar.

A child of balance... Mikey snorted at the absurdity of it all. At the prophecy made by a giant swamp hag thousands of years ago, which said he would save the world.

And with these—Mikey looked down at his palms—*the Devouring will fall.*

Only if he could resist the dark thing inside him that wanted to drain all Source everywhere, bringing the end of the world but offering never-ending pleasure.

Thankfully, it was locked away behind the glove.

"For now," a raspy, sinister voice whispered so faintly that Mikey wasn't sure it was real.

He shook his head, focusing on the present to drown out the spiral of negative thoughts.

Thomas closed his eyes, and Mikey activated his vampiric vision. He could see the tiny red sparks of Source dancing around the fist weapon. They grew brighter and brighter until the light was almost blinding. A vein bulged on the corner of the Mover's forehead. His fists and jaw clenched, the strain visible.

Mikey watched with bated breath, hoping that Thomas would succeed. A sharp, cracking sound suddenly filled the air, and the sparks around Thomas's hand dissipated. His eyes flew open, and he looked at his hand in disbelief.

"It worked," Thomas whispered in awe.

Sabrina let out a whoop of joy.

The brass knuckles glowed like a deep and fiery red sun. Particles of Source swirled around it like solar flares.

Mikey couldn't help but marvel at the power emanating from the relic. He could feel it, even from where he stood a few feet away. It was like a living thing pulsating with energy.

"Let's see what this baby can do," Thomas said with a wide grin, turning toward the concrete wall at the back.

He thrust his clenched right hand outward, and a ball of Source the size of a grapefruit burst from the relic, hurtling toward the opposing cement wall. A deep and deafening boom vibrated within the room as dust and rubble erupted in a cloud.

Mikey couldn't help but feel a sense of awe at Thomas's display of power. The destructive force of the blast had been impressive.

"That was incredible," Sabrina said, her mouth hanging open slightly.

He could feel the knuckles still humming with power. Mikey sensed that the weapon had at least a dozen more punches stored within it.

The dust cleared enough for them to see the gaping hole in the wall where Thomas had struck it. The edges of the human-sized depression were jagged and rough, and Mikey could see cracks spreading from the impact point. He wondered how much damage the relic could cause if pushed to its limits.

Thomas turned to them, a satisfied smirk on his face. "There is plenty more where that came from."

Sabrina huffed, letting out a frustrated sigh.

"What's wrong?" Mikey asked.

She glanced down at the bracers strapped to her leg, her face determined. "I'm falling behind everyone else."

Mikey knew she was feeling the pressure to unlock her relic. They were all feeling it. Even with Thomas's newfound power, it seemed trivial compared to the Devouring. The creatures fed on Source and grew larger and more powerful from their attacks.

Even if they managed to bring all of Otherside together, Mikey didn't know how to stop them. The fae queens had faced them before. Nevra's mother, a Gwyllion and Daughter of Avalon named Beruva, had died fighting them. She had uttered the prophecy about Mikey defeating the Devouring before her death.

But how?

He didn't know. But they needed all the power they could get. And everyone in his Omada unlocking their relic was a good start. Then he remembered Luke and the phone call he had planned to make after breakfast.

I'll have to call him later tonight.

All the talk of relics made Mikey want to see what his could really do. Other than using it to make a giant barrier of ice and heatsink orb when fighting the Edax, he hadn't gotten to practice with his.

Mikey asked Sabrina, "What's it like when you try to unlock it?"

"I already know how to," Sabrina sighed. "It's just tricky."

Mikey frowned. "Tricky how?"

Sabrina bit her lip. "It's hard to explain. When I push my Source into it...a pulse appears. And somehow, I know I'm supposed to follow it through the relic. But the pulse moves so fast, twisting and turning, I lose it every time."

Mikey nodded, understanding her frustration. "So it's a test of agility and speed."

"Yeah. Your theory about the relic tests being geared toward the user seems right," Sabrina said. "I'll get there. I just need to keep at it."

"Of course you will," Thomas said with an encouraging smile. "You've wanted those bracers ever since we were little."

Mikey watched as Sabrina's expression brightened at Thomas's words. He couldn't help but feel a pang of hurt.

He knew he shouldn't be jealous of Thomas, but it was hard not to be. Thomas had grown up with Sabrina, had been her best friend—and more.

And now, with Thomas becoming more of his old self, they had a bond Mikey couldn't compete with.

He shook his head, trying to push the thoughts away.

Mikey took a deep breath and looked at his relic, the metal chain gloves carved with runes. It hummed with power, waiting for him to use it.

He sensed only the surface of its capabilities had been scratched.

"The Conventus probably won't be for a few days, so I'm going to focus on unlocking this thing," Sabrina said determinedly.

"Yeah, I'm going to see what my babies are capable of," Thomas said, clinking the brass knuckles together. Red sparks of Source burst from the relic when they touched.

"All right. It's not like I've got something better to do." Mikey shrugged. He was excited to practice with the gloves but equally sad about his situation with Sabrina.

Hoping that training with the specially made item would be a welcome distraction, Mikey headed to the right corner and sat down.

He closed his eyes, took a deep breath, and focused on his Source. He could feel it coursing through the right side of his body, waiting to be harnessed. Mikey pushed the energy into the metal. The runes etched into its surface began to glow.

Before the relic, when he gathered Source into his core, it felt like riding a bicycle with rusty pedals and wheels. Doing it was challenging, but with his Verdaat-enhanced body, it was easier than for most humans. Now, he was cruising on a brand-new motorcycle. Everything was faster, stronger, more powerful. His Source was more pliant as well. More willing to bend to Mikey's will.

He experimented with the gloves, prodding and manipulating the Source until he realized how much of a difference the relic had made. He could feel the power resonate throughout his body, a surge racing through him, hinting at a potential he hadn't even begun to unlock.

Mikey created ice from thin air by absorbing the heat from his surroundings in a blink.

Incredible...

Time seemed to slip away as he continued experimenting, manipulating his Source through the item.

He focused on the individual aspects of what it took to create a heatsink orb.

Where did the heat go when he absorbed it? Why was wind produced when the heat was pushed outward?

After some trial and error, he answered these questions while practicing. Mikey figured out how to command the cosmic energy to focus on the air instead of heat.

So, if I do this—

A gust of wind whirled from the palm of his outstretched right hand.

Elation rushed through him. The gloves had given tremendous power and control. Mikey was sure with enough practice, all of the elements would be within his grasp, maybe more.

"Mikey," a feminine voice said with a touch on his arm.

Jolting into the present, Mikey registered Sabrina, who wore a stunned expression. Behind her was Thomas and—Mikey grinned—*Marcus*.

They bore the same looks on their faces. His grin disappeared, and he asked, as if everything were normal, "What's going on? What did I miss?"

"I take a quick nap, and now you can control wind?!" Marcus groaned.

Mikey shrugged, still feeling the high from his practice session. "It's one of the things I figured out."

Sabrina's eyes glinted with curiosity. "Can you show us?"

Mikey nodded, standing up. He closed his eyes and focused on the air around him. He pulled Source into his palms, commanded it to create a difference in temperature in the air, and then pushed on the gas, causing a strong gust of wind to blow through the room. His friends had to brace themselves to stay standing.

"Whoa," Marcus said in awe. "I've gotta get practicing with mine."

Mikey opened his eyes, smiling. "I still have a bunch to learn, but I'm getting there. How are you feeling?"

"Not bad." The Shielder shrugged. "I'm starving, though. Can we get dinner?" Marcus asked.

Dinner? Mikey looked at the clock on the wall.

Damn. He'd been at it for almost eight hours.

Mikey's stomach grumbled in agreement. "Yeah, let's go eat."

As they made their way to the dining area, Mikey couldn't help but feel a sense of satisfaction. If he could master the relic, he knew it would greatly help the coming fight. And with his friends and the rest of Otherside with them, they'd have a chance at stopping the Devouring.

Hopefully.

They sat down to eat, and Mikey couldn't shake the feeling of unease. The dark creatures were still out there, growing stronger each day.

And I still have such a long way to go.

A strong gust of wind was practically a parlor trick against a Devourer. His eyes went to his left hand.

Maybe the glove will let me control it? Nope. Terrible idea. He shook his head. The Edax inside him had taken control and changed half his meridians into void. Now, it wasn't just his hand and arm, but the entire left side of his body. A sudden, suffocating wave of panic threatened to overwhelm him at the memory. The fear that he could be slowly turning into one of the Devouring.

Mikey took a few deep breaths, steadying himself before focusing on the present moment. He would continue to work on his relic—*the one that won't unleash a monster that wants to kill everyone*—and hone his skills. And with his friends' support, he had to believe they could win.

After dinner, Mikey waved to Sabrina and the brothers, promising to meet them in the morning for breakfast. The trio had decided to practice for another couple of hours. He wished them luck and headed to his room, picking up the phone the Sect had given him as he sat down.

Let's see how our crazy Healer is doing.

CHAPTER 5

LUKE

"Dammit. Someone better be chopped in half," Luke grumbled as he got out of bed to answer his ringing phone. Though "bed" was a generous word for the small cot in the backroom of the clinic he ran at the Buffalo Sect of Haven.

As morbid as his joke had been, it was necessary. Dealing with death and the mangled bodies of his friends and fellow hunters on the daily forced one to develop a mental toughness. Using humor as a softener for that toughness was Luke's go-to. Without it, he knew he'd soon become one of those angry, disgruntled healers he'd seen too often during his years of training.

Luke rubbed the sleep from his eyes as he answered the phone. "The great and magnificent Luke speaking. Who's this?"

"Hey. It's Mikey," a voice crackled through the speaker.

"Mikey!?" Luke exclaimed, eyes widening. He immediately felt more awake and alert. It had been months since they'd talked.

"Did Sabrina and the others find you? Word on the grapevine is a Conventus is being held. Have anything to do with that?"

Mikey chuckled. "Yep, on all accounts. I'm at SHOP."

"So...what happened?" he asked. "A Conventus hasn't been held in forever, and knowing you, Armageddon is coming, isn't it?" Luke laughed but stopped suddenly as Mikey didn't play along and inhaled a deep breath.

"Kind of spot on there," Mikey replied solemnly. "This conversation is probably being recorded, so I'll fill you in as best I can."

The Source-wielding half-vampire then went on to tell a tale so unbelievable that Luke would've thought it a prank if it weren't for Mikey being the one to tell it. Things seemed to happen around the guy. Luke's instincts had screamed that Mikey was someone important. Even more, they told him he was a good person. Despite his traumatic upbringing, which included losing his parents to Wendigos and spending a decade being alone for fear of hurting others, Mikey had done everything in his power to do what was right. That's why Luke was the first to offer to join his Omada.

And maybe because he wanted to practice healing a vampire.

"Sooooo this Devouring is trapped in a mountain and could break out at any moment to destroy all life as we know it?" Luke asked, whistling when his friend confirmed that to be the truth.

"And you all have relics now?" Luke felt a pang of jealousy at the news. But the Sect needed someone after his mentor and the greatest Healer in hundreds of years, Elder Neema, died to save his life after a horde of monsters ambushed them.

"Yeah. We have a couple for you to try out. Whenever we get to see you, that is," Mikey replied.

Luke perked up at the news.

A relic for me?

A slew of emotions rumbled through him as he processed everything.

Fear for the impending doom that could come upon them, excitement at the thought of getting a relic, and a sense of pride for his friend's bravery and determination. There was also a smidgen of shame that he hadn't been able to help them throughout the ordeal, but he pushed that away.

Time for that to change.

Luke was never one to dwell on the negative. During a hunt, he had also lost his parents, both Movers of some renown. Elder Neema had taken him in after that, for which he'd be forever grateful. Luke smiled at the thought of the old woman. She always tried to look on the bright side of things. To turn every failure into an opportunity.

In the past, when Luke messed up with a patient, cursing his ineptitude, Neema would point a finger at him and say, "In our world of monsters, mistakes are the best teachers. Learn from every battle and let the scars you bear be reminders of your growth, not your defeats."

He hadn't been able to be there for his Omada the past few months. But since then, Luke had trained a few Healers. He felt they were now competent enough to handle things until he got back.

If I get back, he thought. From Mikey's tone, this new enemy was unlike anything Otherside had ever faced.

"I'll get Elder Cassandra to bring me along for the Conventus," Luke said.

"Good. We could use all the help we can get," Mikey said, relief evident in his voice.

Luke nodded, even though Mikey couldn't see it. "I'll start getting everything ready. The clinic needs coverage while I'm gone."

"Thanks, man," Mikey replied.

"Of course. See you soon."

"See you soon."

Just before they hung up, Mikey seemed to hesitate, then blurted, "Luke..."

"Yeah?"

"I—I mean we...we've missed you. The dream team doesn't feel the same without you," Mikey said.

Luke couldn't help but smile at his friend's words. "I've missed you guys, too. Don't worry, I'll be there soon, and we'll kick some Devouring butt together," he said, trying to lighten the mood. "Though from your description, it doesn't sound like they have one."

Mikey chuckled. "Sounds like a plan. Stay safe until then."

"You too, Mikey. You too."

They hung up.

Luke sat back on his cot, mind swirling with everything he had just heard.

With a shake of his head, he immediately got to work, gathering supplies and preparing his clinic for his absence. His friends wouldn't go at it alone again.

Not this time.

As he made a list of things to do in the next few days, Luke couldn't help but feel a sense of excitement. He'd been itching to get back out there, to hunt again. While his friends had been on their adventure, he'd practiced his healing and Source decay with every spare moment.

And if I can unlock one of those relics...

Luke took a deep breath, finishing his list.

"Now I just have to convince the Elder to let me come. Easy peasy," he snorted.

CHAPTER 6

VIKI

Viki paced back and forth in her room, feeling restless and on edge. Several Verdaat guards were posted outside. It was more a show from her father than anything. She'd come back of her own accord. Running away now would be ridiculous.

She had to convince Magnus about the Devouring, the dark creatures that had almost killed her. They would kill everyone soon enough. Unless every living sentient being on the planet banded together to stop them.

But she hadn't had the chance. The instant she came home, her father had ordered her to be confined to her room. Frustration bubbled inside, and Viki couldn't help but feel the weight on her shoulders. She'd spent the entire day waiting.

We're wasting precious time.

Her thoughts were interrupted by a soft knocking on the door. She froze, swallowing the sudden knot in her throat. Too much was riding on this.

"Miss Viki," Mogrin called out. "Your father will see you now."

Viki took a deep breath to calm her nerves before walking over to the door. She could feel the eyes of the guards on her as she walked past them. It was unsettling, but Viki held her head high. Once she reached her father's study, she straightened her spine and took a deep breath before entering.

Magnus, First of his kind and Lord of the Verdaat was sitting at his desk, face unreadable. Viki couldn't help but feel intimidated by him. Hell, everyone felt threatened by the man, for good reason.

Her father was short, standing only five and a half feet tall, yet his presence filled the room like a tsunami. His yellow eyes, shaped like marquise diamonds, seemed to contain an ancient wisdom only attainable after living for millennia. His mere glance could pierce right through her, making her feel as though he could see into her soul.

"Father," Viki greeted him, bowing respectfully.

"Victoria," Magnus replied, his voice rumbling like thunder. He gestured to a chair in front of his desk. "Sit."

Viki sat down, trying to keep her breathing even. She could feel her heart pounding in her chest, and she forced herself to remain calm.

"I take it you returned for good reason?" Magnus asked, his eyes narrowing slightly. "After betraying me yet again."

"Yes, Father," Viki replied, trying to keep her voice steady. "There is something you must be informed of."

Magnus leaned forward, his eyes boring into hers. "This better be good."

Viki took a deep breath before plunging in. She told him everything that had happened—the Devouring, meeting Nevra, the relics—leaving nothing out. Magnus listened intently, his face remaining impassive.

"Do you have any proof?" he asked when she had finished.

"Yes, Father," Viki replied fervently, pulling the scroll from her bag and handing it to Mogrin, who passed it to the Verdaat Lord. "This was discovered in the Dwarf King's chambers that was sealed by a barrier. I could only make out a few words."

Magnus took the scroll from Mogrin and unfurled it slowly, his eyes scanning the text. Viki watched as his expression changed from one of skepticism to one of concern.

After what felt like an eternity, Magnus looked up at her. "This...explains a lot," he said finally, handing the scroll back to Mogrin. "I need to speak with Helena immediately."

"Yes, milord," Mogrin bowed, then gave Viki a slight nod as he walked past them to leave the study.

"What does it say?" Viki asked, curiosity getting the better of her. No matter what the letter contained, she had still betrayed her father and helped Mikey to escape the estate.

"It confirms what you've told me," Magnus replied, his voice grave. "The...Devouring, as you call it, attacked the dwarven source of power, which they named 'the heart of the mountain.' This correlates with this shard you spoke of. King Okskar feared the creatures escaping into the world, so he erected a barrier, trapping them inside the mountain with his people. It also mentions a prophecy uttered by the mother crone that foretells the coming of one who will wield 'The Gloves of Balance' and defeat the darkness once and for all. Okskar gave a key to his son, Orzek, the only other key able to disable the barrier and open their kingdom, Oros. He gave explicit instructions to give the item to the Child of Prophecy."

Viki sat there in stunned silence, processing everything her father had revealed. A prophecy about a hero, relics that could defeat the Devouring and a key that could open up an entire kingdom.

It's all true.

Mikey. Her Mikey—*when he finally comes to his senses*—was destined to defeat The Devouring.

"What do we do now?" she asked, her voice barely above a whisper.

Magnus took a deep breath, then slowly got to his feet. "I will consult with Helena and inform the other ancients tonight. My spies have already confirmed a Conventus is being held among the Clarafae in a few days' time, giving further credit to your claims since one has not been held in quite some time. You will stay here until then."

Before Viki could respond, Magnus called for a guard. A female Verdaat with orange-red eyes and short dark brown hair appeared beside them the next second.

"Escort my daughter back to her chambers. She is not to leave."

The guard nodded, motioning for Viki to follow.

She pursed her lips as if to protest but ultimately stood and bowed. "Yes, Father."

As she left the study, Viki couldn't help but feel a sense of unease settle in her gut. She had told her father of the Devouring and the impending danger. And thanks to Sabrina giving her the scroll, he had believed her.

But Viki couldn't shake the feeling of doom.

What if Otherside couldn't come together? And even if they did, what could they possibly do against the Source-devouring monsters?

No. The negative thoughts would do nothing to help except steal her resolve. *I have to believe in Mikey.*

At the thought of him, her heart ached. She missed him more than she would have liked to admit. She hoped that he and the others were making progress on getting Haven and the Clarafae on board to fight together.

Viki walked over to her window, gazing out at the expansive estate grounds. It was night, but through her vampiric eyes, the gardens before her glowed in a menagerie of color, each plant and lifeform giving off its own hue.

Viki let out a sigh.

I just have to be patient.

She couldn't help her love for Mikey, even if it was one-sided.

But the way he looked at me before I left...

Viki replayed the scene in her mind, her perfect memory recalling the moment in perfect clarity. There was something in Mikey's expression.

Something that made her heart skip a beat. It was a look of longing and affection that gave her hope. Maybe, just maybe, there was a chance for them—one where she didn't have to wait decades for Sabrina to grow old and die.

And for better or worse, Viki knew she would.

Her eyes scanned the room for something to do. They fell upon a DVD case depicting an orange-haired half-breed hero, one who spoke with gods.

Viki hesitated momentarily but then walked over to the case and took it out. She popped the DVD into the player, fondly recalling the memory of Mikey and her watching it together. Then, she went to the door and asked the guard to bring some blood to her room before settling on her bed and pressing play.

I hope you're doing all right, Wonderboy.

CHAPTER 7

MIKEY

—— *ell* ——

Thomas flew backward through the air, gasping after Sabrina's leg connected with his chest. A green barrier shimmered to life behind the Mover, catching him just before he would've slammed into a concrete wall.

"No fair," Thomas grumbled. "That relic is insane."

Sabrina beamed, looking down at the greaves strapped onto her legs. "Why do you think I've been searching for them for years?"

It had taken two days for her to unlock the rune-carved armor, unlocking an agility rivaling the Verdaat. That, and another unexpected ability. One that Sabrina had dubbed 'Source step.' It was that very ability that Thomas was cursing. The relic allowed her to create a platform of energy she could step on, giving her incredible mobility in the air.

Mikey watched the two spar from the sidelines, his heart heavy with conflicting emotions. On the one hand, he was happy for her and the others, at their dedication and progress. On the other, however, was the nagging twinge of jealousy seeing them smiling at each other so...fondly. He didn't miss the longing glances Thomas gave Sabrina or the flush in her cheeks when she caught him. Like they belonged together, making Mikey feel like a wedge.

He shook his head, trying to dispel the thought.

I'm not going to give up on her. And now's not the time.

The Conventus was tomorrow.

Mikey could feel the weight of the upcoming meeting like a physical pressure on his chest. They needed to convince Haven and the Clarafae to abandon this pointless war and join forces. Without them, they wouldn't stand a chance against the Devouring.

Izildora had fought the Devouring before and knew the threat they posed. If that were true, the gold elf fae Queen would surely help.

He focused back on the sparring match, watching Sabrina and Thomas with a critical eye. They were both good fighters, and it was clear that Sabrina's newfound relic gave her an edge. Marcus was on the sidelines, shielding them from serious damage as they fought. The Shielder had improved drastically with his relic.

But Mikey knew they needed more than combat skills to win this war. They needed a plan, a strategy. Hopefully, after the Conventus, they'd have one.

Mikey's thoughts were interrupted by Sabrina's voice. "Hey, you up for taking us on?"

He straightened up, realizing that Sabrina and Thomas had stopped.

"Sure." He nodded.

"Just don't burn us to a crisp or set off a tornado in the room," Marcus chuckled. "My shields can only do so much."

Mikey smirked. "I'll try."

Taking a deep breath, he stepped onto the mat. He could feel his friends' eyes on him, watching with tense, readied postures.

In the past, they often sparred three versus one—except it was Luke instead of Thomas. Mikey's enhanced speed and senses, coupled with his ability to wield Source, made it a pretty fair match-up. That was before his time with the Verdaat, however. Now, Mikey was exponentially stronger. He could now control ice, wind, and, as of yesterday, fire. Though he still hadn't quite gotten the hang of controlling the flames.

But his friends didn't have relics before, either.

This should be interesting.

Mikey waited for one of them to make the first move, his eyes scanning their stances and movements. He could see how Sabrina's body tensed, ready to pounce, and how Thomas's muscles coiled, preparing for an attack. Marcus stood behind them, his hands up in a defensive position. There was no need for the Shielder's staff anymore. The necklace around Marcus's neck had given him potent offensive abilities.

Sabrina was the first to strike, charging at him with incredible speed. Mikey sidestepped her and sent a blast of wind, hoping to blow her away. Sabrina used a Source step, dodging the gust in midair. Mikey jumped backward, barely avoiding the half dozen red fist-sized Source bullets whizzing toward his chest. Despite not hitting him, he winced as the skin on his left cheek peeled back from the projectile's power.

They've certainly improved.

Mikey snorted at the thought.

But so have I.

He extended his right hand and summoned a swirling ice vortex, sending it toward Thomas. The Mover dodged to the side, and Marcus moved to intercept the attack, creating a shield of energy to counter the ice. Sabrina flew in from above, aiming a kick at

Mikey's head. He ducked under the attack and swept her legs out from under her, sending her tumbling to the ground.

The hairs on Mikey's neck prickled, and he ducked. His fine sense of Source warned him of Thomas' attack. He sent a blast of fire at the Mover, who responded with a roll, barely avoiding the flames. Mikey was thankful for the shielding his new gloves provided.

Sabrina leaped to her feet, using her Source step to launch herself at Mikey. He caught her midair, spinning her around and tossing her toward Marcus, who broke her fall with a shield.

Mikey grinned. Sure, the world was on the brink of impending doom. But here and now, in the midst of sparring with his friends, he was having fun.

With a taunting smile, he stuck out his hand and waved them on.

Thomas and Sabrina exchanged a look, then came at Mikey together, but he stopped their combined attack easily, launching a flurry of wind blades at them as they advanced. Sabrina dodged two of them, throwing her ruby-red energy at the third and final one. The attacks collided, canceling each other out. Marcus summoned a shield, blocking the last two from hitting his brother.

They came again.

Maybe just a little tornado, he thought with a smirk.

This time, Mikey gathered the air around him, feeling the power of the currents as they swirled. The wind picked up, whipping around the room with increasing ferocity. Sabrina and Thomas were caught off guard as Mikey unleashed a tiny whirlwind, sending them flying across the room. Marcus's shields held, but the Shielder stumbled backward from the sheer force of the gusts.

Mikey landed on the ground, his eyes scanning his friends. They were getting back to their feet, their expressions a mix of shock and admiration. Mikey raised his hand with a small smile and conjured a ball of ice, twirling it around his fingers.

"Okay, okay, I think we get it," Thomas said, shaking his head before cursing, "Freaking elementals."

Sabrina nodded, her cheeks pink from the exertion. "Okay, THAT's unfair," she huffed. "I'll have to work on my Source step to keep up with you."

"You were doing a pretty damn good job," Mikey replied. "You guys certainly had me on my toes."

Marcus chuckled, giving him a playful push on the shoulder. "I thought we agreed no tornados?"

"It was just a small one," Mikey shrugged, nudging him back. "About the most I could muster right now anyway. If only we weren't stuck here. I want to practice outside to see what these gloves can really do."

"That'll go over well." Marcus snorted. "I've seen the movie *Twister*."

Mikey laughed, feeling the tension and jealousy from earlier dissipate. He was glad to have friends by his side and made a mental note never to forget that.

"All right, let's take a break," Sabrina said, stretching her arms.

They headed to the corner of the room to rehydrate and catch their breath.

Mikey leaned against the wall, his gaze drifting over to where Sabrina was stretching.

She was beautiful—fierce and strong—and the way she looked when she fought. Mikey's heart skipped a beat just thinking about it. He wanted to go to her but knew now wasn't the time. Despite his best efforts, things continued to feel different between them.

He gave her space and tried to act normally, whatever that meant. Returning to how they were before getting together didn't feel normal to Mikey.

But he didn't know how to fix things. How to make her see that he still loved her.

She had brought up a series of valid points. Sure, Mikey was immortal and would live forever.

Until the Devouring kills us all.

But he would love her even if she was old. That kind of stuff didn't matter.

Mikey began imagining a world where the Devourers had been defeated, and they were together.

A knot formed in his throat.

Most likely, the two of them couldn't have a family of their own. Children between the Verdaat were rare to begin with, and Mikey was the only known child born between a vampire and a human.

Did Sabrina want that?

His mind reeled at the reality of what their being together would mean. No children. Mikey imagined himself in Sabrina's shoes. How would he feel watching the person he loved stay young while his body grew old? Would he resent her?

Maybe... Mikey realized. Sabrina had to have been thinking all these things, and the same internal conflict was likely warring inside her.

Then Viki popped into his head. He'd thought of her every day since she'd left, hoping that Magnus wouldn't take out his anger at them leaving on her. That she'd been able to convince the Verdaat Lord of what was coming. More than that, however, Mikey missed her.

"*She loves you,*" Sabrina's voice echoed in his head.

Mikey knew in his heart it was true. And if he was candid with himself, he loved her too.

Dammit, this is so complicated!

Mikey ran his hands through his hair.

"Hey, what's wrong?"

Mikey jerked, snapping out of his thoughts. He looked up to see Sabrina staring at him.

"Oh, uh, nothing. Just thinking," he said.

"You sure? Your face looks kind of...guilty," she said, giving him a knowing look.

Mikey didn't respond.

Sabrina glanced between him and Marcus, then Thomas. She took a step forward, leaning in and lowering her voice. "Are you okay?"

"Do you wanna have kids?" Mikey blurted in a whisper.

The color suddenly drained from Sabrina's face as her eyes widened in utter shock.

"Wha—What?!"

She turned to the Sante brothers, who raised an eyebrow in unison. Sabrina grabbed Mikey by the arm and led him out of the training room into the common area.

"Mikey, what the hell?"

"I know, I know," he said quickly, "not the best time to ask, but I was thinking about our talk the other day about us being together and realized I might not be able to give you—"

"Yes," Sabrina said flatly.

Mikey gulped but didn't respond, unsure of what to say.

Sabrina sighed, her expression softening as she took his hands in her own.

"I've always wanted a family. Not now, of course, but someday."

"Which is something I can't give you...something Thomas can," Mikey finished, shoulders slumping.

"Ouch," he yelped as Sabrina flicked him on the forehead.

"Look, I have no idea if Thomas and I are going to be together, and children are far, far down the road from now," she said. Her lips pursed together as if she was considering her following words. "A family was just one of the things I've been thinking about lately, especially with the end of the world looming. Actually, I started thinking about the future when we were threatened with being kicked out of Haven for coming to find you. Marcus almost had a panic attack at the prospect of not becoming a Jaecar."

This was news to Mikey.

"Marcus freaked out?"

Sabrina snorted. "Yeah, big time. And he asked us what we would do if it happened. At the time, I was so focused on rescuing you that it didn't matter if I was kicked out."

Mikey felt a pang of guilt. "I'm sorry. I know I caused all of this. If you hadn't gotten involved with me..."

Another flick on the forehead. "Ow." He rubbed at his head and huffed a laugh. "It's always violence with you."

"Then stop," Sabrina said firmly, clearly trying to suppress a grin. "Nothing in this world would make me regret meeting you. Hell, if we hadn't, no one would know about the Devouring, and I never would have gotten my relic. Most important of all"—she grabbed his chin, using her fingers to pucker Mikey's lips into a fish. She stroked his cheek with her thumb—"I never would have met one of the kindest, sweetest, most aggravatingly strong guys in the world."

She leaned in, and for a moment, Mikey thought she would kiss him. Then her head turned, and instead, Sabrina planted a kiss on his forehead, leaning on her toes to reach him.

Mikey closed his eyes, feeling his heart swell with warmth. There was a finality to the gesture he hadn't missed, but this was Sabrina. He wanted her to be happy no matter what, be it Thomas or something else that came their way. To have the life she always wanted. Mikey wrapped his arms around her, pulling her close. Sabrina rested her head on his shoulder, her arms around his waist. They stood like that, just holding each other.

"I love you," Mikey whispered into her hair.

"I love you too," she murmured back. "Don't ever think that I don't."

"I know. And I want you to know that I'm okay if—"

The words were more challenging to get out than Mikey thought, but they needed to be said. In his heart, he knew it was the right thing to do. For her sake.

"If you want to be with someone else. Say, for instance...a certain bull-headed Mover with fists for brains."

Sabrina laughed, her chest reverberating against him. "Thanks," she said softly.

They stayed like that for a few more minutes until Sabrina pulled away, wiping at her eyes.

"Don't think I've let you off the hook on being my artist for my Creature's of Otherside book."

"Wouldn't dream of it," Mikey replied.

"Good. Now," she said, taking a deep breath, "let's get back to training. We have a lot of work to do."

Mikey nodded, feeling a weight lifting from his chest. He knew there was still a lot of uncertainty in their future, but he was content with the knowledge that Sabrina loved him and that they could still be there for each other no matter what happened.

As they returned to the training room, they saw Thomas throwing Source punches at Marcus, who tossed up barriers to block the attacks.

The brothers stopped as soon as they saw them.

"Uh, everything all right?" Thomas asked, scratching the back of his head.

"Yeah." Sabrina smiled, looking at Mikey, who smiled back. "I think it is. Who's ready for round two?"

CHAPTER 8

"Guys!" Luke exclaimed as the main door to their common room opened.

"Luke!" Mikey grinned, rushing over to the Healer. The others followed.

"The dream team is finally back together again," Marcus laughed, patting Luke on the back.

Luke chuckled. "It's good to see you all in one piece," he said, looking around at the group. His eyes lingered on Thomas. "So, what did I miss?"

Mikey gestured to the porter watch on Luke's wrist and mouthed, "They're listening." The watches enabled Haven's members to create portals to their Sects in specific locations. Luke nodded slowly, making an "O" with his lips, then unstrapped the device and put it in his bag, dropping it near the door.

The Verdaat had removed Mikey's watch on the day he was taken. He had asked Mogrin about it and was told it could be used as a tracker and a listening device. Sabrina and the Sante brothers had ditched theirs before the drive to Louisiana.

The group huddled together, and Mikey told Luke everything that had happened since he left, from their encounter with Magnus to their training sessions, this time not leaving anything out. Luke listened intently, nodding along, and occasionally interjecting with questions. When Mikey finished, Luke stood, blinking slowly with a dumbfounded look.

"Wow. You met god? Like... THE god?!"

"Well, goddess, but yeah," Mikey said. His mind flashed to his brief encounter with Greel, of the hand bigger than worlds reaching out. The thought made him shiver. He'd left the gods out of their phone call and anything else that might've incriminated or exposed those who had helped. Mikey mentioned Avalon to Arthur as a supposed story, not as a deity he'd met.

"So you think the Devouring, or Edax as you called it, might also be inside you and within the Verdaat. And so far, the one inside you has been the only thing to kill one, except it went out of control, and an...angel saved you."

Mikey nodded. "Yep."

The Healer whistled again and then glanced around the room. "Is Laken here now? Can I meet her?"

Mikey frowned. "No, she left as soon as we got to the Sect, no idea where."

Luke's face fell slightly, but he quickly recovered. "Well, I'm sure I'll get to meet her sometime."

"Is my mother here?" Sabrina asked.

"Yeah, she went to go talk with some other elders. Thankfully, Elder Zuri gave me permission to hang with you guys until the Conventus starts. Do you think they'll let the rest of us attend? This is history in the making."

"Probably." Sabrina nodded. "We're involved in this after all."

The conversation was interrupted by a knock on the door. Sabrina strode over to answer it, revealing a tall, imposing guard. His eyes flicked over their group before settling on Mikey.

"It is time. Follow me," he said in a deep, authoritative voice.

"Speak of the devil," Marcus muttered.

Sabrina shot him a warning glance before turning back to the guard. "Lead the way."

The guard nodded and turned, leading them out through a series of winding hallways. The Sect was abuzz with activity, and Sect Leaders throughout the world were gathering because of him.

Mikey's anxiety began rearing its ugly head. What was said today could very well determine the fate of the planet. Maybe even the universe. His palms started to sweat, and a heavy weight grew in his chest.

Breathe. Just breathe, he repeated.

Despite what people may think, Mikey hated being the center of attention. He'd spent his entire life being as inconspicuous as possible, not wanting to draw people near him for fear of their safety. Now, he was supposed to save everyone. The pressure was too much.

Sabrina noticed his distress and reached for his hand, giving it a comforting squeeze. Mikey looked at her and felt his heart rate slow down. He took a deep breath and focused on the present.

They finally reached a room bustling with activity. People milled around, talking in groups. As they entered, silence fell, and all eyes turned to them. Mikey felt his cheeks heat up.

"This way." The guard led them past the crowd and through another door. As soon as they stepped through the doorway, they were greeted with a plain room. The walls were bare and painted a soft blue, like the color of a clear sky. In the center of the room stood four towering Jaecar, their muscular frames creating an intimidating presence. They faced a raised platform, and behind them, a portal swirled. The air hummed with energy and anticipation as Mikey approached the raised platform.

Mikey could feel the Jaecars' eyes bore into him, and he wondered how much they knew. Were they aware the planet was only weeks, perhaps even days away from being overrun by death itself?

He swallowed and tried to ignore their imposing presence as he ascended the platform. Once he reached the top, he stepped through.

Mikey felt a sudden rush of air as he stepped through the portal. He was transported to a dimly lit chamber. Near him, the stone walls were adorned with symbols and runes that glowed in the dim light. They were the same Source lights they'd found inside the dwarven mountain. The room opened into a hallway with vines growing along the walls facing toward the outgoing path as if pointing the way.

He stepped off the platform, and the others appeared soon after, taking in the space. The guard motioned them down the hallway. When the path split, they went left, down another narrow corridor. Despite being unaffected by the cold, Mikey could tell the air was frigid.

The tense silence between the group was palpable and heavy, broken only by the faint sound of their footsteps echoing throughout the silent halls.

Where are we?

He had his suspicions of whose land they were in. Just not the location.

Oddly, the place didn't smell of old, musky stone one would imagine given the scenery. Instead, it had a fresh, wintery scent like pine and spice.

As they rounded a bend, they came upon two figures guarding a massive, ornate door. The beings had pointed ears and pale silver skin that glistened in the dim Source light. After meeting Helena and Viki's description of the two races of elves in the mountain, he was sure these were gold elves. The vampire had explained that

Helena's people were called silver elves and Izildora's gold. It was a misnomer, however, because the silver elves' skin had a golden hue. In reality, they were Silva, or forest elves, the name changing over time. The same went for their counterparts, the moon or Gol elves.

The two before them were tall and lithe, but much like the Tenefae Queen, their eyes drew Mikey's attention. Instead of the solid black of the Silva race, these were a solid, milky white, making Mikey think for a second they were blind.

That feeling immediately disappeared when the guards saw Mikey and tensed. They motioned for him to stop with a raised hand.

The tallest of the two guards whispered in the ear of the other before the shorter one nodded and went inside.

A moment later, they were ushered through the door.

The five of them looked at each other.

They exchanged nervous glances, feeling the weight of the impending meeting. As they entered the room, a wave of tension washed over them. The air hummed with anticipation, and all eyes turned towards the newcomers.

The Dream Team stepped into the grand circular chamber, eyes widening at the sight before them. Only slightly brighter than the hallways they'd just come from, a soft glow emanated from larger luminescent crystals embedded in the walls. The air buzzed with energy, sparking a sense of both awe and trepidation within Mikey and his companions.

Seating encircled the outer rim of the chamber, accommodating around a hundred of the most influential leaders of various races. Jaecar Sect Leaders, adorned in intricate leathers and armors that glinted under gentle illumination, commanded respect as they observed the proceedings. Alongside them sat leaders of the Clarafae, each exuding an air of wisdom and power unique to their kind.

Standing equidistant along the perimeter were tall, imposing figures wearing black and gold masks with all-black leather armor. A large gold stripe was embroidered across their right upper arm. Within the stripe was an insignia, a scale for measuring weights using a pulley and gravity. The symbol has been used frequently throughout history to represent justice. It was the mark of the Coercitors, an elite band of relic-equipped Jaecar at the exclusive beck and call of the high council of Haven. They wore masks so no one could identify them if they had to do...unsavory things.

They gave Mikey the creeps.

Directly across from the entrance, upon a raised throne, sat Izildora herself. Her regal posture and commanding presence showed she was a force to be reckoned with. Dressed in flowing white robes that looked as if they were spun from moonlight, she radiated an ethereal beauty that mesmerized.

The fae Queen's silver hair cascaded down like a waterfall, glistening under the soft glow of the crystals. Like pools of molten white, her eyes held a captivating depth that seemed to peer into the very depths of one's soul. The way they gleamed in the light gave off an otherworldly aura as if they held secrets beyond mortal comprehension. And given that Izildora was much older than the eight-thousand-year-old Magnus, she certainly did.

As Mikey's gaze locked with hers, he couldn't help but feel a magnetic pull, as if she held the answers to all his questions and the key to his destiny.

It took some willpower to tear his eyes away.

Izildora stood and nodded toward their group.

Her voice echoed through the chamber, rich and melodic, "Welcome, young heroes."

Heroes? Mikey's face scrunched in confusion.

It was the first time anyone on his mother's side of things had said anything positive about him. Sure, in quiet, he'd gotten along with some Jaecar, Chase, and Michelle, for example. If the queen openly declared his Omada heroes, they'd have to take their warnings seriously.

"Please, come forward." She beckoned them with the bend of a slender finger in her outstretched hand.

Once Mikey and the others had reached the middle, Izildora looked up, eyes darting to various dignitaries.

"And welcome to you all, esteemed leaders of the Clarafae and Sourcerers of Haven. We gather here today to discuss matters of great importance. We currently stand at a precipice, on the brink of an unimaginable catastrophe. It is up to us to decide its fate."

The pause hung heavy in the air, a silence settling over the room as everyone waited with bated breath for her to continue.

"You have all sensed it—the encroaching darkness, the rising tide of chaos," Izildora continued, her voice expressing urgency.

From her words, hope began to rise in Mikey's chest. The queen had jumped right into describing the threat of the Devouring.

"The world's fate is at stake from not one, but two great enemies. They are separate, but not entirely so."

Two? Mikey's brow furrowed.

Then he understood.

Oh no...

Helena had warned him what Izildora wanted.

The Clarafae Queen looked toward the Sect Leaders. Mikey saw Sabrina's mother, Elder Zuri, and a few other faces he'd seen during his Omada's tribunal, including Elder Tem.

He tried not to sneer.

"We are currently at war with one of them. Some of you have been made aware of why we must eradicate Magnus and the blight of his ilk. But there is no better time than now to inform the rest. The high council of Haven and even the child of prophecy"—the queen glanced to Mikey—"can no doubt confirm its veracity."

Mikey swallowed, fearing what was to come.

"For thousands of years, the vampires have hunted others, especially humans. The Verdaat would have you all believe it was just for food, for they also have to eat. This is why the Accords were signed. There is, however, a more sinister reason."

Izildora paused, eyeing each member of the Conventus.

She knows.

Mikey knew for certain then. What Simon, the oldest Sante brother who had been imprisoned for two years at Magnus' estate, had shared. The Healer was taken during a fake hunt to find a cure for the Verdaat's infertility and, in doing so, uncovered a dark secret the vampires had kept for thousands of years.

But of course, Izildora knew. Those eyes seemed to know everything.

"To create more of their kind," the queen said. "The Wendigos are not a race on their own. They are, in fact, humans whose blood has been corrupted by the Verdaat Lord. All to create an army to conquer us all."

Murmurs immediately broke out amongst the gathered leaders.

This isn't good.

Why was she focusing on the Verdaat and not the Devouring? What could Magnus have possibly done to Izildora that made her want to risk the end of the world?

A humanoid being to Mikey's left stood up. Something about the act seemed strange until Mikey realized the stout, long-eared fae was standing on its chair to be seen. The being was around three feet tall and had light green skin. It was hairless, save for a short black beard tinged with grey. A black buckled hat rested atop its head. The large oval brown eyes that took up most of its face scanned the room.

Mikey had no clue what the creature's race was.

"Tepen, leader of the simple fae," Izildora nodded.

Simple fae.

Mikey looked to Sabrina and Marcus, who shook their heads and shrugged. They hadn't heard of them either. There was something about Tepen's features that was familiar to Mikey. But he couldn't quite place what.

The short fae cleared its throat, its masculine voice high-pitched yet commanding. It was clear from Tepen's diction that English was not his native tongue.

"Ladies and gentlemen, esteemed leaders of the Clarafae, I stand before you as a representative of the races that have long remained hidden in the shadows, unknown to many. While small in stature, the brùnaidh, sprites, and my ancient elven race, the leipreachán, do not lack determination or resilience. Though those I represent may not possess the magical prowess or physical strength of our esteemed counterparts, our people have always been attuned to nature and its delicate balance," Tepen continued, his voice steady. "There is an even greater darkness within our world. My Queen, is it true the Devouring has returned?"

More murmurs broke out amongst the Conventus members.

A leprechaun.

Mikey's eyes grew wide.

And Brunaidh—he searched for the word in his memory. It meant Brownie.

So, he's their leader.

Almost all of the mythological beings in the folklore of mankind were based in some part on truth. Mikey wondered how much of the lore on leprechauns was accurate.

At least he seems to care more about the real threat over Izildora's vendetta against Magnus and the Verdaat.

The queen's gaze shifted from Tepen to Mikey, her eyes narrowing ever so slightly. The room fell into a hushed silence, awaiting her response. Mikey felt a bead of sweat trickle down the back of his neck. He had no idea what was about to transpire, but it was clear the leprechaun's question had struck a nerve.

"It is true," Izildora finally spoke, her voice low and filled with a mix of sorrow and determination. "The Devouring has indeed returned."

Gasps echoed through the chamber from several fae leaders. The Jaecar looked at one another with confused expressions. Clearly, they had been kept in the dark. Only the Elders that Mikey and the others had informed of their journey seemed to stiffen at the news. The head of the Clarafae just declared his story true.

Mikey felt a surge of validation. Finally, someone of authority acknowledged his claims about the Devouring. He glanced at Sabrina and Marcus, who wore expressions of relief tinged with concern. They understood the magnitude of what they were facing.

"The Devouring," Izildora continued, her voice carrying a note of gravitas, "Is an ancient force threatening to consume everything in its path. It is the flesh of a dark and vengeful being that seeks to obliterate the very essence of our existence. If left unchecked, it will devour our world and countless others beyond. They may very well have already. We have faced the creatures twice before. And twice, we have pushed them back."

Mikey's heart pounded in his chest. She knew everything. More, even.

Earth had been attacked twice? He only knew of the one time.

An unfamiliar Jaecar elder stood. The queen nodded toward him and said, "Sect Leader Lorenzo," before sitting down.

The man had sharp features, short curly hair, and tan skin. He bowed. "Your Grace," Lorenzo replied in a thick accent. Mikey guessed it was Italian. "If this is true, where are the creatures now, and how can we stop them?"

Several of the Jaecar nodded in approval of the question.

Izildora turned toward Mikey and his group. If someone on the outside were looking in, it would be difficult to tell who the queen's milky white eyes were looking at. But Mikey could feel her gaze boring into him.

Izildora spoke, "Child, why don't you tell us again what happened in the mountain."

Mikey straightened his posture, feeling the weight of all eyes in the chamber now on him. He took a deep breath, gathering his thoughts before recounting the harrowing events over the last few weeks, leaving out certain details of those he cared about.

"I urge you all to stop this war and work with the Tenefae to defeat this threat. If you don't, no one will be left to fight anything," Mikey finished.

A loud chattering broke out amongst the Conventus.

Mikey looked around the room, his heart pounding in his chest. The Conventus members seemed divided, their expressions ranging from concern to skepticism. The weight of his words hung heavily in the air as the leaders deliberated their next course of action.

Izildora stood up, her regal presence commanding the attention of the entire chamber. The murmurs quieted, and even the fae skeptical of Mikey turned their attention to their queen.

"The Devouring, according to the boy's own words...is currently contained. And has been for thousands of years," Izildora began, her voice steady and resolute. "I must remind you all that our other threat is not."

Elder Cassandra bolted up in her seat and blurted, "Your Grace, surely you can agree that this new threat is much more dire than the vampires."

The queen stiffened, and Mikey felt the pressure in the air change. He switched his eyes and squinted at the flare of bright silver Source emanating from Izildora. Then the aura was gone in a blink, like someone turned off their high beams. Mikey could see the Gol elf's meridians, a fine and intricate web of innumerable branches, all carrying what looked like molten silver light.

Izildora's lips curled in a strained smile.

"What the boy failed to mention is the Verdaat and Devouring are two sides of the same coin. Within each vampire is the same darkness. It is why they must feed on the Source of others. They are an unnatural parasite plaguing this planet."

No. Mikey began realizing the queen's plan.

"The boy knows this to be the truth. He also has it inside of him."

All eyes turned to Mikey.

His heart raced, anxiety settling over him like a suffocating cloak. He had hoped that his secret, the origin of the darkness he carried within, would remain hidden. But now, it was laid bare in the presence of the entire Conventus.

Whispers filled the chamber as the fae leaders exchanged glances; their expressions ranged from curiosity to fear. However, the majority leaned toward apprehension. Mikey felt his breath catch in his throat. He looked to Sabrina and Marcus, searching for reassurance, but they wore matching expressions of concern.

His shoulders slumped. Of course, they were worried.

The Edax in me almost killed them...

Izildora's gaze remained fixed, her eyes piercing through his very soul. "Do not be afraid, child," she said, her voice laced with authority yet held some sympathy. "The darkness that resides within you is not your fault. It is a burden you have carried unwittingly that, according to Beruva, a great seer, might save us all from the Devouring."

Mikey tried to swallow down the knot forming in his throat. This was not going where he'd hoped.

The queen continued, looking at each member of the Conventus as she spoke. "But we cannot join forces with darkness, for there is no guarantee the Verdaat won't turn on us. Unfortunately, Helena has allied with them. It is my hope that with this newest threat at our doorstep, she will ally the Tenefae to us or at least stay out of our way until the Verdaat are eliminated. Then we can focus our efforts on the Devouring."

"No, you can't do that!" Mikey shouted before he could think better of it.

The air shifted like before, and a sudden, intense weight pressed down on his shoulders. Its strength forced him to one knee.

"You forget your place, child," Izildora said in an icy tone.

Mikey struggled to maintain his composure under the oppressive force bearing down on him. He clenched his fists, his knuckles turning white as he pushed back against the invisible weight. His voice trembled with determination, but he said with clenched teeth, "You're right, Your Grace; I have no idea where my place is in this world. Until just last year, I never knew about Otherside or the Fae. But I am not just a pawn in this game. I have seen firsthand the destruction caused by the Devouring. As have you. And I've spent time with the Verdaat. Not all of them are bad. I hate Magnus for what he did to my parents and others. But the Devouring is a bigger threat by far. It is as much a concern to the Verdaat as it is to all of you. My friend, Viki, is a Verdaat. She was almost killed by one that was free. The same one that I assume took out Elder Zuri's Jaecar. Who knows if more creatures are out there, wandering around?

They aren't mindless; there is a cunning to them. And if the ones in the mountain reach the shard, it will be the end."

The murmurs among the fae leaders intensified, their gazes flitting between Izildora and Mikey. Sabrina and Marcus exchanged worried glances, but they didn't speak.

Izildora remained silent, her milky white eyes fixed on Mikey. The weight pressing down on him slowly lifted, allowing him to straighten himself again. Mikey held his breath, waiting for the queen's response.

After what felt like an eternity, Izildora finally spoke, her voice carrying a hint of consideration. "You speak with conviction, child," she said.

Mikey felt a glimmer of hope ignited within him. Maybe, just maybe, he had managed to sway the queen's decision.

"But I was there when Magnus was created. I've witnessed the atrocities he and his kind have committed for thousands of years. Their very existence goes against nature." For just a moment, he saw Izildora's face contort in an amalgam of emotion. Disgust, hatred, bitter sadness, and so many more Mikey couldn't even imagine for someone as old as the elven queen. But the ones he did recognize touched his heart. Izildora had lost someone very dear. And she blamed Magnus for it. Then it was gone, her serious, regal façade back in place as she continued, "He and his kind must be eliminated before they can raise an army. Then we will face the Devouring together."

Mikey couldn't hold his tongue. He didn't care if the queen's power could crush him to a pulp. Someone equally dear to him was an older vampire.

"I won't let you do that," he said.

The queen looked at him, her face tilting and eyebrows rising in surprise as if the idea of someone talking to her so brazenly was absurd.

Elder Tem stood suddenly, pointing a finger at Mikey. "You insolent, vile thing! How dare you speak to the queen so disrespectfully!"

Izildora held a hand toward the high councilman, who cut his words off immediately and sat back down. But her gaze never left Mikey.

"Tell me, child. How will you stop us?"

"I don't know," he exhaled, shaking his head and throwing up his arms in frustration.

The entire situation was ridiculous. Who was he? A cursed kid who grew up with no friends, wishing every day for his parents to be alive and a normal life. Instead, he discovered that the supernatural world, Otherside, was real, and he was an energy vampire destined to fight against the same darkness he was carrying inside himself. If Mikey's life were a story, whoever wrote it was clearly insane. Now, he threatened the queen of the Clarafae, a being so ancient and powerful that her complete and utter lack of fear of his threat was understandable.

It's funny how I sometimes wish for the days of being a lonely nobody. The world wasn't ending then, and I wasn't smack dab in the middle.

Mikey considered the queen's question, asking himself what he would do.

It's not like I can attack everyone here.

Not that he'd even have a chance of winning. And even if he could, what would that accomplish? The prophecy was nonsense if it meant he had to fight the supposed good guys. He'd have to let out the thing inside him even to stand a chance. And all that would do is let two monsters battle it out until one wins before destroying everything and everyone.

Mikey took a deep breath, his mind racing for a solution. He couldn't let his anger and frustration cloud his judgment. The fate of the world rested on his shoulders, and he needed to find a way to convince Izildora and the Conventus that working together was the only option.

"I understand your hatred for Magnus and the Elder Vampires," Mikey said, his voice filled with emotion. He stepped toward the queen, and the elven guards beside them began to raise their spears, but Izildora signaled them to let him pass. This time, he did not break eye contact. Holding back the whirlwind of feelings those thoughts of the past did to him, Mikey continued in a husky whisper, "He took everything from me. *Every-thing*." The last two syllables came out angry and bitter. "I know you've lost someone. I understand the pain." His fists clenched at the rage he felt for all he'd lost. Then, with a strained sigh, he let the hurt go, shaking his head.

For a second, the queen's dry expression wavered. Hoping he wasn't imagining it, Mikey continued.

"But this...what you're doing—it isn't right. If we let our vendettas blind us, the Devouring will consume us all. There must be a way to find common ground. To forge an alliance against the true enemy. What you want is genocide, and to that end, you'd be no better than the dark things trapped in that mountain."

The fae leaders exchanged glances, their expressions shifting between skepticism and consideration. Mikey's heart pounded as he waited for the queen's response. Sabrina stepped forward, her voice filled with unwavering conviction.

"Mikey is right, Your Grace," she said, meeting Izildora's gaze. "We cannot afford to be divided. I've met some decent vampires." She winked at Mikey, and a smile crept on his lips.

Marcus put a hand on Sabrina and took a step forward, looking to the leaders. "You didn't see what was in that mountain." Marcus turned to the Jaecar. "These things are... unlike anything we've ever fought before. They make the Verdaat look like garden gnomes."

Realizing his blunder, the Shielder gave a slight bow to a gnome sporting a particularly pointy head with brown hair wrapped around its base like a furry ring. Atop it rested a silver crown.

"No offense," Marcus added.

The tiny king rolled his eyes.

Luke held up a finger and exclaimed, "And let's not ignore what happened to the dwarves. I believe they trapped the creatures with them to protect us. What would that say about us if we let their deaths be in vain?"

There were several more nodding heads now.

Mikey smiled at his friends proudly.

Yes! Way to go, guys.

The queen's eyes narrowed at seeing the change in the group.

"You know nothing," she seethed at Mikey through clenched teeth, just loud enough for him to hear. "Magnus must pay for what he's done."

Then, her mouth contorted into a wicked smile as if a great idea came to mind.

She stood, and the chamber grew quiet.

"While the sacrifice of the dwarves brings me great sorrow, their efforts would be meaningless if we don't eradicate the vampires who carry the same darkness they tried so hard to stamp out," Izildora said.

"No, that—" Mikey started.

"Do not interrupt me again!" the queen spat, and Mikey fell to the ground with a cry of pain and surprise as it suddenly felt like a semi-truck was thrown on top of him.

The oppressive power vanished as quickly as it came.

A shiver ran down Mikey's spine as he got to his feet. The sly smile had never left Izildora's face.

"For all your speak of trust and alliance, let me ask you one question," she said, raising a slender finger. "Have you ever tried to kill your friends?"

CHAPTER 9

The color drained from his face.

Izildora's question cut like a sharp blade, leaving Mikey reeling.

"I...I've never *tried*," he stammered, enunciating the last word while guilt etched his features. The loss of control was coming to haunt him yet again.

The queen's eyes bore into him, unwavering as a winter storm. "The darkness you carry, Mikey, is the same that resides within these Devouring creatures. You claim to be fighting against it, yet you remind me of a snake eating its own tail, destroying itself from within."

Mikey's mind raced as he tried to find a counter to her argument. He knew she had a point; the Edax was a part of him, a horrifying testament to the powerful beings he was destined to face. But he also knew he was different—more than the Verdaat. Izildora had the right of it when she used the word parasite. But it was the substance inside them, a piece of the dark god Greel, not the people themselves.

Mikey had never told anyone about what he'd felt when the God's hand had reached for him. The part that terrified him more than anything. He felt a connection, a kinship. Like Avalon said, *"Greel is as much a part of you as I am."* At that moment, he'd realized what it was dwelling within. A Devourer. Except it wasn't separate, like something foreign that had taken residence inside him. He, Mikey Black, WAS a Devourer. At least in part. His father, a regular man infected with Magnus' tainted blood, and his mother, a Jaecar, humans with the ability to wield Avalon's essence, a cosmic energy known as Source. He was born of the two, the first in history.

All this time, he'd been fighting that fact.

No, not fighting, he thought. *Denying.*

I'm the child with life and death in each hand. Not the child with life and a deathlike parasitic infection.

His resolve hardened with that revelation.

I can't let the queen's desire for revenge blind her to the reality of the situation. They need to see what they are up against.

"You're right," he said steadily despite his racing heartbeat. "Several times, the thing inside of me has broken free and tried to hurt my friends. And several times, they've saved me. I'm a being of death, just as the Devouring is. But that doesn't make us the same, any more than the dark things that can be found within your hearts. We must band together before it's too late. I'm telling you, once these creatures get the shard, no one, not even me, the 'supposed child of prophecy,'" Mikey said, forming air quotes for the last bit, "will be able to stop them. United, we stand a chance. Divided, we will fall. And it's time I accepted who I was."

Gods, I hope this works.

Mikey lifted his left hand and opened the doors to his void. He latched onto the Source of Death, using the relic to hold it in place. It resisted, fighting with all its might, but Mikey's will was iron.

You will come out. We will take all the ambient Source within the room, nothing more. If you disobey me, you are never coming out again. Understand?

The reply he received from it was best described as a resigned hiss.

Black tendrils of darkness erupted from the center of Mikey's outstretched palm like hungry serpents released from their cage.

The room erupted with the sounds of chairs scraping against the floor, weapons being unsheathed, and the heavy thud of feet hitting the ground as the leaders prepared for a fight. Mikey's own heart thundered in his ears, almost drowning out the voices of the others. He could see the Coercitors' relics bursting with a rainbow of fiery color from the corner of his eyes, ready to strike him down.

"It's okay. I've got it. I can control it now," he said.

Holy hell, I'm freaking doing it!

Elation filled him, but he shoved it away, afraid to lose focus of his will.

The room fell silent as the tendrils of darkness twisted and writhed, the cavernous chamber becoming a sea of inky blackness. The Conventus leaders, their faces a mixture of shock and fear, exchanged uneasy glances. The queen's expression was unreadable, her eyes never leaving Mikey.

With a deep breath, he focused all his willpower on the darkness within, steering it with his mind. The tendrils began to slow down, bending to his command, and Mikey could sense the room's Source being funneled into the void like paint down a drain, feeding it to his control. The feeling was incredible. Delicious morsels of Source filled his body with strength and energy.

Enough, he stated, closing the doors of the meridian. Mikey would not be lost to the pleasure again.

The tendrils snapped back into his hand like a rebounding rubber band, leaving nothing behind but stunned silence.

Mikey lowered his arm, glancing around the room.

No one moved.

"So...uh." He cleared his throat. "The Devouring are pretty much like that, except bigger, and with the uncontrollable desire to consume everything."

Elder Tem slammed both fists down as he stood up and spat at Elder Cassandra, "You let that monstrosity into our order?!"

Zuri rose to her feet. "That Jaecar," she said as if correcting the man, "saved my brother's life and the lives of everyone here by bringing us this news. And in case your memory fails you, Tem, Mikey is supposed to defeat the creatures locked in the mountain to prevent the world's end. If I recall, he was almost killed because you meddled in their Tribunal."

Mikey's heart swelled with gratitude as Zuri defended him.

"He what?" Izildora glowered at the high councilman.

Tem bristled and then looked pleadingly at the queen. "Your Grace...we didn't know about a prophecy. Just that a half-vampire was trying to join Haven. Members of the council sanctioned the change to the tribunal."

Zuri raised an eyebrow and said, "Yes...members. It was only until after you had done the deed that I was begrudgingly informed of what had occurred."

Mikey noticed three Elders turn their heads abashedly. He was glad to hear Zuri hadn't been involved in the fiasco of their Tribunal.

Tem cleared his throat. "It was a matter beneath your attention. The—"

"Enough," Izildora interrupted with a wave of her hand. "If the boy had died to a pitiful vampire, then he would not be the one of prophecy. The fact he was seen with the Treasurer proves that enough." Whispers broke out again at Laken's revelation, but the queen continued, "Now, you have all seen the darkness lurking within the Verdaat. We cannot take the chance of unleashing it upon us when facing the Devouring. I vote that we exterminate the Verdaat while our other enemy is contained and then, with our combined might with the Tenefae, destroy the remaining darkness as a united front. We will take a vote. All those in favor of my plan raise a hand."

Immediately, most hands rose into the air save for Zuri, Cassandra, two other Jaecar, and Tepen, the leprechaun.

"A vote?" Mikey snarled. "You are taking a vote on whether or not to kill an entire race of people!? My father is one of them. He never harmed anyone!"

"Oh?" Izildora said, bringing a finger to her lips, a sly smile playing across her face. "In all of his six thousand years? Are you sure of that?"

"I—"Mikey hesitated. He guessed the queen knew of his father from her snide tone, probably more than he did.

"I assure you he has. The Verdaat are not people. Not anymore. They are monsters," Izildora replied in an icy, cold tone. "Ones who kill others to survive. And what did I say about interrupting?"

The pressure appeared again around Mikey, and he felt it start to push him down. But he was done being pushed around. The doors to his left hand opened, and he drained the energy. Immediately, the weight lifted.

Izildora blinked slowly as if trying to register what Mikey's abilities really meant. With control over the Source of Death, he was practically invincible.

Mikey finally understood Elder Neema's fear and awe when she'd first examined him. He had the speed, strength, and agility of a Verdaat, with the powers of a Jaecar. No, that wasn't true. Mikey was stronger than a Jaecar. He could control the elements, and soon, he knew, even more.

After being struck repeatedly by Izildora's Source, he started getting a feel for what it was.

The queen could control the very gravity around her.

Elves of the moon...

But even a power so mighty was nothing if he drained it away. And with some practice, Mikey felt he'd be able to mimic her ability.

As the room filled with murmurs of shock and awe, Mikey leveled an unwavering gaze at the silver-skinned fae.

"Izildora," he said, feeling a never before confidence after finally coming to terms with his nature. "I may be young, but I am not a toy to be thrown around at your whim. Or anyone's for that matter." His eyes darted to Tem. "I understand the Verdaat are dangerous and have taken many lives. But you can't exterminate an entire race because of the actions of a few. We need to set aside our biases and face the real evil in this world together." His voice echoed through the chamber, ringing with determination.

The queen's lips pursed into a white slash, her finger tapping on the dais.

"Does anyone wish to change their vote?" she asked those gathered.

Silence.

"You can't—"

"I am queen! I ruled on this earth long before mankind first emerged from the Source! Do not think to tell me what I can or cannot do. Unless you wish to use your dark powers to kill us all here and now?"

He realized what her endgame was.

"No, I'm not going to kill anyone..." Mikey sighed.

What can I do?

Izildora was bent on wiping out Magnus and his people. And she knew he couldn't force these world leaders to do anything.

Then, the queen would accuse me of being a dictator. And most here would start believing Tem that I'm a monster.

The whole point of coming here and holding a Conventus was to bring the people together.

"Good. Then you will stay here with your Omada until we have dealt with the vampires. Afterward, we will unite and rid the world of the Devouring once and for all."

"What?! I'm not staying here," Mikey said, eyebrows drawn close together, snorting in disbelief. "And you can't keep me here."

"You're right. We cannot." Izildora nodded. "I doubt anyone in this room, including me, could stop you. Nor would I want to risk my people in doing so. You are"—a chilling grin appeared across the queen's face—"free to leave."

I don't like that smile on her face...

But he didn't have time to work out what the conniving fae was hiding up her sleeve.

"But your Omada will stay here," she finished.

"Like hell I will. Simon is still Magnus' prisoner," Thomas blurted.

"One more outburst like that, and you will be removed from the order!" Elder Tem snapped. "After your betrayal, you should have been already."

"I don't care about the order," Thomas replied, not backing down against the councilman's sneer. His comment elicited a few melodramatic gasps that made Mikey want to roll his eyes. "Not after seeing what it's really like. And if you morons think you're making the right choice here, let me tell you, you're going to be in for a rude awakening once those things get that Source. I'd at least like to see my brother one last time before I die."

"Same for me," Sabrina joined in.

"And me," Luke said.

"You know what? You have a point, bro." Marcus clapped his brother on the shoulder. "Their plan is going to get us all killed.

Might as well see Simon before we get turned to dust. That's what happens, by the way." Marcus shivered. "You get turned to dust."

Several people and fae squirmed in their seats.

Elder Tem stood. "This is a direct order from a Conventus vote, and thus the high council itself. You do not have the option to disobey. Before you agree to join the order, we make it abundantly clear that no matter if you are still a member or not, you must obey the high council. And we are authorized to use force if necessary."

"With Mikey here, I doubt you'd be able to," Sabrina said, coming next to him. She leaned in and whispered from the side of her lips, "I can't believe you controlled it. You're like...unstoppable now."

"Thanks, I had an epiphany," Mikey replied in the same hushed tone.

"Then we will die trying," Izildora said matter-of-factly before her expression grew serious. "Is that something you'd like to pursue?"

As if to solidify the sentiment, the guards took a few steps toward them, weapons drawn. Mikey felt Source begin to gather around several of the Jaecar.

Dammit, Mikey swore to himself. *What the hell am I supposed to do?*

If he fought against the queen of the light fae and the high council of Haven, he'd never unify everyone.

It all keeps leading back to here. Someone's always gotta be a prisoner.

Elder Cassandra stood abruptly, her chair grinding against the floor. "Are you suggesting we fight a bunch of teenagers?" She scoffed.

"They are...or I should rather say were Jaecar, save for the acolyte," Tem hissed. "That makes them subject to our laws."

"No harm will come to them," Izildora said. "But we need assurances that you will not interfere in our war. Warn Magnus, if you please, that will not make a difference. But I will not have you attack my people. As Avalon is my witness, you will regret it."

"Sabrina," Cassandra said her daughter's name with a pleading edge. "Just cooperate. All of this..." The Elder exhaled, shaking her head. She looked around the room as if searching for the words. "It's just not worth it. They are serious about this. And I can't protect you. Mikey, I appreciate all that you've done. You're a good person like your mother, and I respect you. But you're in a different league than they are. Then all of us are. Think of their futures. Even if we win the fight, what will be left for them after?"

"You're in a different league."

The words stung, reminding Mikey of what Sabrina had said, the reason for their breakup. It was yet another reminder of how alone he was.

No. That's not true. That's old Mikey talking—his anxiety. In reality, Mikey had the best friends anyone could ask for. Most wouldn't give up everything for each other like they did for him.

And what kind of friend would I be if I let them get kicked out of Haven? The organization was as much a way of life for the Jaecar as a job.

Besides, there was nothing they could do to stop the war, and he believed Izildora that they'd be well taken care of. Cassandra wouldn't let her daughter be mistreated.

Mikey didn't know how, but he needed to think of a plan to prevent Izildora from getting her way. First, he would warn Magnus. As much as that idea left a bad taste in his mouth.

With a sigh, knowing what to do next, Mikey addressed his Omada and said, "You guys need to stay."

CHAPTER 10

Thomas interjected first. "No way. I meant what I said about seeing Simon."

"I'll make sure he's okay. Besides, Magnus isn't going to just let you visit him," Mikey replied. Then he added, trying to sound more confident than he felt, "I'll think of a way to free Simon, stop this pointless killing, and bring everyone together." The task seemed as impossible as actually beating the Devourers.

"We can help," Sabrina said.

"Not if helping leads to fighting all of the Clarafae's and Haven's leaders. Stay here, train, and get ready for the battle to come."

"But—" she started, but Mikey held up a hand.

"You know it's the right thing. They aren't going to let you go, and there is not much you guys can do right now except get stronger."

After taking a few seconds to mull over his words, Sabrina deflated.

"He's right," she *tsked*.

"Dammit, we just got together," Luke said. "Who is gonna be the guinea pig for my new and improved decay?"

Mikey snorted a laugh.

"Well, now you've got a relic to unlock and practice with. And I'm sure Marcus would love to volunteer."

"Not it!" Marcus exclaimed. Then he put a hand on Mikey's shoulder and asked, "You sure you're gonna be all right?"

"Yeah. Keep an eye on everyone for me, will ya?"

"Of course, you know they can't function without me," the Shielder quipped.

"I know," Mikey nodded, putting on a smile for his friends. The weight of what he had to do felt more crushing than anything Izildora had thrown at him.

He was grateful for them. They were the reason he was still here. The reason he was able to keep struggling through the chaos that had become his life.

Thomas walked over and whispered, "You better do what you said." He gave Mikey a light tap on the chest. "And"—the Mover looked off to the side, and Mikey swore his cheeks looked redder—"be careful," he mumbled.

Mikey thought about teasing the guy and asking, "What was that?" but thought better of it. Thomas was trying.

"You too," Mikey replied before turning to Izildora and nodding.

"Excellent," the queen said. "I hereby declare the Conventus concluded. I will meet with the war council tomorrow to discuss our next steps. Guards, you may take the young warriors back to Portum's headquarters. I trust you understand your orders, Elder Zuri?"

"Yes, Your Grace," she replied.

The gold elf guards came to usher Mikey's group out of the chamber.

"Not the child of prophecy; I wish to speak with him privately," Izildora commanded.

At seeing his friends about to protest, Mikey assured them, "I'll be fine, go. I'll see you all soon."

The Conventus leaders began making their way around the chamber to the exit. Elder Cassandra leaned in as she passed Mikey and said, "Thank you."

He gave a curt nod.

Tem wasn't nearly as grateful. The man sneered at Mikey the entire thirty seconds it took him to exit the room.

Mikey gave him his best winning smile.

It was forced at first, until he saw a bulging vein appear on Tem's forehead at seeing the smile.

Soon, the chamber was empty save for the queen and two guards behind her. The now sudden quiet was eerie.

She motioned for him to approach.

Mikey swallowed, then did as he was bid.

"Where is the Treasurer?" Izildora asked.

The question was so unexpected it took a second for his mind to register it.

"Uh, I don't know. She left as soon as we got to SHOP."

The queen's unnerving eyes narrowed as if trying to discern whether his statement was true.

"Very well," Izildora replied, straightening. Her tone suggested she believed him. "Laken is the last daughter. It pleases me to hear she is still alive. I've not heard news of her in many years."

"The last?" he said, frowning.

In the vision Avalon had shown him, hundreds of angels were sent out.

They've all died?

"Yes. At least on Earth," Izildora said.

That implied there were others out there in the universe. A fact too big for Mikey to grasp at the moment. They had enough problems on this world.

"Our mother was among the first to perish when the Devouring initially came. And then my sister to"—Izildora's fists clenched as she stared off in the distance as if lost in memory—" to him," she said with derision.

But behind her expression, Mikey could see terrible pain.

He reached out, placing his hand on top of hers in comfort—the guards startled at the gesture, hands immediately on their weapons.

The queen bristled at the contact but waved them back with her free hand.

Her skin was cool and soft as silk.

"I'm sorry," Mikey said with all sincerity. "I know you're older than me in ways I can't even begin to wrap my head around, but all that means is you've had that many years to feel the pain."

Izildora looked down at her hand, then back at Mikey, her eyes softening. She blinked, shaking her head as if trying to wake from a dream. The impassive expression returned.

"Thank you," she said, straightening. "I hope you don't think me a monster for what must be done."

Mikey cursed internally. He felt a fool for hoping that, with the two of them alone, he'd be able to convince the queen to stop her vendetta against the Verdaat.

He sighed, meeting her gaze. "And I hope you won't think the same of me when I put a stop to this pointless war."

Izildora smirked, then nodded. "Very well. You may leave. Until we meet again, Mikey Black."

He inclined his head, and two guards entered to escort him away.

As Mikey was led through the labyrinthine corridors of the palace, he couldn't help but marvel at the opulence around him. The ambiance was entirely different from the area around the portal room. Gold-encased tapestries flanked the walls, each one depicting celestial bodies and mythical creatures in awe-inspiring detail. The floors were inlaid with precious stones of every color imaginable, and the air was heavy with the scent of exotic spices and incense.

It was as if he had been transported to another world entirely—a world of magic and mystery where even the shadows seemed to hold secrets.

The guards opened two large doors. A gust of wind blew at him, and all he saw was white.

The snow outside was thick and pristine, falling gently to the ground in a steady rhythm. It felt like walking through a dream.

He stepped out and turned around, wanting a good look at the building.

The queen's palace stood alone in what appeared to be wilderness, its towering spires disappearing into the gray above.

The doors started to close.

"Wait—" Mikey called out.

Were they just going to throw him out here?

I don't even know where here is.

"Civilization is that way." The pale-eyed elf pointed directly behind Mikey. "I suggest you start walking."

The doors closed with a loud click.

"Of course," Mikey threw up his arms. He understood why Izildora had grinned at saying he'd be allowed to leave.

She probably wanted him to get lost. To wander around the woods while she carried out her plan of annihilating the Verdaat.

He glanced around, trying to get some sort of bearing, but there was only snow and trees.

Mikey knew he couldn't just give up. Not when he still had friends to protect and a world to save. With renewed determination, Mikey set off into the snowy wilderness, hoping to find his way back to civilization and a phone. Ahead of him, the darkness stretched on, and the weight of the world seemed to grow with each step. But he wouldn't stop. Not even the Queen of the Light Fae could keep him down.

Mikey trudged through the seemingly endless white; his footsteps muffled by the powdery blanket that covered the ground. The woods around him were dense, the trees creaking and groaning in the cold wind. He stopped and shook off the snow that had clung to him after what felt like hours of walking, grateful that the cold did little to him.

"This is getting nowhere! I can't see my own hand in front of my face!" he grumbled to the wind.

Everything looked the same, and there was no guarantee he was heading in the right direction. Mikey felt like screaming, frustration climbing up his throat. The weight of the snow that now reached up to his waist seemed to be slowing him down, making it difficult to move with any haste.

The cold wind continued to howl around him, and the snowflakes became dense, blinding him from seeing beyond his immediate surroundings. Mikey took a deep breath and tried to think of a solution as he was pelted by the blizzard.

Blizzard! You're an elemental, duh, his mind said.

Mikey gathered the Source in his right hand and converted it to heat, to fire.

The energy quickly melted the snow, creating a small clearing in front of him.

Now we're talking!

With renewed determination, Mikey continued his walk, using the vague outline of the queen's palace behind him as a guide.

The gnawing hunger came shortly after. Using his Source continuously to create flames quickly drained his reserves. He'd absorbed the ambient Source in the air but that only gave him a few more minutes.

You will obey. Take only a little from these three trees, Mikey commanded, opening the void.

"Yessss," a raspy, sinister voice said from within.

Black tendrils burst forth from the palm of his left hand, wrapping around the base of several trees. They began to wilt as vitalic euphoria filled him.

It might have been his imagination, but Mikey could have sworn he felt their pain through the pleasure.

Enough! He shut off the dark meridian, eliciting a screech from the Edax.

"Sorry," he said, patting the trunk of one of them. It was tall and majestic, and he assumed very old. Several of the branches had turned black and shriveled.

Mikey squinted his eyes, using his vampiric vision to try and see ahead into the night.

There was nothing—just endless trees and snow.

Though using his elemental abilities had greatly improved the trek, it wasn't enough. For all Mikey knew, he was hundreds of miles away from civilization.

Think! He made a list of his abilities and tried come up with a better plan.

Maybe I can—No. Mikey shook his head.

Opening the void and draining all around him while he ran on using the flames was too risky. He didn't feel confident enough of his control of the Edax. Having it out for that long could spell disaster. Besides, it would put the plants and animals around him at risk of dying, and Mikey didn't want that on his conscience.

"Oof," he blurted as a giant pile of snow fell from a tree above, hitting him on his head and shoulders.

Mikey looked up at the now bare branch, and an idea began forming in his mind.

That's it!

He remembered the queen's power over gravity. The crushing weight that brought him to his knees.

What would happen if I used it in reverse?

The idea was crazy but worth a try. Mikey concentrated on the Source within him, focusing on how Izildora's manipulation of it felt.

Slowly, he began to manipulate the force of gravity, gently pulling the snow from the branches above and sending it down toward the ground. It was a delicate balance, but Mikey felt excited by the prospect of the ability.

He practiced again and again, at one point accidentally causing a large tree branch to break off and plummet toward him.

Mikey stepped back, watching it crash into the ground with a loud thud.

"Okay," he whispered to himself, "I'm getting the hang of this."

With newfound confidence, he decided to try the opposite, directing gravity upward. The action was more like blocking the gravity holding him to the earth.

"Whoa!" he exclaimed, throwing his arms outward as his feet began to rise off the ground. But there was no balance. Mikey tried to lean forward, thinking it would propel him in that direction. Instead, he started flipping in the air like an astronaut in space.

Mikey panic-laughed, releasing the gravity control and falling face-first into the chilly white powder below. The snow crunched beneath him as he stumbled to his feet, a big grin splaying across his face.

I did it!

The exhilaration surged through Mikey's veins as he continued experimenting with his newfound ability. He marveled at the thought of soaring through the sky, leaving behind the relentless snow and the endless trees. His friends would be in awe at the sight of him flying. The thrill of defying gravity, like a bird breaking free of the chains that kept it grounded, beckoned him.

Mikey began to practice in little spurts.

He discovered it was possible to split his Source, commanding some of it to wind and some to gravity. After raising a dozen feet in the air, he directed a gentle breeze to push him forward.

It worked. Mikey slowly moved toward his intended direction.

I'm flying. Holy hell, I'm flying!

He increased the intensity of the wind and let out a yell of surprise as he flew through the air in a burst of speed.

Straight ahead was a large Hemlock, with a trunk wider than Mikey was tall.

Stop. Stop. Stop!

He cut off the energy, but not before slamming into the tree with a grunt.

Pain shot through Mikey as he lay sprawled on the ground beneath the Hemlock. He gasped for air as he struggled to catch his breath; the wind knocked out of him. A sharp sting in his left wrist caught his attention, and he looked down to see a small wound bleeding slightly.

"Oops," Mikey muttered, grinning despite the pain. With his vampiric eyes, he saw the stars through the blizzard. They twinkled in the inky black sky above him. There was a newfound sense of freedom in his heart.

He could fly!

Marcus is going to be so jealous.

The elation in Mikey's heart couldn't be contained as he continued experimenting. He played with different combinations of wind and gravity, testing the limits of his control. Each new attempt brought a sense of wonder and excitement as Mikey pushed himself further and further into the skies.

The storm that had been tormenting him for hours began to calm, as if the universe itself was recognizing his newfound power. The snowflakes that still fell became lighter and less menacing as Mikey soared higher and higher, leaving the cold world below.

As darkness fell, the night sky opened to him like a canvas painted with myriad stars. It felt like the cosmos was now within reach as he flew through the heavens, humbled and empowered by his new gift.

Lights in the distance caught his eye.

Civilization! Finally.

It felt like he'd been lost in the wilderness for days, though it was probably only a few hours.

Time to figure out where I am.

The wind whipped through his hair as he descended. Mikey was grateful for not crashing this time. He landed gracefully on the forest floor, taking a moment to ground himself and absorb some Source from the surrounding fauna. With renewed vigor, he shot back into the sky, destination in sight.

CHAPTER II

LORD MAGNUS

"Why have you kept this from me?" Magnus demanded.

Finding out that he'd been kept in the dark about a prophecy, the boy, and what was put inside of him all those years ago had left the Verdaat Lord in a foul mood, especially because one of the very few he trusted—to the extent he trusted anyone—was at the heart of it all.

"For several reasons. Many of which I'm sure you can figure out for yourself," Helena replied. The Queen's gaze, with eyes black as obsidian, bore into him like an arrow.

They have always done that, ever since Magnus could remember. Before he was made into the creature he is now.

"I'd like to hear them from you," he said.

"Fayna—"

"Leave her out of this!" Magnus snapped, long-buried emotions rising like a tempest at the name.

He took a deep breath to calm himself before nodding his head.

"My apologies. I know the pain of your sister's loss is not mine alone."

"But it is still pain that we share," Helena replied softly, her voice tinged with sorrow. "I kept this secret from you because I was afraid. Afraid of your reaction, of what it would mean for my people, for our world. If you had known, it might have changed the course of History. Mikey may not have been born."

"I'm sorry for what I've done to you! But you aren't a monster. Please, stop this, Magnus. Please, live. The world depends on it..." Fayna's words echoed in his mind.

This is what she'd meant.

Through him, Mikey had been born.

The boy who would save us all.

Memories of her, the third and oldest elven sister, his love and greatest sin, had never left him despite all of Magnus' efforts. It was the curse of perfect memory.

"And were it not for the prophecy," Helena continued, "Izildora would have ended your life long ago. She looked up to our sister so much..." She sighed, her expression pained. "So much so that she'd risk the end of the world to avenge her."

The two of them were quiet for a time until Magnus spoke, a sly grin on his face.

"I am not so easy to kill."

He glanced at Excalibur mounted on the wall in his study.

Helena laughed, then said, "As tenacious as you are, my old friend, she could have done it easily enough."

"Well, according to my informants at the Conventus, she will get her chance," Magnus said.

"No. I'm still holding out hope that will change," Helena replied.

"Hope," Magnus snorted, "is no different than a wish, a prayer, a desire. All meaningless."

"Perhaps not to you, but to others, hope is everything," Helena said, her voice soft but firm.

"You can't let yourself believe that," Magnus retorted.

"Why not?" she asked, her eyes challenging him.

He shook his head, the memories of all the pain and betrayal "hope" had brought him over the years flashing through his mind.

"What good would hope have done in curing the infertility of our women? Would a solution have appeared out of thin air? How about these Devourer creatures? If we hope or wish hard enough, will they go away? No. Terms like that lead to inaction, and inaction leads to our downfall. Hope is a seductive illusion that blinds us to the harsh realities of our world."

Helena's expression hardened, her eyes narrowing in response to his bitter words. "You may have lost faith in hope, Magnus, but I haven't. Hope gives us strength when all seems lost. It fuels the determination to fight for a better future. Do you think Okskar was without hope when he sealed the Devourers with his people, guaranteeing the end of the dwarves? Or did he have hope that in their sacrifice, we would be able to stop the creatures and save the world?"

Magnus was silent for a moment, contemplating his friend's words. He knew she had a point, but the bitterness in his heart made it difficult to accept her perspective fully.

"I understand your point, Helena, but hope is not something I can afford to have. My position as leader of the Verdaat requires me to be rational and pragmatic, to make decisions based on facts and not emotions. If hope is an illusion, then I will not be seduced by it."

Helena sighed. "It's a difficult path you walk, my friend. But remember, even in times of despair, there is always a glimmer that can help guide us to a better tomorrow."

Magnus nodded, knowing that Helena would continue to hope for a brighter future, even if he could not join her in that belief.

Action was the only thing that had gotten him anywhere in life. It was when he did nothing that those he cared for suffered.

"Have you heard anything about Mikey?" Helena asked.

"You mean your hope?" Magnus smirked.

The fae Queen's lips pressed together, and she gave him a look of annoyance.

He couldn't help but tease her. The fact Helena put so much faith in the boy was laughable. Yakub's son was talented and yes, his powers unique—not to mention that his DNA might hold the key to his people's flourishing. But Magnus couldn't believe one teenager held that much power. They'd sparred before Mikey left, leaving Magnus impressed but wanting. Besides, if that were the case, the boy would probably see him dead before Izildora.

Magnus could see the irritation in Helena's eyes but quickly realized that he had pushed her too far. He sighed, realizing that he needed to choose his words more carefully.

"I apologize, Helena," Magnus said sincerely. "I did not mean to belittle your belief in Mikey. I understand you see something in him that I cannot. For the sake of us all, I *hope* you are right. The last I heard, he was released from Izildora's custody."

Helena cocked her head. "Released? Interesting..." she said before closing her eyes and lifting a hand toward the slightly open window to her right.

Golden Source streamed from the queen to the outside.

Helena's eyelashes fluttered erratically, eyebrows drawing together in concentration.

Magnus sat across from her, patiently waiting. He'd always envied her ability to commune with nature.

With her eyes still closed, the fae Queen *tsked*, shaking her head. Then, the corner of her lips began to turn up, and she smiled.

Helena opened her eyes and blinked several times until they focused on Magus.

"I take it you found him?" he asked.

She nodded, the sly smile still on her face. "Yes. I believe we'll see him soon enough."

Magnus sighed, knowing Helena all too well. "You're not going to tell me what you found out, are you?"

The fae were fond of games and riddles.

Helena's smile widened. "Where would be the fun in that, Magnus? Besides, some secrets are best kept until the right moment."

Magnus rolled his eyes, but there was a flicker of amusement. "You always did enjoy tormenting me so."

The fae Queen had been cold and callous back then, especially to humans. She'd constantly berate Fayna for taking care of his bedridden frail body.

Oh, how one loss can change everything.

Helena should have hated him for what he'd done. Instead, it had brought them closer. Made them allies.

"I still do, even before you were...altered," she replied with a mischievous glint in her eyes. "But don't worry, I believe now more than ever that Mikey will come through for us all. *If* we lend him our strength."

Magnus leaned back in his chair, studying Helena's face. Her unwavering faith in the teenager intrigued him. If there was anything he knew about the woman, it was that she was no fool. Though none of the sisters had ever divulged the information, Magnus guessed the queens were at least three or four times older than he.

Perhaps there's something to the boy I'd dismissed too easily.

Magnus pondered Helena's words, the possibility of Mikey holding some kind of power he had underestimated. His ability to drain Source was formidable but couldn't be used with precision.

Was that it? Had he figured out how to control it?

That would be a serious threat indeed. Mikey was already a decent elemental Sourcerer. It had been some time since Magnus had fought one of those. The most unfortunate thing was his being raised as a human. Immortality was not a trifling thing. If the mind wasn't prepared and made strong...then madness could follow. The Verdaat Lord knew from firsthand experience.

And with his help, we might be able to figure out how to cure my people and ensure their survival.

"Very well," Magnus said, nodding. "If you believe in this boy so strongly, then I will support him."

Helena inclined her head. "Good."

Magnus clasped his hands together, placing them on top of his desk. "Now, let us prepare for war."

CHAPTER 12

MIKEY

Fairbanks?

Mikey read several signs with the name.

He didn't want to make a scene, so he landed in a thicket of trees on the city's outskirts. It was much larger than he'd originally thought. Tall buildings several stories high rose from the ground, their windows illuminated with a warm glow. People walked hurriedly on the streets, trying to avoid the slow trickle of snowflakes bombarding them.

So, Izildora's domain is in Alaska.

Mikey shook his head, clearing off the snow that clung to it before re-tightening his ponytail and heading toward a gas station.

Thankfully, he still had a few dollars in his wallet from his trip to see Nevra.

"Are you okay, man?" the cashier, a tall, lanky guy who looked barely older than him, asked.

Mikey looked down at himself. His clothes were soaked, and every step brought a squeaky, squishing sound from his sneakers.

"Uh...yeah. Just out for a run," he replied with a shrug. The name Brett was pinned on his shirt, sporting the company's red and white colors.

Brett's eyebrows furrowed together as if he wasn't buying the explanation. "In a blizzard?"

Mikey grinned. The adrenaline from flying still hadn't left his veins. "Yeah. I'm into all that extreme stuff. Jumping out of planes, rock climbing, you name it. Makes me feel alive, ya know?"

"Not really," he snorted. "But whatever floats your boat."

Mikey bought a jerky stick and exchanged a dollar for some quarters.

"Thanks." He waved, then headed outside to the payphone. Arthur needed to know what was going on.

Wait, what time is it?

There was a digital clock against the window of the station. It was almost eleven p.m. With the time change, that put it at two in the morning for Arthur.

His foster father wouldn't care, but Mikey did. The man didn't get enough rest as it was.

Then, an idea came to mind. Mikey returned to the gas station and quickly found what he was looking for.

"Back already?" Brett asked, ringing up the map. "Trying to figure out your next adventure, eh?"

"Something like that," Mikey replied.

He was going to New York to warn the Verdaat anyway. And flying was a much faster way of travel.

Mikey opened the map and memorized his route to get home.

Then, he walked back into the night, draining some nearby Source before shooting off into the sky.

Arthur is gonna freak when he sees me!

Arthur

Arthur woke up to shattering glass, followed by a loud thud in the room above him. He bolted out of bed and reached for his gun. Source gathered around him, solidifying in a shield. The disturbance came from Mikey's room. He hadn't slept well since he'd left, and dreams of the boy being in danger haunted him.

Arthur gingerly stepped out of his room and peered at the top of the stairs.

Quiet cursing reached his ears, followed by the sound of shuffling footsteps.

"Hello," he called out, hope filling his chest.

"Sorry," a familiar voice replied in a guilty tone before Mikey's head and shoulders poked over the railing.

Arthur's heart skipped a beat.

"I tried to fly in through the window to not wake you up. I crashed into it instea—"

Mikey's words were cut off as he lunged up the stairs, wrapping his son in a crushing embrace. Arthur was delighted to hear that Jacob Black was still alive, but it didn't change the fact he would always consider Mikey one of his own.

"I'm so glad you're alright."

Mikey returned the hug, deflating as tears welled up in his eyes. "I missed you, too."

"Wait," Arthur pulled back, tilting his head. "Did you say fly?"

Mikey nodded, lips curling in a wide grin. "Yeah. I did."

CHAPTER 13

MIKEY

"See!"

Mikey could barely contain his excitement as he changed gravity, rising a foot off the ground in their living room. He had learned how to control his Source, to fly and manipulate the elements. Powers he never thought he'd possess, and now, they were his.

Arthur whistled, shaking his head. "Boy, if you were one of those cheesy product ads, it would read: 'Now with all kinds of something else!'"

He laughed. "What gave you that idea? Was it me meeting the goddess of all creation or the fact that the left side of my body is part Devourer?"

Arthur raised an eyebrow. "Don't remind me. I still remember the recluse who wanted nothing more than to stay home and draw monsters."

"Gosh, that feels like ages ago." Mikey shook his head, running a hand through his hair. "Hard to believe it's almost been two years."

He looked around the room, memories flooding back to him. To the days when he was just a normal kid—well, never normal. But there was a quiet life here with Arthur. Now, everything had changed. Mikey had been thrust into a world of gods and fae, which was both exhilarating and terrifying.

"I never imagined that my life could turn out like this," he said, his voice filled with a mix of awe and disbelief.

Arthur nodded, a proud smile on his face. "You've come a long way, son. And I do not doubt you will continue doing great things."

Mikey's excitement was quickly replaced by determination. He knew he had a responsibility now, not just to himself but to the entirety of Otherside. And not just to them, but also to the Saps—the regular people who had no clue what was happening behind the scenes, woefully ignorant of the magical world around them.

"I can't just sit idly by while Izildora starts a genocide and the Devouring gets ever closer to the shard," Mikey said, his voice filled with resolve. "I'm going to Magnus' estate to force him to free my dad and the Jaecar he has prisoner."

An image of Viki popped into his head, and he hoped she was doing okay. It had been almost a week since he'd heard from her.

She's all right, he decided. The Verdaat Lord's daughter was strong and resourceful.

And beautiful...

"Uh, Mikey?" Arthur looked at him quizzically.

His cheeks grew hot, flushing. "Oh, sorry. In my head."

"Thinking about Sabrina?" he asked.

Mikey shook his head. "No...we kind of broke it off. It's a long story, but it's for the best. We're still Omada."

Arthur placed a hand on his shoulder. "Wanna talk about it?"

"No. It's all right, really."

"So you were thinking about a different young woman then?" The Shielder raised a questioning brow, a sly, boyish grin creeping on his face.

Mikey's blush deepened, and he looked away sheepishly. "Well, maybe..."

Arthur chuckled, patting him on the back. "Ah, well, I approve. She's good at keeping you on your toes."

More like off them, he thought, remembering the countless times they'd sparred and she sent him flying.

"That's for sure," Mikey grinned. "But right now, I need to focus on the bigger picture."

"Agreed," Arthur said.

Mikey took a deep breath, his determination resurfacing. "I'm going to Magnus's estate tonight. It's time I end this madness once and for all."

Arthur's eyes gleamed with mirth and pride. "Who are you, and what have you done with my shy, awkward teenager who lives off Pop-Tarts?"

Mikey grinned. "He's still here, just with a few more tricks up his sleeve."

Arthur scratched the grey and white stubble on his chin and snorted, "That you do. That you do. Whelp, I may be old, but I was still a Shielder and an Elder Jaecar of Haven. Let me know how I can help."

"For now, I want you to see if you can get in touch with your contacts on the council and find out what their plans are for the Verdaat."

"Consider it done," Arthur replied with a nod. "I have a few friends who might be able to shed some light on the council's next move."

Mikey's heart swelled with gratitude for the man's unwavering support. They had been through so much together, and Arthur had always been there for him.

"Thanks, Arthur," Mikey said sincerely. "I couldn't ask for a better parent and friend."

The old man swallowed, eyes growing misty. "We're family, Mikey. And family sticks together, no matter what."

Mikey felt a lump form in his throat as he looked at Arthur, overwhelmed by the depth of their bond. It was true—they were family. Their connection went beyond bloodlines and genetics; it was forged through shared experiences, trust, and unconditional love.

"What are you going to do right now?" Arthur asked.

"Sleep," he replied. The night's excitement had begun to wear off, leaving Mikey feeling drained. He needed rest, both physical and mental, for what was to come.

"Good idea. I'll order pizza tonight before you head off."

"Don't forget—"

"I'll order the giant cookie," Arthur interrupted with a laugh. "Get some rest."

After a delicious dinner and a difficult goodbye, Mikey was soaring through the night sky on his way to Magnus' estate. It would only take ten minutes to get there at a moderate speed, and he used that time to solidify his plans. Magnus *would* listen to him. He would make the old vampire if it came down to that.

And what are you going to do after you defeat the Devouring?

Mikey shook his head, trying to clear away that pesky, persistent thought.

A deep-seated anger that would never go away still roiled within him. His teeth and fists clenched at the memory of his mother and that night. At the pointless death.

All because of me.

He let out a pained laugh that disappeared into the whooshing wind.

Sabrina would smack me for thinking like that...

But Mikey couldn't help it. The anger was a part of him now, fueling his determination to protect others from experiencing the same tragedy.

For months, his burning desire to exact revenge on Magnus had been the primary fuel keeping him going. Would he finish the job once it was all said and done?

As Magnus's estate came into view, Mikey descended gently onto the lush courtyard in front of the sliding glass door. The moon cast an eerie glow upon the mansion, its modernized Gothic architecture symbolizing power and dominance.

To the Verdaat's credit, several guards appeared around him.

Mikey raised his hands in surrender, his eyes scanning the guards. Their claws were out, ready for a fight, but he didn't want to resort to violence just yet. He had come here with a purpose and hoped reason would prevail.

"Please," Mikey said, his voice steady but filled with urgency. "I need to speak with Magnus. It's very important."

The guards exchanged uncertain glances, clearly conflicted about whether to let him through or not. The tension in the air was palpable as they weighed their options.

Just then, an authoritative voice echoed from behind them. "You all may go."

Mikey turned to see Magnus walking from the mansion's entrance, his cold eyes fixed on him. The Verdaat Lord looked as imposing as ever, dressed in a tailored suit that seemed to enhance his aura of power. The guards vanished as fast as they'd come, leaving the two of them outside alone.

"Mikey," Magnus said coolly. "You've certainly"—the ancient vampire looked up at the sky where Mikey had come from—"improved."

Mikey met Magnus's gaze, unflinching. "I have, thanks to the help of some very capable people."

Granted, it was mostly from them beating the crap out of me.

"That's not why I'm here. I need you to release my father and the Jaecar you have prisoner."

A smirk played at the corner of Magnus' lips as he stepped forward, his presence commanding. "And why would I do that?"

"Because it's the right thing to do," Mikey replied firmly. "Holding them captive won't solve anything. It only gives the others a reason to perpetuate this war. Bigger things are going on."

Magnus laughed, a cold, heartless sound that sent shivers down Mikey's spine. "The right thing to do? Oh, Mikey, you haven't learned a thing, have you? In this world, there is no such thing as right or wrong. There are only those who hold power and those who don't."

The Verdaat Lord raised an inquiring eyebrow.

"And it seems now that you do. Show me."

Before Mikey could say anything, Magnus lunged toward him with supernatural speed. Mikey's instincts kicked in, and he dodged Magnus' attack, narrowly avoiding the sharp claws that came swiping at him.

"I don't want to fight you, Magnus," Mikey shouted, his voice laced with determination. "But I will if I have to."

Magnus chuckled darkly, circling Mikey like a predator closing in on its prey. "You think you can challenge me? I am the first. You were made from my blood."

Mikey stood his ground, his fists clenched and his eyes filled with fierce determination. "Yes, Magnus, I was made from you. But I am not defined by you. I'm not weak anymore, and I won't let you control me or anyone else."

He tried to push away the anxious knot that formed every time he used the "other" part of him. Despite it seeming to work now, Mikey had never truly felt in control.

No. Not 'other." Just you. It's only you.

He gave the order: *Come out and absorb the Source in the air. Nothing more.*

Mikey didn't know whether ushering the commands actually did anything. But it made him feel more in control.

He opened the void in his left hand. Instantly, dark tendrils erupted from his palm, swirling around Mikey like an oily, obsidian wave. Delicious Source was pulled into the blackness, filling him with energy and euphoria.

Magnus froze, eyes wide.

"*This*, is what we're up against!" Mikey exclaimed, ignoring the rush. "Giant creatures made from death that want to drain all the Source in existence! The same thing inside you and me. Except they're not picky about who they feed on. And if they get to that shard, we're all dead. So goodbye to your little plan to find a cure, rule the world, whatever the hell stupid thing it is you want to do."

Come back.

Mikey pulled at the Edax with his mind, willing it to return. The darkness seemed to resist, if only for a moment, before it reluctantly obeyed.

Black tendrils zipped back into his hand like a recoiling snake. He could feel the raw power coursing through his veins, fueled by the absorbed Source. It was exhilarating and intoxicating, but he knew he had to maintain control.

Magnus stared at him, a mix of astonishment and begrudging respect evident in his eyes. "So it's true. You've learned to control it."

"Yes." Mikey released some of his Source, molding it to manipulate the gravity around him. He rose a foot in the air, hovering. "Among other things."

Mikey cut off the energy, landing on the ground with barely a sound. "Let them go. We can choose to break free from the darkness that consumes us."

The ancient vampire's expression shifted as those words seemed to strike a nerve. The Verdaat Lord's face contorted with a mix of emotions. Then, with incredible speed and strength, he grabbed the sides of Mikey's shoulders. He was about to fight until he saw the mixture of fury, guilt, and sadness in the man's eyes.

"You can never break free!" Magnus snapped. "I know now the plague of my kind. From what the Healer reported and Helena's admission, there is no cure for the countless deaths of our children, for death itself runs in our veins. It is a wonder we can have children at all. They are truly a miracle."

Mikey felt a pang of sympathy for Magnus despite everything. He could see the torment etched in his eyes, the weight of centuries' worth of guilt and regret. But he couldn't let that cloud his purpose, nor could he ever forgive the man for what he'd done.

"Maybe there isn't a cure for what we are," Mikey said, his voice softening. "But that doesn't mean we can't try to make amends, to do better for ourselves and those around us. We can choose to break the cycle of violence and destruction."

Magnus released his grip on Mikey's shoulders. "You speak of ideals, but ideals won't save us from the Devouring," he said, his voice filled with resignation. "Only power."

Mikey stepped forward, his eyes locked with Magnus's, a fierce determination burning.

"Power alone won't cut it, Magnus. It's what we do with that power that matters. We can use it to protect, to heal, to create. We can shape our destiny and change the course of our world."

Magnus scoffed. "And what makes you think you have the answers? A boy less than twenty years?"

Mikey held the ancient vampire's gaze. "Because I've seen the destruction caused by our own choices, our thirst for power. And I refuse to let it continue. I may be young, but I've learned true strength lies not in dominating others, but in finding common ground, in forging alliances. My whole life was spent being rejected by others. I could have become resentful and angry...truth be told, maybe I was a little bit. But I tried to understand what they were going through. Being around me made them sick. Were they wrong for lashing out at me? What would I do in their shoes? Hurting them would have solved nothing. We need to unite, Magnus, against the real threat in that mountain."

The Verdaat Lord regarded Mikey for a long moment before he let out a heavy sigh, the weight of his centuries'-old existence evident in his weary expression.

"Alliances are fragile constructs in this world. They can crumble as easily as they are forged. Even if Otherside could somehow be united and the Devouring vanquished, Izildora would simply seek our eradication afterwards."

"I—" Mikey realized that was probably true. The Clarafae Queen was hellbent on taking out the Verdaat.

"I won't let that happen," he finished.

Magnus put a hand to his chest, stepping back and feigning surprise. "Oh, does that include me? You'll fight for my life?"

Mikey paused, considering Magnus's words carefully. Despite the atrocities committed by the man and his kind, Mikey couldn't deny there was a sliver of humanity buried deep—way deep—within him. Magnus had shown a flicker of vulnerability just now, a glimpse of remorse for the choices he'd made. Perhaps there was a chance for redemption after all.

"I won't make any promises, Magnus," Mikey said, his voice steady. "But I believe people can change. If you're willing to fight alongside us, to protect innocent lives and work towards a better future, then yes, I'll fight for your life as well."

The right corner of his lip turned up slightly. "Interesting. You've definitely *changed*."

Mikey shrugged. "I just accepted who I am and what I'm supposed to do. Since it seems no one else will."

Magnus stared at Mikey for a long moment, his gaze piercing and searching. There was a flicker of something in those ancient eyes, a glimmer of hope amidst the darkness. Slowly, he nodded, a subtle acknowledgment of the path that lay ahead.

With a sharp inhale, Magnus nodded. "Very well. You'll be glad to know that your father and the sorcerers have already been released."

"Just like that?" Mikey asked, genuinely surprised.

"As I said before, I've come to the realization there is no cure for my people, so the Healer's captivity is pointless," Magnus shrugged. "Normally, I would kill them to prevent word getting out, but..."

"Let's just ignore that last part and focus on the fact you did the right thing," Mikey said, trying to resist the urge to drain the man.

"All right. And your father will be needed for the fight to come. Helena and I have put the word out to all of our allies to prepare for war. Already, several of my people have been slain. I had my suspicions the Clarafae have been keeping track of the Verdaat, and now they've been confirmed. My orders are for everyone to make their way here. It will take at least a day or two for most of our forces to gather. That way, they'll have to come to us to fight."

Mikey nodded, a sense of urgency washing over him. He knew their time was limited, and every passing moment brought them closer to oblivion.

They needed to act swiftly.

Then, an odd thought occurred to him, and Mikey snorted a laugh. He thought if anyone had joined him, it would be the light fae and Haven. Instead, it was Magnus himself who had agreed to fight alongside Mikey.

He even released my dad and the others. The world certainly had a funny way of surprising him.

"I take it you have some sort of plan?" Magnus asked.

"Yeah," Mikey exhaled, nodding. "But it might just doom us all anyway."

CHAPTER 14

Mikey had a plan—a desperate one. But part of it was so terrible that he wasn't sure he'd be brave enough to go through with it.

Regardless, he needed Laken for that part. Where had the little angel disappeared off to?

I'll deal with that choice when the time comes.

Mikey shook his head, focusing on the present.

"Mikey!" a voice called from behind, and the worries slipped away.

He turned, joy flooding him.

"Dad!"

Mikey's heart swelled with relief as he rushed toward his father, Jacob Black, enveloping him in a tight embrace. The weight of their separation seemed to dissipate at that moment.

"I'm so glad you're all right," Mikey choked. "Part of me doubted that Magnus actually let you go."

His father pulled back slightly, a wistful smile etched on his face. "He did."

Mikey nodded, his eyes shining with gratitude. "I'm glad you're here. We're going to need every ounce of strength we can muster."

Jacob's gaze shifted toward Magnus, who stood in the doorway, observing the reunion with an inscrutable expression. Mikey could sense the tension between the two, but he also saw a flicker of understanding pass between them. They'd been together for thousands of years, a length of time Mikey couldn't really fathom.

Yet.

But only if they could save the world.

"Thank you," Jacob said, his voice filled with sincerity as he extended a hand toward Magnus.

The ancient vampire hesitated momentarily before reaching out and clasping Jake's hand. It was a simple gesture, but it held a weight that went beyond words.

"We have a common enemy," Jacob continued, his voice unwavering. "Despite our past differences, we must put them aside and fight together once again."

Magnus nodded solemnly. "Agreed."

"So," his father said, clasping his hands together, "how bad are these things?"

"World ending," Mikey said. There was no embellishment in his voice.

"That bad, huh?"

Mikey nodded, taking a few steps back. He took a deep breath, squelching the anxiety before uttering the words of command to himself and lifting his left hand, unleashing the Edax.

His dad leaped back wide-eyed and stunned as he witnessed the dark, serpentine energy pouring from Mikey's hand. The Edax twisted and writhed, hungry for power and eager to be unleashed upon the world. Still, it whispered, trying to entice him.

Mikey fought against the pull, tightening his grip on the power. His voice wavered slightly as he spoke to his father, trying to steady himself.

"It's the Devouring. Or at least a small part of one. Some are as big as this mansion, born from the god of death, Greel, and their only desire is to consume all Source. They get bigger and stronger as we fight them, draining the energy from our attacks."

Mikey closed off the void, bringing the tendrils back into him.

Before he could continue, several familiar faces began entering the room: Brittania, Mogrin, and a few of the oldest Verdaat he'd been introduced to when he was a captive. Not wanting to give anything away about the help the goblin and Amazon had given him to escape, Mikey gave them all respectful nods as they filed into the space Magnus had called his War Room.

Just in time.

He was concerned about whether the others had seen his display but shrugged it off. They'd see it eventually, anyway.

Maybe I should show everyone to get them prepared for a Devourer?

Then, Viki strode into the room, and all his thoughts disappeared. He'd asked Magnus about her after their talk in the courtyard. Of course, she'd been fine, just as he had predicted.

But seeing her in person, the relief was overwhelming. Viki's eyes widened as she took in the sight of Mikey standing there, alive and well. Her ruby lips curled into a small smile, a mixture of disbelief and happiness shining in her gaze.

"Mikey," she breathed, crossing the room in a few swift steps to throw her arms around him. He held her tightly, burying his face in her jet-black hair, taking in her scent. The world around them seemed to fade away, leaving only the two of them and their shared moment of solace amidst the chaos.

"Viki," he whispered, his voice filled with a longing that had been pent up for so long. "I missed you."

Tears welled up in Viki's eyes as she pulled back to look at him. "I missed you too," she admitted, her voice trembling with emotion.

She stiffened suddenly, pulling away.

"You have a girlfriend. I'm sure Sabrina wouldn't—"

"That's...over," Mikey interrupted. It felt strange saying those words, yet at the same time, they felt right.

Viki's eyes widened in surprise. "Oh."

Mikey could see the questions swirling in her mind, but he didn't have the energy to explain everything just yet. Bigger things were at stake, and he needed Viki by his side for what was to come.

"Viki," Mikey said firmly, taking her hands in his. "I need your help. Besides me, you're the only one here who really knows what we're up against."

Viki nodded, her gaze filled with determination. "Whatever you need, Mikey. I'm with you until the end."

His heart swelled with gratitude and...*love?*

Mikey squeezed Viki's hands, feeling a warmth spread through his chest. He had always cared for her deeply, but now, in this moment of imminent danger, he realized just how much she meant to him. She'd been there for him through everything. She defied her father, twice—a man who would lock a family member away for decades as punishment for disobedience.

"Thank you," he said softly, squeezing her hands. "I don't know what I would do without you."

"Neither do I," she said, a sly smile playing at her lips.

They released each other and joined the others in the War Room, where Magnus stood at the head of a long table covered with maps and strategic documents. Mikey took his place beside his father, feeling a strange sense of unity as they gathered around their common goal.

Magnus cleared his throat, commanding everyone's attention. "Now that we're all here," he started, then looked at Mikey, "it's time you to explain your plan. I've already informed the ancients on what happened to the dwarves."

The letter!

In the chaos of the last week, he'd practically forgotten about it.

"So, you could read it?" Mikey asked.

"Yes." Magnus nodded before filling him in on its contents. It was pretty much what he and the others had already assumed.

"Well..." Mikey stammered as all eyes were on him, waiting to hear the plan.

He froze, his mouth suddenly feeling dry.

"I—" All thoughts flew out of his mind like birds startled from a tree.

Their expectations bore down on him, threatening to drown him in doubt and uncertainty.

But then, Mikey felt Viki's hand slip into his, her fingers intertwining with his own. A rush of warmth and reassurance coursed through him, reminding him that he wasn't alone. He met his father's eyes. Jake gave an encouraging nod. Together, they could face anything.

Mikey took a deep breath, summoning the courage that lay dormant within him.

"Izildora wants the Verdaat eradicated. Her hatred for Magnus runs so deep that she's willing to risk the world's fate to get revenge. I tried to convince her to put that aside but I failed."

Mikey paused, studying the faces of those gathered around the table. Determination filled his heart as he continued, his voice steady and resolute.

"The dwarves sacrificed themselves, knowing that if the Devouring escaped, we'd be done for. We can't let that be in vain. Because they were right. There is only one way we get out of this alive: if Otherside, and I mean all of Os, bands together to fight."

"How do you propose we do that, given what you just said? And how do we kill these creatures? I heard you defeated one?" Brittania, always direct and to the point, asked.

Mikey smiled, glad to see the Amazon was doing well. He glanced at each person in the room, his eyes locking with theirs, one by one.

"Yes, I did. Inside a Devourer is a crystal of Source that grows as more energy is taken in. The only way to kill them is by shattering it, which is easier said than done. They can move it around inside their hulking forms. Attacks with Source seem to scatter the void-like ichor they're made of, but it also strengthens them as they absorb it. We'll have to devise a way for the Verdaat to help fight them. Claws and strength will do little unless we can expose the crystal."

"I see," Brittania nodded, absorbing the information.

"And to answer your first question, we'll bring Otherside together by giving Izildora an opportunity she can't resist," he answered before turning to the goblin who had done so much for him. "Mogrin, can the goblins make a portal to a specific location?"

CHAPTER 15

It turned out they could make a small portal, but it would take half a day to prepare it. Creating pathways between different locations on the physical plane was " tricky business," in Mogrin's own words.

There was only one person who had seemed to do it effortlessly.

Mikey wished they'd be able to get it done faster, but, to quote something Arthur would often say, "it was what it was."

Instead, he focused on spending time with those he loved.

Viki stood beside Mikey, her hand firmly clasped in his. Jake walked beside them. They wandered through the lush gardens of the mansion, finding solace in the fragrant blooms surrounding them. The air was thick with anticipation and uncertainty, but at this moment, they allowed themselves a reprieve from the weight of it all. It was an hour or so before sunrise, but thankfully, the forecast was cloudy. Already, the nimbi began to creep their way above.

As they walked, Mikey couldn't help but steal glances at Viki, her beauty illuminated by the moon's soft light that had yet to be blanketed. He marveled at her strength and resilience, her unwavering faith in him and their cause. Viki was a constant presence, a source of comfort and hope in all the chaos and danger surrounding them. And after finding out what happened between Sabrina and him, the yellow-eyed vixen continued to wiggle deeper into his heart. She'd inserted herself by his side, and somehow, it just...fit.

"So," his father started, inclining his head to the both of them. "When did *this* start?"

"Oh, it started a while ago." Viki grinned, nudging Mikey with her shoulder. "Wonderboy here just needed to realize it."

"Is that so?" His father laughed. "Well, I'm happy if you're both happy."

Mikey blushed, but a smile tugged at the corner of his lips. He couldn't deny the truth in her words. Their connection had been building over the last several months, even if he hadn't fully recognized it until now. He'd always have a place in his heart for Sabrina. No matter what, they were Jaecar, an Omada, hunters, and protectors of the innocent. And most important of all, friends. But she had been right; he wasn't human, not entirely. Mikey belonged in both worlds, three if you counted the blissfully ignorant one of the Saps. It wasn't so long ago that that world had been all he'd known. Yet, Mikey also felt like he didn't actually fit into any of them. Viki was similar in that regard. A young woman thrust into modern society, surrounded by ancients who lived in the past.

But in each other, they had found a kindred spirit, someone who understood the complexities of their existence in a way no one else could.

"I'm going to head back inside and get a drink," Jake said, putting a hand on Mikey's shoulder. From the corner of his eye, he caught his father's wink.

Mikey watched him disappear back into the mansion, his footsteps echoing faintly in the quiet of the night. He turned to Viki, a soft smile playing on his lips. "I can't believe how much everything has changed in such a short amount of time," he murmured. The weight of their impending battle loomed heavy on his shoulders.

"And I can't imagine going through all this without you," Mikey confessed.

When her dazzling yellow eyes met his, a softness in their depths made his heart skip a beat.

"Well, since you've finally come to your senses, now you won't have to," she quipped, smirking.

Mikey chuckled, feeling a warmth spread through him at her teasing. She always had a way of lightening the mood, even in the darkest times.

He reached out and gently brushed a strand of hair away from Viki's cheek, his touch tender and full of unspoken emotion.

Viki's eyes sparkled as she leaned into his touch, a gesture that filled Mikey with an overwhelming sense of affection and longing. In that fleeting moment, the world around them seemed to fade away, leaving only the two standing in the moonlit garden, lost in each other's presence.

"I never thought I'd find someone who truly understands me," Viki whispered, her voice barely above a breath. "But then you came into my life, Mikey, and everything just... brightened."

The last ray of moonlight seemed to cast its beam on her, illuminating Viki's face with an ethereal glow. Mikey was captivated by her beauty, feeling a surge of emotions. At that moment, surrounded by the fragrant blooms and the hushed whispers of the night, he knew he had found a love he had never experienced. It was a love born from understanding, acceptance, and shared destiny. When the darkness had almost taken hold, she'd loved him. When he'd pushed her away, she'd given him space. Over and over, no matter what, Viki had supported him.

He reached for her, gingerly caressing her cheek before grabbing the back of her neck. Mikey pulled her close, their lips only inches apart. "I love you, Victoria Moon Shooting-Star Philopator."

She laughed, "That's not—"

Her rebuttal was interrupted when his lips touched hers.

Viki's laughter melted into a soft sigh as she returned the kiss, her arms wrapping around Mikey as though she never wanted to let go. Everything froze, the world falling away around them as they lost themselves in each other. Viki broke off the kiss. She smiled a beautiful, wide grin that made his heart yearn to see it again. "I love you too, Mikey Wonderboy Black." She flicked his nose before pulling him down for another kiss.

The last flicker of moonlight bathed them in its gentle glow, casting a romantic aura over the garden as their hearts beat in unison. The light was snuffed out as they pulled away, the dark clouds finally engulfing the sky. Their eyes met, and a silent understanding passed between them.

They stood there, hand in hand, a sense of peace settling over them, anchoring them in the present moment. The weight of impending doom threatened to overwhelm Mikey, but with Viki by his side, he could push it away and enjoy the moment, the solace in the simple beauty of being together with someone he loved.

CHAPTER 16

"I forgot how stuffy this place was," Viki said, tugging at her already-dampening shirt.

"Yeah, it's times like these that I'm grateful I don't have as sharp senses as you," Mikey replied.

The stench of mud and stale water made even more pungent by the heat still wasn't pleasant with his duller faculties.

"Do you think she'll be happy to see us?" Viki asked as they began their way through the swamp.

"If last time was anything to go off of...probably not," Mikey chuckled.

It had been a few weeks since they'd last seen the Gwyllion. So much had happened since then.

"She seemed to be good friends with Laken," Viki said.

"Yeah," he nodded, his mind going back to the last time he'd seen the fairy.

Where is she?

Without the key, Mikey wouldn't be able to carry out his kamikaze plan. He just had to hope they'd find her or that she'd show up soon.

They reached a familiar land bridge surrounded by a dark, murky marsh. Bubbles appeared on the water's surface to his right, and a shell appeared in its stead.

"Not these guys again," Viki *tsked* as more ripples appeared followed by corresponding green and brown domes. The shells moved toward them before several boggarts stood in front and behind.

"Take us to see Nevra," Mikey ordered.

One of the turtle-frog creatures, the one closest to Mikey, narrowed its eyes.

"Tek huk!" it shouted, stomping its feet.

"Oh no you don't!" Mikey snapped. He poured Source into his right hand, manipulating the gravity around them. The boggarts fell to the ground as energy pressed down. Croaks and grunts of protest filled the air. Mikey maintained his concentration, determined to show them he meant business.

A loud banging sound came from the other side of the land bridge.

He looked up to see the Boggart Chief, rapping his staff on what looked like a primitive drum, alligator hide stretched over a large wooden bowl.

Mikey released the Source, and the boggarts eagerly dove into the water. The Chieftain turned and disappeared deeper into the marsh.

"Well, it's a warmer welcome than last time," Viki snorted. "And that power of yours is something else. Do you think the goddess had anything to do with that?"

Mikey knew she had. Something changed when Avalon touched him and calmed the raging void within. Not only could he feel the Source more intensely, but also what the energy was doing, how it was being used. And he could copy it.

Mikey nodded. "Yeah, she did."

Avalon bestowed upon him a gift he had yet to fully comprehend. But it was yet another thing to separate him from everyone else. The more unique he became, the greater the burdens that piled onto his shoulders.

Viki put a calming hand on his arm. Mikey didn't know if she guessed how he felt, but it didn't matter.

The act was just the reassurance he needed.

Mikey was grateful for the opportunity to be with her. His father had been called upon to lead one of the Tenefae armies. A role he'd apparently filled in the past as the third oldest living vampire. That fact was still hard for Mikey to wrap his head around.

And it's up to me to make sure those armies are fighting for the world, not for slights of the past.

Gods, why did it have to be him, though?

"Chance," Nevra had told him. *"Complete chance."*

You're just the lucky winner of the worst lotto in the world, Mikey.

He shook his head, looking toward the basin's center and his goal.

They reached a massive mangrove tree with a hut carved within its base a few minutes later. The wooden front door was open, and a giant elderly woman with horizontal slits for eyes stood in the entryway, arms folded.

"I was wondering when you would come back," Nevra said.

"You know us, always fashionably late," Mikey replied with a grin, trying to lighten the mood. He needed the Gwyllion's power to form portals if his plan had any chance of success.

Nevra's expression didn't change as she stepped aside to let them enter the dimly-lit hut.

"What brings you back to my humble abode?" Nevra asked, her voice deep and resonant.

"We need your help," Mikey said, stepping forward. "The Devouring has returned, but Izildora would rather start a war to wipe out the Verdaat than band together to fight it."

Nevra's eyes darkened at the mention of the Devouring. She paced back and forth in her hut, her long, gnarled fingers tapping against her arm. The atmosphere grew heavy with tension as she contemplated Mikey's words.

"So my sister's words are true." The swamp woman looked down, lips pursed. "I've got no love for the vampires, but the Devouring...that is a threat that transcends anything else. What is it you'd have me do, young one? Know that I will not be a part of harming any fae. It is not my place."

Mikey nodded, relieved to have Nevra's support despite her reservations. "We need your help to fight the Devourers at the dwarven mountain. Where you sent us last time," he explained earnestly. "And—" he continued, uncertain how the Gwyllion would react, "I'd like to get a sense of how your power works. I...think I can copy it."

Nevra's slitted eyes widened in surprise at Mikey's request. She studied him for a long moment as though searching for the truth in his words. Finally, she nodded slowly.

"I see the goddess has truly gifted you. Good. Perhaps you are The Child of Balance."

There was something about those words that irked him. The words that Avalon had said.

Child. That was it. After everything he'd been through and the terrible things yet to come, putting that responsibility on a kid was cruel. And would that kid still be one afterward?

Mikey's thoughts were troubled as he absorbed Nevra's words. Being labeled as the "Child of Balance" only added to the weight on his shoulders.

Nothing was balanced. The whole damn world was in chaos. But there was little time for self-doubt or hesitation in the face of their impending threat.

Nevra observed the conflict in Mikey's eyes, the burden of his destiny evident in his troubled expression. She reached out a hand, larger than his head, and placed it gently on his shoulder; her touch was surprisingly warm despite her appearance.

"Do not underestimate the power within you, young one. Embrace it, for it is the key to restoring this world," she said softly, her voice filled with ancient wisdom and reassurance.

Mikey felt a surge of determination coursing through him at Nevra's words. He nodded, resolve solidifying within him. If he was to fulfill his so-called destiny, he knew he had to confront the challenges ahead with courage and conviction. Even though what he really wanted was to be back in his room, drawing monsters and the macabre, with no knowledge of Os. In a world where his mom and dad were both happy and alive. With Arthur, the man who had saved his life and given him a family again. No Devouring, no gods, no evil thing inside him that, if he was completely honest with himself, he sometimes wanted to give in to.

But that also meant no powers or flying through the air. No Mogrin, changelings, or even Viki...The world would be so much duller if the supernatural weren't real.

No, that couldn't be his life. Mikey had a world to save, responsibilities to fulfill, and a destiny to embrace. He straightened his posture, meeting Nevra's gaze with newfound determination. "Let's do this," he declared, the weight of his words echoing in the dimly lit hut. "Can you make a portal? It doesn't matter where. I just want to get a feel for how you're using Source."

The Gwyllion nodded in approval, the corners of her eyes crinkling in a semblance of a smile. With a wave of her hand, the air around them shimmered, and a gateway began to materialize before them. It glowed with a soft, ethereal light.

"Now, manipulating time and space requires a delicate touch," Nevra cautioned, her voice stern yet reassuring. "As well as extensive knowledge of the physical world. But something tells me that won't be necessary with you."

Mikey stepped forward, feeling the pull of the portal's energy tugging at his very core. Closing his eyes, he walked around it and tried to sense what was happening. The Source was ripping at—no, punching through the fabric of reality, creating a hole to another location.

With a deep breath, Mikey focused on the sensation, letting whatever it was that Avalon altered inside him do its thing. The air crackled with static electricity as Mikey's right hand hovered near the portal, his brow furrowed in intense concentration. After several moments, his hand began to emit a soft blue light mirroring the portal's glow before him. The energy flowed from him and intertwined with the Source, harmonizing in a symphony of power.

Amazingly, just as he'd done with gravity, Mikey was able to manipulate his Source to alter space and time. Nevra waved her hand, and the portal vanished.

The temporal power in Mikey's palm did not, however. A bolt of energy arced from his hand, shattering a large clay pot in the corner. Smoke rose from the irregular, charred pattern on the mud brick where it struck. Another bolt burst free, breaking a chair leg.

Crap! The Source was growing more unstable. There was one tiny bit of information he should have asked before trying to copy Nevra's ability.

"So," Mikey shouted over the increasing crackles. "How do you set the portal's location?!"

Nevra shook her head. "The science of that answer would take too long to explain. I'd wager all you need to do is imagine where you want to go. But it must be somewhere you've been before. Use your Source to open a path there!"

Mikey's mind raced as he tried to envision a location he had visited before. The memory of Arthur's cozy living room flashed before his eyes, filled with warmth and safety. With a surge of determination, he focused on that image, channeling the power of the Source within him to open a path to that familiar place.

The air crackled with energy as Mikey's hand glowed brighter, the temporal power pulsating increasingly. With a final push of will, he directed the energy flow toward creating a direct connection to his home.

The room quaked with power as the portal began to form, its edges shimmering with a light blue light. Mikey swallowed, his heart racing with anticipation as he took a step forward. "Wait," Viki said, stepping up beside him and taking his hand. "Let's go together."

"Together," he nodded with a grin.

He'd made a freaking portal!

Oh no.

Panic rose in his chest. *He* made the portal.

What if I screwed up and we disintegrate?!

She squeezed his hand, and he drew strength from her presence.

"On three?" Viki said, taking a deep breath.

He nodded, noting how cute it was she held her breath like he did.

Together, they stepped into the portal. There was a slight feeling of displacement, but nothing more.

Mikey looked around at the familiar items that decorated his living room.

"Dammit, son! How many heart attacks are you gonna try and give me in one week?" Arthur snapped from the corner of the room.

He suppressed a laugh at his foster father's reaction. The man was a legendary hunter but probably never had a portal appear in the middle of his house.

"Sorry," Mikey said, grinning sheepishly. Even though he felt bad for startling Arthur, it was comforting to be back in his own home, even if only for a moment.

But more importantly...

It worked!

Arthur's grumpiness couldn't calm the rising tide of excitement that filled him.

Mikey couldn't contain his elation as he realized the extent of his newfound power. The ability to manipulate the Source and create portals to different locations opened up a world of possibilities. He turned to Viki, a wide grin spreading across his face.

"I did it! I really can copy abilities!" he exclaimed, his words filled with triumph and wonder. Though he could feel the act had taken a tremendous amount of Source. A hunger for more of the energy started to gnaw at him, but Mikey shrugged it off, too excited.

Viki beamed at him, her eyes reflecting pride and admiration. "I knew you could do it," she said, squeezing his hand affectionately.

Arthur, though still grumbling about the unexpected portal in his living room, couldn't hide the glimmer of pride in his eyes as he watched Mikey's accomplishment. "Well, I'll be damned," he muttered under his breath, a hint of a smile playing on his lips. "This was you?" He inclined his head toward the dissipating portal.

Mikey nodded.

"Amazing," Arthur scoffed, shrugging and shaking his head as if nothing could surprise him anymore. "Looks like you're starting to figure your abilities out."

"Hopefully, it'll be enough," Mikey replied.

Arthur gave a solemn nod; then, he turned to the young woman at his side. "Oh my, where are my manners? Nice to see you again, Miss Viki. You make sure to look out for each other, all right?"

"Yes, Mr. Cafferty. Good to see you. Don't worry, protecting Mikey is my top priority." She smirked at him and added, "Even though he makes it really tough sometimes."

Arthur chuckled at Viki's words, his eyes twinkling with a mixture of humor and fondness. "Well, I can see that hasn't changed then," he said with a shake of his head. Turning back to Mikey, he became serious once more. "You've got a lot ahead of you, son. Is the plan still on for tomorrow?"

"Yeah," Mikey replied. "Be ready."

Arthur snorted. "Oh, I will. It's not like it'll be tough to spot the swirling portal in my living room."

"True," Mikey chuckled, shrugging.

There was a moment of quiet tension between the three as the reality of tomorrow's events hung in the air.

A loud grumble broke the silence, and Mikey winced, embarrassed.

"Sorry, I'm starving. Creating the portal took a lot of Source."

Arthur laughed, then headed toward the kitchen. He grabbed a box from the cupboard, and Mikey's mouth started to water.

"Are those wild berry?" Mikey asked.

"Sure are," Arthur said, grinning. "Seems like the one thing that will never change is your sweet tooth." The Shielder opened the box and removed the silver foil wrapping, before popping the delicious pastries into the toaster.

"Guilty," Mikey chuckled.

Thank goodness for that. If he had to subsist on nothing but the Source in blood like Viki and his father...

Arthur looked to the yellow-eyed vampire, then frowned. "I'm sorry...I don't have anything that would—fit your tastes," he finished. By the expression on his face, it was clear the old man was trying not to offend.

She waved him away. "Oh, it's fine. I filled up before we left. Wonderboy here is the one who's hungry all the time."

At the mention of a sweet tooth, Laken came to mind. He'd meant to ask Nevra whether she'd seen the tiny fairy and reminded himself to do it when he returned to her swamp.

But first, Pop-Tarts.

CHAPTER 17

"No, I've not seen her," Nevra answered, pouring herself a drink from a pot hanging over the firepit in her hut. "Though from what you've told me, it is likely she is resting near the other piece of the goddess."

Mikey's mouth fell open.

"There's another piece?"

The Gwyllion nodded. "Very small, about the size of a fist."

Mikey noted that a fist to the large woman was more like a boulder to him.

"It is in my sister's domain. Our mother placed her in charge of it because she's older," Nevra *tsked*, then huffed, "Bah, by only a thousand years!"

Mikey's mind raced with the new information. Another piece of the goddess existed, and it was under the care of Nevra's elder sister, a Gwyllion Arthur had dealings with in the past. The thought of different pieces scattered throughout the world filled him with a sense of urgency. Each piece held immense power, and if the Devourers got a hold of one...

"Are there any more?" Mikey asked.

"Not that we know of," Nevra replied. "I haven't spoken to Orsa in ages, but she contacted me the other day and said a Devourer had returned and that she killed it trying to get the piece."

Mikey's stomach lurched at the news. Had they escaped the mountain already? Or was this a rogue creature like the one they'd fought? If it was the latter, were more coming?

No, he'd know if they escaped. Magnus had people watching the mountain to make sure. Mogrin had given him a special, unhackable phone just in case. If the Devouring had broken free, it would be ringing incessantly.

A flicker of hope rose in his chest at the revelation that Nevra's sister had killed a Devourer. His entire Omada, himself included, had barely survived fighting one. If one of the powerful fae was able to defeat one by herself—

I need to find Laken and get Orsa's help.

Time was running out. How perfect it was then that he now had the ability to create pathways to anywhere he'd been and the support of an ancient and powerful half-angel fae who could do the same?

"Can I talk to Orsa? I also need to see Laken. She has something important."

Nevra hesitated, her gaze flickering with uncertainty. "I'm not sure that's a good idea, Mikey. Orsa is...unpredictable."

Mikey's determination hardened in his eyes. "I have to try. Laken has the key to open the mountain. Without it—"

Nevra sighed. "Fine. I'll send word to her." She eyed him warily before adding, "Just be careful. Orsa is not as sweet as I am."

Mikey thought of Marcus. The Shielder would have made a quip at Nevra's comment. A pang shot through him. He hoped his friends were doing okay.

Mikey nodded to Nevra in thanks.

The Gwyllion walked over to a small shelf and gingerly plucked out what appeared to be a round purple crystal, nestling between her thumb and forefinger. Nevra poured Source into the item, and it began to glow.

Mikey and Viki shared a glance as the large woman appeared to have a silent conversation with who they presumed was her sister. Nevra's face flashed with annoyance several times and Mikey was pretty sure he caught an eyeroll.

Orsa must be quite a character, Mikey thought as Nevra finished the communication with a frustrated sigh. The purple crystal dimmed, returning to its normal state. Mikey cleared his throat, shifting his weight nervously from one foot to the other.

"So...?" he prompted, wanting to know what Orsa had said.

Nevra fixed him with a stern look before speaking. "Orsa has agreed to meet with you. But she is very tired. Fighting the Devourer took much of her strength."

Mikey felt a surge of gratitude towards Nevra for convincing her sister to meet with him despite her exhaustion. He knew the importance of the mission at hand and didn't want to waste any time in gathering information that could potentially save their realms from the threat of the Devourers.

"Be careful what you say. My sister is especially cranky when she's tired. Wouldn't want our savior being turned into a toad right before the big fight," Nevra added.

There was an awkward pause, and Mikey scratched his head, laughing, "The Source can do amazing things, but it can't do that, right?"

Nevra didn't laugh.

Mikey's brows furrowed. "Right?"

Nevra's expression remained serious, and she simply replied, "You'd be surprised at what the Goddess's essence can do. Tread carefully." With that caution hanging in the air, she gestured for them to follow her outside. The cool breeze carried the scent of damp earth.

Nevra waved her hand, materializing a portal.

"I'll need to conserve my Source for the battle tomorrow. Remember, I will *not* fight the fae. On *either* side."

He nodded, then replied, "If my plan works, no one will. Thanks for your help."

Mikey gave Viki's hand a squeeze and stepped through.

They found themselves in a dimly lit cavern. The air was thick with the smell of moss and damp earth, and a faint glow emanated from clusters of bioluminescent mushrooms growing along the walls. Various shelving and pieces of furniture were scattered about them.

Mikey felt a surge of Source from behind. He turned swiftly, activating his vampiric vision and lifting out his left hand, opening the void. A twisting whirl of violet energy was sucked in. Mikey shivered blissfully at the sensation. Gods, it felt so good.

"*Mooorrrre,*" darkness whispered from within.

"Mikey, there's someone there!" Viki's voice cut through the euphoria, bringing him to the present. In the pleasure, he'd entirely missed the glowing purple silhouette hidden in the cave's shadows.

"Hmm," the figure croaked. The voice was raspy yet high-pitched and clearly feminine. "Of course, my sister would bring you right into my living room." The figure snorted. "Your abilities seem potent enough. Had you not stopped that attack, you'd be slithering on your belly right about now."

Stepping forward cautiously, Mikey tried to make out the woman's features. The purple glow surrounding her made her seem ethereal and otherworldly. Her eyes were like twin orbs of amethyst, piercing through the darkness. Oddest of all was that the woman was only a few feet tall. Mikey returned his vision to normal, and details of her came into focus. She was sitting on a bed carved into the rock. Small in stature, Orsa had gnomish features with an oversized, bulbous nose and wavy grey hair that fell to the middle of her back. Though not as pronounced as a gnome, the top of her head came to a rounded point. All the Gwyllion needed was some missing teeth, and the term "swamp hag" would be truly fitting. She looked nothing like her large, burly younger sister.

Maybe they have different fathers?

That wasn't a question he felt comfortable asking.

"Orsa, I presume?" Mikey said, bowing his head respectfully.

The ancient Gwyllion regarded him, her expression a mixture of annoyance and curiosity. But behind her eyes, Mikey could see exhaustion.

That fight must have taken a lot out of her.

Orsa tilted her head. "Interesting. Most would not take being attacked with a curse so nonchalantly."

"Curse?" Mikey raised a brow.

Orsa waved her hand dismissively. "The name humans give to powers they don't understand. The act of stopping my Source in such a way gives credence to who you are, Child of Balance."

Mikey was curious to know what kind of "curse" she could create and how that would work. He was tempted to ask Orsa to show him, but they were on a crunch for time.

He shrugged. "Well, I'm used to getting attacked."

Viki laughed, bumping into him, then she nodded at Orsa and said, "Yeah, Wonderboy here has pretty much been a punching bag for the last year."

Mikey rolled his eyes, lips pursed. The truth in her statement was irksome.

"I am in no mood for idle chatter, boy. Why have you come before me?" Orsa demanded, her voice dripping with ancient power. Mikey stood his ground, meeting her intense gaze with unwavering determination. "I need to see Laken to retrieve the key that opens the dwarven mountain. The Devouring is trapped inside, desperately trying to break through a shield to get at a Shard of Avalon. I understand you were attacked by one here." Mikey looked around. "Wherever here is."

"The humans call this place the Great Dismal Swamp," Orsa stated.

Dismal? What a name.

As if sensing his thoughts, Orsa grinned wickedly and added, "They say it's cursed, you see."

Mikey shared a glance with Viki; she had the same "this fae is a bit crazy" expression.

"Uh—that's great," he said. "I'd love for a tour sometime...but right now, I need your strength to fight the Devourers, and I need to talk to Laken."

Orsa leaned back on her bed, her eyes narrowing as she studied Mikey intently. After a moment of silence, she let out a long, drawn-out sigh that seemed to fill the entire cavern with its weight. "Very well," she finally said, her voice low and gravelly. "I will aid you, for there is no choice, but know that defeating an agent of Greel has weakened me. I will do what I can. Regarding the Treasurer, however, I cannot bring you to her. She is resting. Fighting with you has left Laken in a state of exhaustion I haven't seen in centuries."

"Really?" Mike said, feeling a pang of guilt. Laken had saved his life, calming the Devourer within him and causing the fairy to lose consciousness. Even now, the memory pained Mikey greatly. He thought she'd died. She'd woken up a bit later, seeming no worse for the wear. Then she'd fought the creatures again in the mountain.

All to protect me...

Orsa's gaze softened slightly at Mikey's expression of concern.

"Do not blame yourself, Child of Balance. Laken made her choice willingly, knowing the risks involved. The Treasurer's strength lies in knowledge of all things. She will be there when needed."

Mikey shook his head.

Knowledge of all things?

"If Laken knows everything, then why didn't she know about the dwarven mountain or the creatures inside?"

"The Devourers are beings made of Greel, of the void, of death and nothingness," Orsa replied. "They exist as a blind spot in reality, leaving only the sensation of absence and emptiness in their wake. Even the Treasurer can't pierce that veil."

"I see," Mikey said. "So other than the Devourers, Laken can see everything everywhere? Can you?"

Orsa cackled. "A little," she said. "Though nothing like the Treasurer. Imagine the universe as the sand on a beach. From far away, you can't make out much. But as you get closer, the grains become more visible, more prominent. Closer still, and you can see the intricate details of each grain, every speck of sand unique, a tiny crystal. Laken sees all grains on the beach, while I see a handful at a time. Enough to know when a storm is coming or if some foolhardy boy stumbles into my swamp uninvited. But even for a Daughter of Avalon, she must focus her sight, and rest assured, it is on you."

Mikey absorbed Orsa's words, feeling a newfound respect for his tiny friend and the ancient fae.

"Now"—Orsa sat down, giving the same dismissive wave she had before—"I know of the mountain and can guess your plan. Tomorrow, the fate of all will be decided once again. Until then, go, let me rest."

Mikey nodded in understanding, grateful for Orsa's assistance despite her weariness. He turned to Viki and gestured toward the cavern's entrance, silently signaling that it was time to leave. As they made their way out of the dimly-lit chamber, Mikey couldn't shake off the weight of the impending battle against the Devourers. The fate of everything, even the goddess of creation herself, rested on their shoulders. And even with all the support in the world, the odds seemed daunting to Mikey.

Once outside, hot and humid air greeted them, making Viki wince in discomfort.

"I hate swamps," she grumbled.

"One sec," Mikey said, sympathetic to her plight. "Be right back."

The "curse" he'd drained from Orsa had taken the edge of his hunger. But Mikey wanted a bit more Source for the portal. He still didn't feel completely comfortable with the ability and thought being at full charge would be best.

He walked a safe enough distance away and opened the void just enough to drain the energy around him, not letting out the tendrils.

Then, fighting the bliss that threatened to overcome him, he walked back to Viki and began opening a portal to Magnus's estate.

Viki whistled, shaking her head in amazement. "I'll never get tired of that."

Mikey forced a smile. The gravity of what was to come hit him like a bugbear punch.

Even as the portal shimmered into existence before them, Mikey couldn't shake the heavy feeling of dread settling in the pit of his stomach. The impending battle and the terrible choice he'd have to make if he couldn't make peace between the fae and Verdaat loomed like a dark storm on the horizon, casting a shadow over his soul.

As they stepped through the gateway, leaving the Great Dismal Swamp behind, Mikey couldn't help but wonder how many wouldn't make it tomorrow. He wasn't naïve to the world anymore. The Devourers were death incarnate. People would die—people he loved, people others loved. Of course, he'd do everything in his power to prevent that.

But what if I'm not strong enough?

As they emerged from the portal into the serene grounds of Magnus's estate, Mikey's thoughts were consumed by the weight of responsibility resting on his shoulders. The cool breeze carried whispers of uncertainty and fear, swirling around him like specters from a forgotten past. Viki glanced at him, her eyes filled with unspoken concern, mirroring the apprehension that gripped Mikey's heart.

"I can't shake this feeling of impending doom," Mikey confessed to Viki as they walked toward the grand manor at the heart of the estate. The lush gardens surrounded them in a cloak of tranquility that starkly contrasted with the turmoil brewing within him.

Viki placed a reassuring hand on his arm. Her touch was a grounding force amidst the storm raging in his mind. "We've faced crazy odds before, Mikey. And we've always come out together. We'll beat them."

Her words were a balm to his anxiety.

He looked into her mesmerizing yellow eyes and found solace in their depths, a silent promise of unwavering loyalty and steadfast companionship. Mikey reached out, pulling her close to him.

"I'm a lucky guy," he whispered, brushing his lips against hers.

Viki's eyes sparkled with affection as she returned the kiss, her arms wrapping around Mikey in a comforting embrace. The world around them faded away, leaving only the two of them entwined in a moment of shared understanding and love amidst the chaos that threatened to consume them. Mikey felt a surge of determination rise within him. Tomorrow would not be the end.

When they broke apart, she grinned, pecking him on the tip of his nose and giving a wink. "Yes, you are, Wonderboy. But so am I. Come on, let's go tell the others what happened and get ready."

Mikey nodded, grateful for Viki's unwavering support and the brief respite from his worries. Unfortunately, the anxious knot returned as soon as they approached the automated sliding glass doors leading into the estate. He took a deep breath, steeling himself for the time being, and walked in with Viki. They were greeted by Mogrin. The goblin was, as always, dressed in a crisp blue and black tailored suit that fit his slightly plump, three foot frame perfectly.

"Ah, Mikey, Miss Viki, you've returned. Will Nevra help us? Any word on the Treasurer?"

"Hey, Mogrin. Can you gather the leaders together? We'd like to fill everyone in all at once and go over the plans for tomorrow. And then I'd like to get some rest," Mikey said.

That last part wasn't true. He knew there was no chance of sleep tonight, not with the choice he would have to make the following day. Countless lives rested on his shoulders. But he couldn't let his fears show, not now. Mikey's weakness wasn't theirs to bear.

Mogrin gave a quick nod, his sharp eyes betraying a hint of concern beneath his professional demeanor. "Right away, right away. I'll round everyone up in the war room. Take all the time you need to rest afterward, Mikey." With that, the goblin scurried off, his polished shoes clicking against the marble floor.

As Mikey and Viki made their way to the war room, the faces of his friends and allies flashed through his mind, each a reminder of what was at stake. Despite Viki's unwavering support, doubts gnawed at the edges of his resolve.

Oh how he wished he could turn that part of himself off. The anxious part that was always waiting for the next shoe to drop.

Entering the war room, Mikey found himself surrounded by a diverse group of fae from different realms and walks of life. There were several beings he hadn't seen in their first meeting. The yeti king, Hesh, was among them, as was a woman with green skin that looked like interlocking scales. Tom, wearing the appearance of Justin Bieber, leaned against a wall in the corner of the room. The changeling winked at Mikey when their eyes met.

Will they all die because of me? Because I'm weak and terrified?

It didn't matter that he could conjure the elements, could fly, or make portals. What good would any of it do against an army of death that grew stronger from the very powers wielded against them? How could the Verdaat fight such creatures? They couldn't even use Source. Physical strength, speed, and cunning were useless. One touch from a Devourer and the body began to wilt, drained of its life essence.

Mikey's thoughts swirled in a maelstrom of doubt and fear as he stood before the gathered fae leaders in the war room, their expectant gazes fixed on him. He could feel the suffocating weight of their hopes and trust pressing down on him, threatening to crush his already fragile confidant facade. Despite Viki and his father's reassuring presence, a sense of isolation crept into Mikey's heart, a chilling reminder of the immense burden he bore as the reluctant hero chosen to lead them in the impending battle.

"I won't lie to you," Mikey began, his voice steady despite the turmoil raging within him. "Tomorrow will be the greatest challenge we've ever faced. The Devourers are unlike anything encountered before. They are the embodiment of death. You can't let them get a hold of or touch you. They'll drain all the Source in your body in a matter of seconds."

The fae leaders exchanged uneasy glances, their expressions reflecting a mixture of fear and determination in the face of the grave threat looming over them. The green-skinned woman stepped forward, and Mikey could see her eyes were also a vibrant green, with black slits for the pupil. "Though we are few in number now, the dragons will fight with you. We stand ready to do whatever it takes to protect our lands and those we hold dear. The Dragorafen remember the darkness."

Mikey's gaze shifted to the yeti king, who nodded solemnly in agreement. He spoke in his own tongue, a language of grunts and growls. The rumble of his deep voice resonated with a primal strength that belied the fear lurking in the hearts of those present. Mogrin translated, "The mountains will not yield to the darkness. We are with you in this battle against the Devourers."

Mikey's heart swelled with gratitude for their unwavering support and determination. Each word spoken, each pledge made, strengthened his resolve to face the impending storm head-on.

He informed them all about what had transpired with Nevra and her sister before they devolved into a discussion of tactics.

Their talks eventually ended, the war room falling into a heavy silence as the fae leaders dispersed to prepare for the battle ahead. Mikey watched them go, a knot of anxiety tightening in his chest. A sense of resignation settled within him as he excused himself, his mind swirling in a myriad of emotions.

Sensing something was off, Viki and his father tried to comfort him. Mikey waved them away, saying he was okay and just needed some rest. The lie only served to deepen the ache. He made his way to his chambers; the corridors seemed to stretch endlessly, each step echoing with the weight of his doubts and fears.

Alone in his chamber, Mikey sank onto the edge of his bed, the heaviness of his responsibilities bearing down on him like a crushing weight. His thoughts spiraled in a chaotic whirlwind, each passing moment bringing him closer to the inevitable confrontation that would determine the fate of not just his world but countless others. He clenched his fists, frustration, and fear intertwining in a tumultuous dance within his heart making it hard to take in a breath.

Why me?! he screamed in his head, looking up at the sky. *How could you let this happen, Avalon!?*

No one answered.

Something wet fell on his arm, and Mikey looked down at the teardrops that had escaped his eyes, betraying the facade of strength he had tried so hard to maintain. He was a teenager, a regular kid. Well, not entirely regular, but not some world-saving hero, that was for sure. All Mikey wanted to do was crawl into a ball and wait for the world to end. He couldn't stop a war, and he couldn't defeat the Devouring. In that moment of vulnerability, a soft knock on his chamber door broke the deafening silence. Mikey hesitated for a breath before wiping his face and calling out, "Come in."

The door creaked open, revealing Viki standing in the threshold, her expression a mix of concern and determination. Without a word, she crossed the room and sat beside Mikey on the bed.

She scooched toward the middle and patted her lap.

"You don't have—" Mikey started, but Viki put a finger to his lips and patted again.

Mikey hesitated momentarily, his heart heavy with unspoken emotions as he looked into Viki's eyes. Gods, she was beautiful. And so strong. Stronger than he'd ever be. With a sigh, Mikey relented and shifted closer to her, resting his head on her lap. Her hands went to his temples, and she began massaging, trying to soothe the knots of tension that had taken root in his mind and body. The gentle touch of her fingers worked like magic, easing the weight of his burdens and offering a moment of respite from the storm raging within him. Mikey closed his eyes, allowing himself to be enveloped by the warmth of Viki's presence, the rhythm of her touch lulling him into a sense of calm he hadn't felt in what seemed like an eternity.

"I know you're scared," Viki murmured softly, her voice a soothing melody in the stillness of the chamber. "I am, too. Hell, the thought of facing one of those things again terrifies me. But you're not alone in this, Mikey. We're all here."

He nodded.

"We're all here," Viki repeated, her voice barely above a whisper. "I'm here. Close your eyes and rest. I'm here."

"I love you," Mikey breathed.

Viki's touch paused for a heartbeat, then she whispered, her voice soothing but filled with emotion, "I love you too."

He smiled, eyes closed as the tiny circles resumed on his temples.

"Now sleep, Wonderboy. You're gonna save the world tomorrow."

Miraculously, Mikey did just that.

CHAPTER 18

IZILDORA, QUEEN OF THE CLARAFAE

"My Queen." Erendiel bowed. "I bring news."

Izildora, Daughter of Lunasha, the goddess's firstborn, already knew what Erendiel would say. She did not need to infer from the negative tone in his voice what was occurring across the continent.

"The enemy is gathering," Izildora said, her pale eyes looking to the east. "Including the Tenefae." She didn't know their plans, only that they were amassing.

Erendiel nodded, not a hint of surprise on his face. He was her *Buzur*, after all, the Queen's Hand. The man knew she had the sight, though it was not as great as Beruva or her mother's had been. Izildora could truly see the Source, a vast network of holy energy spanning across the universe. Its intricate branches and patterns pulsed with vibrant colors and seemed to stretch endlessly, each path leading to new possibilities. It was a living entity pulsating with a powerful desire to expand and create.

There were perhaps a dozen on the planet who could do the same, including her sister, which was why she found it infuriating that Helena and the others had not joined her in eradicating the vampires and all agents of the dark god, Greel. They were a blight, a black hole in the divine pattern. An evil that had taken Fayna's life. The world had not deserved a woman so beautiful and filled with light.

And that man had killed her!

Magnus.

Even after thousands of years, the name still made her jaw clench. The vampire had ripped out Fayna's throat while she begged for him to stop, consuming her essence and gaining power through her death.

Izildora had found him, *feeding*. She grimaced at the memory. All because her sister believed he would bring forth The Child of Balance, a being prophesized by the mother crone—one who would finally defeat Greel and the Devouring, freeing the goddess.

Fayna had believed it so strongly that even as she was dying, her sister had begged Izildora not to harm Magnus.

The Clarafae Queen had never forgiven herself for honoring her sister's last wish. She spared Magnus, allowing him to escape into the shadows, slipping through her fingers like smoke.

But the memory of Fayna's death haunted her every waking moment, a reminder of the cost of mercy in a world filled with darkness. Her sister had been right, though. Mikey Black was the child of prophecy. Laken's involvement left no doubt. And now that he had been found after eight thousand years, nothing was keeping Izildora from killing Magnus and his kind, finally ridding the world of them. There was no better opportunity. The Child of Balance had control over the death inside him. He *would* defeat the Devouring. Beruva's prophecies were never wrong. Once the Verdaat were gone, Helena would see reason, and Otherside would be united.

Erendiel cleared his throat, bringing Izildora back to the present. "My Queen, what are your orders?"

Izildora's jaw clenched, and her steely resolve hardened in her gaze. "Gather our armies and the gnome engineers. Be ready to deploy at any moment. I want all our informants on high alert. The moment they move, we strike."

"It will be done, my Queen." Erendiel bowed before hastening out of the chamber.

Izildora stood from her throne and moved to the window over-looking the vast fields of snow.

"What are you planning, child?" she said under her breath.

Already, her agents had eradicated hundreds of Verdaat. They hid among the humans like wolves in sheep's clothing. Thankfully, Izildora had ordered the vampires to be documented and tracked. It was a small pleasure each time one of them broke the Accords, allowing her people to dispense justice. That was all gone now. With Magnus's twisted experiments on humans finally in the spotlight, the treaty was broken, leaving Portum and the Clarafae free to act. How convenient it was that the vampires were gathering from all over the world in one place?

Izildora watched the snow fall softly outside, her mind consumed with thoughts of strategy and vengeance.

Soon, she thought. Soon, her sister would be avenged, the god-dess would be free, and the void would be defeated once and for all.

Yet, despite all that, the emptiness she felt at Fayna's loss would not be filled by revenge or victory. Fayna's laughter, her gentle touch, her unwavering belief in the goodness of all beings lingered in Izil-dora's memories, a bittersweet ache that no amount of bloodshed could soothe. As the snow continued to drift down from the leaden sky, Izildora's heart felt heavy with the weight of millennia-old grief and longing.

But duty called, a relentless drumbeat demanding her attention. With a final glance out at the snowy landscape, Izildora turned away from the window and strode purposefully out of the chamber. It was time for war.

CHAPTER 19

MIKEY

Mikey awoke with a start, a feeling of unease settling in the pit of his stomach. The dreams that haunted his sleep were still fresh in his mind, images of shadowy figures, screams, and the shriveled husks of all those he loved. He sat up, running a hand through his tousled hair, trying to shake off the remnants of the nightmares that clung to him like a shroud.

Viki was already by his side, concern etched on her features as she reached out to touch his arm gently. "Are you all right?" she asked, her voice soft with worry.

Mikey forced a small smile. "Just a bad dream," he murmured, not wanting to burden her with the details of what he had seen.

The real nightmare was yet to come.

Mikey could sense it, a foreboding darkness looming on the horizon. As he got up from the bed, a sense of urgency gripped his heart.

We have to hurry.

He looked out the window and saw the sun was close to setting.

"What is it?" She asked.

"I dunno..." Mikey shook his head. "I just have this...feeling. We need to get to the mountain as soon as possible."

"Well, the armies are mostly gathered so—"

There was a tap at the window.

A familiar and tiny, red-haired fairy was waving from outside.

"Laken!"

Mikey hurried over and unlatched the lock, letting her in.

Laken fluttered into the room, her wings glistening in the dim light. She gave him a quick hug on the side of his arm. But her emerald eyes held a spark of urgency as she looked at them.

"You can feel it too, can't you?" he asked.

She nodded solemnly, gazing to the west.

"Okay, okay, okay," Mikey said, trying to take in deep breaths to calm the rising tide of crippling anxiety and think. "Do you have the key, Laken?"

The Daughter of Avalon lifted up her palm, and a gold, rune-es-cribed key flashed into it.

"Good," Mikey exhaled. "I need to get Arthur and the others."

Haven be damned. It might have been selfish, but he didn't care about their stupid rules. The Devouring was about to get the shard; Mikey could feel it in his gut. And all he wanted were his friends by his side.

"I'll bring them here, and then we need to go to the mountain." He turned to Viki. "Can you have Magnus ready the armies in the next hour?"

Viki nodded, her eyes reflecting the gravity of the situation. "I'll make sure everything is set for when you get back."

Mikey turned to Laken, his expression serious. "Are you okay? Orsa said you were pretty exhausted."

Laken gave an affirmative nod and raised a fist, flexing her bicep.

"I'm glad," he said before summoning his Source and shaping it to form a gateway to their room back at SHOP.

I hope they're still there.

A few moments later, the portal solidified.

"You coming?" he asked Laken.

The angelic fae zipped through in answer.

Mikey followed, glad to have her back.

The experience was always the same; one moment, he was in one place, the next, his destination. This time, however, Mikey walked into chaos. The blaring of an alarm blasted in his ears. He found Sabrina and the others, minus Marcus, surrounding the portal in a defensive stance. They relaxed as soon as they saw him.

"Mikey?" Sabrina looked confused. "What—"

"We need to go," he interrupted. "The Devourers are close to getting the shard."

"How do you know?" Thomas asked.

"I just...do," he answered, noticing the Mover's hand resting at the small of Sabrina's back. Mikey felt a twinge of something but shrugged it off. He was with Viki now; it was for the best.

"Where's Marcus?" Mikey asked, looking around.

"Well, hopefully, he's on his way back since you triggered a defensive alarm with this portal," Luke replied.

The door to the room flew open, and the youngest Sante brother burst in, holding the hand of a man Mikey recognized as one of the guards who had stood watch outside during their time here. His name was Percy.

Marcus's eyes widened when they took in the scene. "Mikey? What's going on?" his voice was tight with worry.

Mikey wasted no time in explaining the urgency of the situation. Marcus exchanged a quick glance with Percy, a silent communication passing between them.

"Go," the guard said. "I'll just say a portal appeared, and you all slipped through it."

"Thanks," Marcus said, giving Percy's hand a squeeze.

Without wasting another moment, the group gathered their belongings, and they stepped through the portal, one by one.

"Whoa! Is this where you were staying with the vampires?" Luke said, looking around at the large space once they'd all gone through. "I imagined you were in a dungeon or something."

"Is he here?" Thomas asked, eyes and nostrils flaring with anger. "Magnus? Is he here?!"

"We don't have time for that," Mikey said. "There are bigger things—"

"Bigger things?! After what he did to Simon, I'll kill him! I don't care if he let him go. With my relic, I'll—"

Mikey blurred, grabbing Thomas by the shirt and lifting him up several inches above the ground.

"You'll do nothing!" he hissed through gritted teeth. "I am done playing these stupid games of revenge. Magnus killed my mother. He imprisoned my father for ten years! There is no one who wants to see him punished more than me. But the WORLD is at stake. As much as you hate or despise him, we need the Verdaat. We need EVERYONE to fight."

Tears began to well behind Mikey's eyes as emotions threatened to overwhelm him. This was too much. The weight of it all was more than one person could handle.

Sabrina and Marcus rested a hand on either side of his shoulder. "It's okay," Sabrina said. "We're here."

Mikey released Thomas and breathed deeply, trying to regain control.

"You're right, Mikey," Thomas said softly. "I'm sorry."

"No, I'm sorry," Mikey exhaled, rubbing his temples. The soothing motion made him think of Viki and last night. It helped quell the anxiety enough for him to regain composure.

"I'm just overwhelmed with everything," he said. "If the Devourers get that shard..."

"We're all a bit shaken right now," Sabrina said, trying to keep the group calm. "What do you need us to do?"

Mikey took a deep breath, nodding. "Right." He filled them in on his plan. Surprisingly, none of his Omada so much as batted an eyelash at what he'd decided to do. Viki came in just as he was finishing up.

There was an awkward silence, which Luke finally broke.

"Viki! Long time no see." The Healer walked up and gave the vampire a hug.

"Hey, Luke," she gave an awkward smile and returned the gesture. "Glad to see you're okay."

"I need to get Arthur," Mikey said, his tone urgent. "Everything set on our end, Viki?"

"Yeah. They're gathering out on the field."

"Good. I'll get Arthur, and we'll head there together," Mikey said before opening a pathway. He was starting to feel hunger pangs from using so much Source.

Several gasps erupted around him.

Marcus threw up his arms dramatically. "We were gone for a few days; of course, you can create portals now. Of course."

Despite all that was at stake, a small smile crept at the corners of Mikey's lips.

"Oh, you'll be amazed at what Wonderboy can do. Did you know he can fly?" Viki smirked.

Marcus's jaw dropped, and he started shaking his head vigorously. "That's not fair. That's just not fair."

Mikey snorted. "If we survive the next twenty-four hours, I'll take you flying, Marcus." His expression grew serious. "I'll be back in a few minutes. Don't get into any fights or anything. Please."

They nodded, and Mikey stepped through.

CHAPTER 20

Mikey walked with his foster father and the others to a large field adjacent to Magnus's mansion. The sight was breathtaking. Thousands of supernatural beings gathered in one place united against a common enemy. Vampires, elves, goblins, dragons, and even more creatures stood together in solidarity. Mikey even saw some bugbears, though most kept their distance from the large and burly troll-like creatures. Around the goblins were weapons that looked like modernized cannons. The machines rested on four wheels, and Mikey was curious what they did.

"Whoa..." Luke muttered, conveying the sentiment everyone present felt.

Sabrina, standing beside Mikey, looked on in awe, her fingers drawing to her lips. "This is a sight I'm sure no one has seen for thousands of years,"

"It's a good thing we have a historian here, then," Mikey said, nudging her arm.

She grinned and leaned in to whisper, "Thanks...for everything." She glanced at Thomas and said, "I know none of this is easy for you. I can't imagine what kind of pressure you're under. So whatever happens, just know—thank you."

He nodded, not knowing what to say. It wasn't they who should be thanking him—quite the opposite. Sabrina and the others had finally given him a sense of belonging. Mikey had almost given up before Arthur found him. But the old man was right: having friends and doing something worthwhile was the first thing that had ever made him feel alive.

Before Mikey could respond, Magnus, along with Brittania, his father, and Helena, came to greet them.

"Can you feel it, too?" Mikey asked the elven queen.

"Yes," Helena nodded. "A wrongness. The shield must be weakening."

Mikey pursed his lips, a solemn expression marring his face.

"We need to go. Are they ready?"

"There are more coming, but this is all we could gather in the short time," Magnus said. Mikey noticed a sword at the Verdaat Lord's hip. The end of the pommel was shaped like a dragon, and the hilt was wrapped in metallic ribbons with runes etched along its entirety.

Wonder why he has that? It looked like a relic.

"Understood," Mikey said. "We'll make do with what we have."

He glanced back at Thomas. The Mover was glaring daggers at Magnus, who pretended he didn't notice. Sabrina was doing her best to keep him calm, and thankfully, it seemed to be working.

Yay for small victories.

"We're with you, son," Jake said, placing an arm on his shoulder.

He nodded, sucking in a determined breath and exhaling. "Let's go."

Mikey headed toward the diverse army of fae a few hundred yards ahead. As they walked, he heard his father. "Nice to see you again, Arthur. I wish there was more time, but I need to thank you for all that you've done for my son."

Arthur simply nodded, a small smile playing at the corner of his lips. "I appreciate that, Jake. But Mikey saved me as much as I him. He's a fine young man."

Mikey rolled his eyes at their comments, but the conversation was a welcome reprieve from the heavy sense of dread that was gnarling in his stomach.

"I'm Marcus, Mikey's best friend and Arthur's protege," the Shielder said, stepping beside Jake.

The ancient vampire gave Marcus a small grin as he stretched out a hand to shake his. "Nice to meet you. I've heard a lot about you. Thanks for being there for Mikey as well." Jake looked behind him. "And that goes for all of you."

As they neared the army of fae, Mikey told the group to wait for a moment. He darted into a thicket of trees and drained Source from the nearby life. Creating a portal to the mountain for an Army would take a lot.

Mikey gathered his resolve after his reserves were full, knowing this was a crucial moment. He felt honored to have such wonderful friends and family who would face death itself alongside him. But with that feeling came dread. Dread that everyone here would die. That he'd fail them and the world itself. All those years alone, thinking he was radioactive and would forever be so. Now, there was so much to lose.

No, I'll save them.

He had to. Deep inside, Mikey knew his family was why he had not given in to the Edax. Even now, the desire for more Source pulled at him like a gnawing itch that could never be fully scratched. He was an addict surrounded by his vice. Mikey guessed the Devourers felt much the same, except without humanity.

He took a deep breath and focused on his goal, his heartbeat quickening as he returned to the gathering.

As Mikey emerged from the thicket, he saw everyone standing, waiting for him. They were ready to face the Devourers together, with the weight of their shared resolve and determination heavy upon them.

"All right," Mikey said. "Let's go face the minions of a god."

He gathered his Source to create the portal and poured more of the cosmic energy into it than he had before. The gateway needed to be big enough to fit the various fae, which drastically ranged in size. Once it had solidified, Mikey turned to his companions, nodding. It took little energy to keep the portal going once formed.

"Ready?" he asked.

"Uh...should we give a speech or something? To get the armies motivated?" Marcus asked, then shrugged. "It's what they do in the movies."

Helena raised an eyebrow. "That isn't a bad idea, human. My people know what we fight, but a little encouragement never hurts." She turned to Mikey.

Dread filled him.

Me? They want me to give a speech?

For some reason, that seemed more terrifying than facing the Devouring. If he hadn't been so nervous, he might have laughed at the absurdity.

Viki came to his side. "You don't have to do—"

Mikey held up a hand. He did have to. It was him all these people were following.

"I do." He nodded.

Helena's golden wings unfurled, reminding Mikey of a mystical butterfly. Bright, gold Source swirled around them like glitter in a vortex.

"All gathered will be able to hear you now," the queen said.

Mikey nodded in thanks, then took a deep breath, gathering his thoughts and steeling himself. He unleashed Source and manipulated the gravity around him, rising into the air before the army. Upon seeing him, the crowd's muttering quieted like a switch had been flipped.

"I am Mikey Black, son of Angela and Jacob Black. You all stand here today to defend your homes, your loved ones, and your very existence. We are united in this fight against the Devouring. No doubt you've been told what we face, but seeing the darkness up close is a different story altogether."

Mikey opened the void, unleashing the Edax within. Black tendrils erupted from his palm like a hundred hungry serpents. They writhed around Mikey, seeking Source, its prey. With some effort, he kept them under control and away from the others.

Just as he had at the meeting before, Mikey explained what they faced and urged the army not to engage Haven or the Tenefae. He closed the void, ignoring the hiss of protest from deep within.

"No matter how powerful or hopeless the enemy may seem, we will not back down, we will not falter, and we will fight until our last breath to protect all that we cherish." He glanced down at Viki, who gave him a thumbs up.

His eyes scanned the faces of his friends, family, and the brave souls gathered before him. "Each and every one of you, from the smallest pixie to the largest dragon, holds a part of the shield that stands between annihilation and our world. We are in this together, the living against death incarnate. And though I may not speak as eloquently as some of you here, I can promise you that I am as determined as the rest. Twice, this world has pushed back the Devouring. The dwarves sacrificed themselves to give us another chance. This time, we will stop it once and for all. You have my word and my strength."

With that, Mikey ceased his speech and looked out at the masses, his eyes shining with determination. There was a deafening silence for a moment before a chorus of roars, chants, and applause broke out. The army was ready, and Mikey felt a swell of pride and gratitude.

Marcus beamed, waving at Mikey as he came down. "Yeah, you definitely have to take me flying. And I think you got them motivated."

He smiled, took a deep breath, and said, "Let's go," before walking through the portal.

CHAPTER 21

A large quake greeted Mikey as he stepped away to let the others come through. The feeling of impending doom was even more potent here.

Izildora has to sense it. She'll do the right thing.

He'd created the gateway to bring them to the base of the falls. The once beautiful scenery was marred by death. All the animals and trees in the area had died, shriveling to dust or blackened husks, courtesy of the Devourer they'd faced outside the mountain. This, and the attack at Orsa's swamp proved that not all the creatures had been trapped.

Or maybe they were sent to investigate?

At least it made a good clearing for an army.

As Magnus and the other leaders came through, they began giving orders to their people on where to position themselves for battle. Mikey paused for a moment to observe the gathered fae, taking in the sheer number of creatures that had banded together to face the Devourers. They were a sight to behold, each group forming intricate formations under their respective leaders' guidance.

Fifteen minutes later, all available to fight had come through. Mikey cut off the energy keeping the portal in place, and dashed to an area that hadn't been devastated, refilling his reserves. The ground continued to rumble, and the mountain trembled with increasing frequency. Mikey could feel the ominous aura of death like a suffocating fog. He tried his best to ignore the sense of familiarity it brought.

"Are you sure they're going to come?" Sabrina asked, sounding nervous.

Mikey nodded, looking around at the gathered army. From their mannerisms, it was clear many of the fae could sense the darkness, too. They stared at the mountain, shivering as if something abhorrent had touched their skin. Even the ones who couldn't wore expressions of concern as the earth shook like a restless beast. Arthur, his dad, and the others were gathered around him, waiting. Viki grabbed his hand, squeezing it. He was grateful for that, for all of them. The people whom he trusted with his life. Except Magnus, of course.

"They'll come," Mikey said.

At least, he hoped they did. An anxious thought came to mind, and Mikey's chest started pounding.

What if Izildora didn't come? What if she let them face the Devouring alone, coming after the battle to get her revenge and exterminate the Verdaat when they were weakened? Would the Clarafae Queen be that reckless and risk total annihilation just to kill Magnus and his people?

No, he thought, trying to reign in his anxiety. *She's not that far gone.*

As if in answer to his inner debate, he felt a gathering of Source off to his left.

A portal shimmered into existence.

Mikey's breath caught in his throat as he waited.

A tiny woman appeared, wearing ragged, brown robes. One that Mikey instantly recognized.

"Orsa," he muttered, a wide grin spreading across his face. He ran toward the gateway, getting there in seconds.

Another appeared through the portal.

Mikey craned his neck, looking up at a pair of slitted eyes.

"Nevra!"

"Mikey Black," Nevra greeted him with a deep, rumbling voice.

Mikey felt relief flood through him at the sight of them. Orsa and Nevra, the only two of their kind on the planet. Though, it was hard to believe they were of the same species given how completely different the two looked from each other. The presence of these formidable allies bolstered his confidence.

Orsa and Nevra exchanged a glance that crackled with unspoken history, their eyes narrowing in a silent challenge before returning to Mikey.

"At least the end of the world hasn't started yet," Orsa cackled.

"Nope. Just in time," Mikey laughed.

"Laken!" Nevra beamed at the fairy hovering next to him.

The Treasurer's wings shimmered, reflecting the dim light of the setting sun. She smiled and zipped up to the Gwyllion before giving her giant cheek a hug.

"You baby her too much, Laken!" Orsa snorted.

Mikey watched the interaction between the three powerful beings with a mix of amusement and relief.

They're probably the oldest beings on the planet.

"You're just upset I'm her favorite," Nevra teased.

The banter between the ancient beings lightened the heavy atmosphere that had settled over the army preparing for battle. Mikey was grateful for their arrival, knowing that Orsa and Nevra brought not just immense power but also a sense of wisdom and experience that could prove invaluable in the upcoming fight.

"Perhaps I was wrong about you," a familiar voice said behind Mikey.

He smiled, then turned around to see a goblin dressed all in black.

"Daygan."

"No one has been able to gather such a force in eons," Daygan said, motioning to the army.

Is he smiling?

It was slight, but Mikey was sure the goblin's lips were slightly curled upward. "Just stay away from Grinwine, and we might actually stand a chance against the darkness. Better yet, all inebriating substances."

Mikey laughed, nodding. "No worries, I've given up the stuff. How've you been?"

"Busy," Daygan replied, glancing around at the assembled army. "This is...impressive, Mikey. You should be proud. You've brought our queen, Magnus, and the Gwyllion sisters all to your side."

"Yeah, well, it's not like they had a choice, what with the prophecies and the world ending, ya know?" Mikey said with a shrug.

"Indeed." Daygan nodded, his expression grew solemn. "We are with you. I must go speak with my brother and the others before we make our final preparations. We will stand by your side."

Mikey nodded, grateful for the goblin's support. He turned back to face the others as they began to prepare for the battle ahead.

The clinking of armor, the sharpening of swords, and nervous murmurs filled the air, creating a symphony of anticipation and fear. Mikey's gaze swept over the assembled army, taking in the varied and determined faces, each with their own story and reasons for standing by his side. The weight of their trust and support settled heavily on his shoulders as he turned to face them, determination shining in his eyes as he took a deep breath and prepared for the battle that could determine the fate of their world.

The sun dipped lower on the horizon, casting long shadows over the desolate landscape. It took over an hour after they'd arrived before half a dozen portals began to form a short distance away. Figures wearing gold and black masks stepped through.

The Coercitors.

They moved together, taking places on either side of the portal. Then Izildora appeared, wearing elegant silver armor, a half-moon emblazoned on the middle of her chest plate. She was followed by an army of humans and Clarafae.

Mikey gathered his closest allies around him.

"Don't do anything. I'll handle this," he stated.

The newcomer's army was larger, bolstered by a significant number of Jaecar.

Both groups stood opposite one another, the entrance to the mountain in the center.

Izildora began walking toward them, several guards and Coercitor members trailing behind. Mikey did the same, with Helena at his side. Magnus had also started, but they'd thought it best if he stayed with the army. It was clear Izildora hated the man with every fiber of her being. Now was not the time for instigation. Thankfully, the Verdaat Lord obliged, opting to stay near the front of his gathered people.

As they neared each other, Mikey could feel the air crackle with tension. He could sense Izildora's anger and hatred. The elven queen's milky white eyes never left Magnus. Mikey knew that if he didn't handle this correctly, there would be no way to stop a devastating conflict.

"Izildora," he said calmly, despite his racing heart. "I'm sure you can feel it. The Devourers are close to the shard. If that barrier goes down, we're all done for. We need to band together. Please."

Izildora stared at Mikey, her pale eyes unreadable. For a moment, it seemed like she was considering his words, weighing the fate of her people and the world against her burning rage. But then, she turned her gaze back to Magnus. "It was nice of you to bring the Verdaat all in one place. It will make eradicating them that much easier. Stand aside, Helena, let me avenge our sister by killing Magnus and his kind. Then, we will unite and finally rid this realm of the dark god's influence."

Helena sighed. She looked at Izildora as someone would an injured puppy. There was pity, love, and what Mikey thought was sympathy.

He could see the Tenefae Queen felt it, too, and understood the depth of Izildora's pain and loss, but she couldn't condone her actions.

"Izildora, sister," Helena began, her voice firm and unwavering, "I will not fight you. Nor will I stand by and do nothing, for it was Fayna's last wish that Magnus live."

"Her last wish?!" Izildora hissed, a cold fury brewing underneath her calm, regal facade. "That was only so the boy could be born, and here he is, standing before us."

"You know it was more than that," Helena said, lips pressed in a thin line. It was clear the topic bothered her as well. "She loved him."

That comment broke Izildora's resolve.

She spat, "And he *killed* her! Right before my eyes!"

It wasn't loud enough for a normal person to hear, but Mikey saw Magnus look over at them, utter sorrow on his face.

Damn him! Mikey thought.

That man wasn't allowed to make that expression. Not after all he'd done. The lives he ruined. Mikey wanted nothing more than to take Izildora up on her offer against Magnus. But deep down, he knew that wouldn't make him feel any better. Mikey didn't know whether that was the same for Izildora. Still, the silver-haired queen wanted to kill all the Verdaat, and he wouldn't let that happen.

There were several among them he loved, and others he considered a friend. Not to mention the looming threat of life-devouring creatures right beside them created by the God of Death.

"I understand your pain, Izildora," Mikey said, his voice calm and steady. "I know you've lost so much, but it's now that we must stand together. We can't let our grief consume us, or we'll lose everything. We need to work together." He pointed to the mountain. "There are dozens, if not hundreds, of Devourers in there!"

Izildora's eyes narrowed. "You'll never understand."

"Maybe not," Mikey admitted. "I haven't lived for thousands and thousands of years. But I have lost, too. I've seen my friends and family killed, and my own demons have nearly torn me apart. But I won't give up. I won't let hatred consume me."

He didn't say it, but Izildora reminded Mikey of Greel in the vision Avalon showed him. The goddess had done something to enrage the deity, enough for him to capture Avalon and send forth minions to destroy all she had made.

Guess it doesn't matter if you're man, god, or fae; we're all vulnerable to our emotions and desires.

"Heed his words, sister," Helena urged.

Izildora scowled deeply, shaking her head. The ground rumbled violently as if to match her expression. "You would have me listen to a child and join forces with our sister's murderer? A man filled with the same darkness that took our mother and so many more? No, Helena, it is you who should heed my words. You are weak and have always been so. Too timid to do what must be done."

Helena's eyes widened, her expression one of deep hurt. Then it was gone, replaced by a cool, regal poise.

Mikey gritted his teeth, fighting back the urge to lash out at Izildora for the harsh words. But he knew it was pointless. The Clarafae Queen was lost in her grief and rage.

Helena stared at her sister with eyes like molten obsidian. Then she sighed, a sound Mikey was all too familiar with: exasperation.

"Izildora," she said, her voice dripping with disappointment, "you know that was not what Fayna would have wanted. Her desire was to unite the fae and the humans, not to be pulled apart—"

"They are not fae!" Izildora spat, pointing to Magnus. "They are an abomination. I have united us. You are the one who would tear our people apart over those monsters!"

Helena's stance remained unwavering, her voice echoing with a depth of sorrow and resolve. "Monsters are not born; they are made. But even the darkest souls hold the flicker of light within them. We choose to nurture that light or let our hatred snuff it out."

Izildora's face contorted with a mix of fury and anguish. She raised a hand, readying her Source to strike at the Verdaat, but Helena stepped forward, a hand outstretched in a gesture of peace.

"Izzie, do not do this. The world is—"

"Damn the world," Izildora cursed. "If that's the price to eradicate evil, then so be it."

The air crackled with an impending clash of forces as both queens stood at an impasse.

Mikey's heart sank as he faced the decision he had been avoiding.

He knew deep down it was inevitable, even though he didn't want to admit it. Izildora was blinded by her quest for revenge, and they were running out of time.

"If you want to see real darkness. Then I'll have to show you," Mikey growled bitterly. It wasn't enough that his mother had been killed for nothing. Or that he'd been thrust into utter chaos and had to bear the burden of responsibility far beyond his years—anyone's years. No, now Mikey had to do something unthinkable. He hated that he was forced to do this. Hated that no matter how hard he tried, still, it wasn't enough. If Otherside wouldn't band together, he'd have to force them.

Numbness filled him as he began walking toward the mountain.

"What is he doing?" Mikey heard Izildora call out.

"What must be done. You've forced his hand, sister," Helena replied.

The pale-eyed queen must have realized what Mikey planned to do because she shouted with a panicked voice, "No, stop him! Don't let the boy get to the doors!"

There was a shift in the air, and he felt Izildora's Source gather around him. Mikey opened the void. Black tendrils sprang free and drained the energy.

Magnus and the others moved toward him as if to help, but he waved them away.

There was so much senseless fighting. So much death and sorrow. Mikey was sick of it.

A flash of Source erupted from his left.

An arrow?

The snake-like tendrils lashed forward, and it, too, was absorbed. Mikey glanced over at the projectile's origin. A Jaecar wearing a black and gold mask held a bow carved in runes.

The sweet bliss of the energy threatened to overthrow his numbness. But Mikey wouldn't let it. He just wanted this to be over.

More projectiles began flying toward him, but none reached their target. With his relic and control over the Edax, there wasn't much anyone could do to stop him. That realization only bolstered Mikey's sense of hopelessness at the burden on his shoulders.

The mountain groaned and shook violently. This time, it did not stop.

Oh no. No. No.

Mikey flew up to the large stone doors behind the waterfall with all the speed he could muster. The barrier still covered it, disappearing into the stone on either side. He grabbed the key and, with shaking hands, reached toward the lock. But before he inserted it, the shield waivered, blinking like a light bulb on its last leg, and then it vanished. The ground stopped shaking. Everything was quiet except for the whoosh of the tumbling falls.

Mikey froze as he stared at the keyhole, his breath caught in his chest.

The mountain exploded.

CHAPTER 22

Mikey lept backward, taking to the air as a cascade of stone and soot came barreling toward him. A loud, deafening roar filled his ears as a giant plume of smoke erupted into the sky. Everything around him blurred as ash filled his vision. Haunting shrieks, so loud he felt their vibrations sent chills down his spine. The Devouring was free, and they'd gotten the shard.

I was too late.

Cries of panic and flashes of green Source erupted all around him.

Shielders blocking the falling rubble, he guessed.

"Mikey!" Viki's voice called out through the fog, snapping him to attention.

With barely enough time to react, he dodged a large boulder that nearly caught him and followed the voice. Mikey found her, eyes wide with fear and concern. She reached out to him, and he squeezed her hand.

Magnus came to his side and had to yell to be heard through the chaos. "Dammit, the volcano has erupted! We need to do something about the ash cloud!"

But it seemed several of the fae were already on it. A great gust of wind blew by them, carrying the dust and debris away enough for them to make out their immediate surroundings.

Sabrina and the rest of their group hurried over, and Mikey exhaled in relief that they were all safe and unharmed.

"Are you okay, son?" his father asked.

"No," Mikey said, shaking his head. "I failed."

"You didn't fail. This isn't all on—" Jake stopped, looking up as the sky cleared.

Viki's grip tightened on his arm as she saw it too.

The top of the mountain had blown off, and rivers of magma were flowing down its side.

Above that was a writhing swarm of darkness.

The earth rumbled beneath their feet as a never-ending stream of Devourers poured from the crater like a dark and unstoppable tide. Their wraith-like forms had grown several times over, no doubt fueled by the power of Avalon's shard. The armies of Otherside could only stand in frozen terror as the screeching mass descended the mountain, leaving a trail of death and destruction in its wake. The air was thick with the stench of decay, and the ground quaked as if the earth itself was afraid of the oncoming horde.

"Good Lord, I can't believe you kids faced these things..." Arthur said, eyes widening.

"We're dead," Thomas muttered, the color draining from his face. "What can we do against that?!"

Looking at the expressions of those around him, Mikey could see they agreed.

"I've got to find Percy. No way am I going to die without kissing him," Marcus blurted before taking off toward Izildora's Army.

"Wait—" Sabrina called out to him, hand outstretched. She tsked, pursing her lips as his silhouette disappeared a second later.

The sky became dark red as the swarm grew larger, and the devourers' diabolical shrieks grew louder. The ground shook more violently, and a wrongness permeated the air.

"To arms!" Magnus bellowed, pulling forth the sword at his hip and pointing it upward.

The weapon pulsated with a fierce, yellow energy that seemed to radiate from within. The black void surrounding it churned and swirled like a vortex, drawing in all the light and warmth around it. It was a formidable sight, both beautiful and terrifying at the same time. The weapon seemed to hum with power, ready to unleash death upon anyone who dared stand in its way.

What. Is. That?

Magnus continued, "Do not let the enemy frighten you. We are all that stands between this world and the end. Think of your people, your families. You are the strongest amongst us. Let's show them the power of Otherside!"

There was no eruption of cheers, not with death charging at them. But the Verdaat and Tenefae began to organize into ranks around their leaders, readying their weapons.

Then, the darkness came upon them.

CHAPTER 23

IZILDORA

What have I done? Izildora thought as she stared at the oncoming horde.

The Jaecar Shielders had protected the army from the falling debris

"So many," Helena gasped beside her.

The Devourers were larger, both in size and number than the last time they'd faced this foe—much larger.

The thunderous roar of the approaching tide shook the ground, and the sky above turned a deep shade of red. A chill ran down Izildora's spine. This was not just a battle; it was an apocalypse. There was nothing that could be done against this. There were perhaps over a hundred.

So, the boy spoke the truth...

Deep down, Izildora knew the children hadn't been lying. Which meant she'd never get the vengeance she sought. If they were all going to die anyway, then what was the harm in finally getting her revenge? After eight thousand years of pushing down the boiling rage that had taken root, festering like a poison deep within her core, she could no longer contain it. But now, staring at death itself come for them, and all those around her willing to fight...

Her resolve wavered.

She could feel the tremors beneath her feet, and the air around her had turned thick with a feeling of emptiness.

Or maybe that is just me?

Izildora could hear the wails and moans of the Devourers as they approached. She felt fear rising within her but pushed it away, instead focusing on the fury. Greel had taken her sister away. The dark god's evil infected this world and men like Magnus.

She gripped Helena's hand and looked into her eyes, "I was wrong, sister. However, I doubt joining the boy would have changed anything. But I will fight until my last breath and send as many of these creatures back to the abyss until so. For Fayna."

Helena pursed her lips, then nodded, "Don't die, Izzie. Otherwise, you won't be there for the tongue-lashing I'm to give you after this is done."

Izildora had to laugh despite the circumstances. "That tongue-lashing might be a fate worse than death."

Before she could respond, a voice cried out through the smoke, "To arms!"

Izildora's blood boiled.

Magnus.

If there was one positive in this, it was that he would die, too.

There was a glowing light near the opposing army.

Izildora used her power to lift the ash and smoke further into the air, where several fae and Nora, an elemental Coercitor, created gusts of wind to clear the area.

She could see the Verdaat Lord wielding a sword that radiated with fierce energy. It hummed with power and drew the light and warmth around it.

"Excalibur...so Okskar did make it for him." Izildora was about to curse the dwarven king, but she held her tongue. Okskar had made the ultimate sacrifice, trapping those monstrosities in the mountain to buy them time. Even though the king had not heeded her warning never to create a weapon for the vampire, speaking ill of the man would not do his memory justice.

Magnus's voice boomed, and the vile man rallied those around him.

Izildora watched as he prepared to face the onslaught of death.

A shiver ran down her spine as she realized how hopeless their situation was. There was no way they could stand against this over-whelming horde.

Dammit! Izildora's body tensed in frustration. The thought of fighting alongside Fayna's murderer left a taste her heart could barely stomach. But she could not deny they needed all the strength they could muster to survive. It was a decision she loathed to make, but the boy had been right, their only chance was to stand together.

With a heavy heart and fierce determination, Izildora stepped forward, facing her army. "We will ally ourselves with the Verdaat and our fae kin, for it is our only chance of prevailing against such an enemy. It pains me so, but we must stand with a lesser evil to defeat a greater one. May the goddess give us strength!"

The fae Queen charged toward death to fight alongside her greatest enemy.

CHAPTER 24

MARCUS

Marcus sprinted through the chaos, dodging and weaving his way through Izildora's army. No one seemed to pay him attention, what with the end of the world staring them in the face. The ground beneath him shook with every step he took, and he could feel the fear and desperation of those around him.

"Percy!" Marcus yelled, his voice hoarse from shouting.

He'd finally found a guy he liked, which was difficult in an order of rough and tough monster hunters. Surprisingly, eligible guys were slim pickings. And it was virtually impossible to be with a Sap. Eventually, they'd start asking questions he couldn't really answer.

So that left no prospects. Not until Marcus had defied Haven, gotten placed on house arrest, and had a particularly cute Jaecar assigned to guard his Omada. He and Percy had been exchanging looks for days until he'd asked Marcus to go on a walk through the unrestricted areas of the Sect.

Marcus had joked that that pretty much meant to the cafeteria and back—after which, he accepted the offer.

They'd totally hit it off, and there was no way he was going to face the apocalypse without at least kissing Percy. Marcus had worked up the courage to finally do it just before Mikey had teleported in with his never-ending procurement of new powers, setting off an alarm and ruining the mood. The guy was great as a best friend and world savior but an utterly terrible wingman. But Marcus wasn't worried. Either the prophecy was true, and Mikey would save them all, or they were goners. Regardless, he wasn't going to die with regrets.

Percy, where are you? Marcus thought to himself, frantically searching for short blonde hair and dark, piercing eyes. Unfortunately, he could barely hear his own thoughts over the mayhem. Shrieks from the Devourers, sect, and fae leaders bellowed out orders, and the rumble of the earth erupted all around.

Marcus spotted a large section of Jaecar and ran over.

Percy was standing near the edge of the group, his eyes scanning the battlefield with a mix of determination and fear.

When he heard Marcus call his name, he turned around, a flicker of surprise and relief passing over his face.

"Marcus, what are you doing here? Shouldn't you be with—"

He was cut off as Marcus pressed his lips to Percy's, silencing any further questions or protests. The chaos of battle faded into the background as Marcus poured all his pent-up emotions into the kiss. Percy hesitated, then gave in, wrapping his arms around Marcus and pulling him closer.

Worth it. If I die, at least I had this.

The Shielder's eyes darted open, a sense of purpose filling him.

No. No one's dying until I've gotten a proper date.

Marcus stared at the black, twisted horde bearing down on them.

With Percy's lips still tingling against his own, Marcus felt a surge of determination unlike any he had experienced before. Pulling away from the kiss, he met Percy's gaze with a newfound strength in his eyes.

"After we survive this, we're going to an arcade for a real date," Marcus stated.

Percy blinked in surprise, staring at him like he was crazy. Then he laughed, nodding. "Deal."

The Jaecar began to move toward Magnus's army. He thought they would attack the Verdaat for a moment and was relieved to see they joined them in the fight.

Guess the queen saw reason after all. Better late than never.

Marcus patted the relic pendant around his neck for luck and took a deep breath before giving Percy's hand a squeeze and charging into battle.

CHAPTER 25

MIKEY

Just before the wave of darkness hit, Helena appeared, wielding beautiful golden energy. The queen lifted her arms, and the ground rumbled before rising into a massive rock and stone wall. It rose higher and higher, like a tidal wave, before crashing into the oncoming horde. The act had bought them a few more seconds, enough for Izildora and her people to join them.

Thank goodness.

They needed all the help they could get.

The Clarafae Queen glanced his way and nodded before scowling at Magnus. She then began giving orders to her leaders.

Ahead, Mikey could see the rock barrier begin disintegrating in various places, the Devourers draining the Source holding it together. Moments later, they broke free, and Mikey's world was thrown into chaos.

He'd never been in a war before, not like this, with armies fighting monsters from nightmares. Thankfully, Magnus and the others had.

A loud bang erupted from his right, and balls of Source erupted from the goblin cannons to slam into the horde, exploding in a dazzling array of colors that elicited shrieks. But the energy was drawn into the Devourers, and they grew in size.

"Remember, we need to find their cores! Focus your attacks to expose it!" Magnus shouted, zipping away and cutting at a giant black tendril. The Devourer flinched back, roaring in anger. Another appendage took its place and was cut down again.

That relic is something else.

Magnus expertly danced around the monstrosity, his sword flashing with spectral precision. The Verdaat Lord's orders were relayed to the rest of the army. Sabrina and Thomas joined in, throwing relic-fueled projectiles in coordination with the goblin's cannon blasts. Several times, he'd seen a glowing core deep within the nightmarish creatures. But it would quickly disappear into the black mass. The Bugbears were picking up large boulders to throw, though it had little effect. The wraithlike forms of the Devourers barely budged from physical, Source-less attacks.

"I'm going to help," Viki said, kissing his lips.

Mikey wanted to say no, that she should run and hide to stay safe, but that wasn't like her.

With pursed lips, he begrudgingly nodded. "Be careful, please."

"You be careful, Wonderboy." She took off.

He watched her leave, and the further away she got, the larger the anxious knot in his gut grew. Mikey muttered a prayer for her safety and gathered his surroundings.

Where is Laken?

He hadn't seen the fairy since he went to talk with Izildora. But there wasn't time to search for her. She was an enigma with motives that were impossible to know.

Mikey flew into the air to survey the battle and where he could best help. A part of him was still nervous to use his void against the creatures. The horror of losing control and almost killing his friends still lingered.

He saw Arthur joined by other Shielders as they did their best to protect those around them with powerful, well-timed barriers.

Mikey's father and the other Verdaat were moving quickly, passing messages and rescuing fae from danger. Their superhuman speed had proven useful for avoiding harm. He saw one vampire grab a man, saving him from being drained just in time.

Six dragons took to the sky. They encircled the horde, blasting it with Source fire. The battlefield was a cacophony of shrieks, roars, and cries of pain.

What can I do?

The strongest of Otherside were fighting a losing battle. Their Source attacks kept the armies from being overrun, but they were gradually strengthening the Devourers while those fighting weakened. The creatures were already huge, making the dragons seem no more than pesky flies.

"Mikey, over there!" Magnus pointed to a section of the army.

He saw Elder Ryan with his sister, Zuri. The SHOP leader's bracelets were glowing purple, and two whips made entirely of Source sprouted from them into the Elder's hand. Zuri was using her relic to keep the tendrils from taking out a group of gnomes whose focus was on a device that looked like a small tube.

Several Devourers were upon them. Mikey's eyes widened in horror as one broke through a shield, slamming its black appendage down onto four Jaecar. They turned to dust in an instant.

NO!

Mikey began gathering Source, forming a condensed orb of ice. He flew over to them and hurled the sphere at the creature while forming an ice barrier around the group to deflect any ricocheting shards. The attack exploded, sending icy shrapnel in all directions. The Devourer let out an ear-splitting screech as its form shuddered and cracked, revealing a pulsating core within its dark mass. Elder Ryan launched a massive Source blast at the core while a tiny red dagger covered in runes whizzed past his ear to slam into it. The sphere cracked but did not break. The weapon stopped glowing and fell to the ground as the core shifted deeper into the growing Devourer.

Dammit!

The hearts of the creatures were tougher. If only he'd been able to bring Otherside together *before* they'd reached the shard.

Elder Cassandra came to his side and clicked her tongue in annoyance before reaching toward the dagger with her Source. The relic flew back to her like a magnet. The woman glanced at Mikey and seemed like she was going to say something, but there was no time.

Mikey nodded at her in gratitude before returning to the battle. The Devourers were relentless, their dark forms twisting and contorting as they absorbed more and more Source. They grew stronger as those around them grew tired or, worse, crumbled to dust as their very essence of life was drained away.

"Hitthemagain! We'vealmostgottheblasterready!" A grey-haired gnome shouted to him, speaking so fast it took a second for his mind to catch up.

One of them picked a small object from their pocket, and Mikey had to squint at the bright, pure glow of Source emanating from it.

A shard?

The Devourer's around them screeched upon seeing it, attacking with renewed vigor.

Bright blue energy began to coalesce in Mikey's right hand as he formed another attack and then hurled it at the black masses before him.

The blast hit with a sound of shattering glass, freezing all that came into contact with it. The Devourers recoiled, howling in fury.

"There!" One of the gnomes pointed at an exposed, glowing heart within the void. Another placed the tube on its tiny shoulder as if—

A beam of pure Source erupted from the bazooka-like tube, lancing straight into the heart of the Devourer. The creature convulsed, a deafening wail escaping its maw as it disintegrated from within, crumbling into a cloud of fine black dust that scattered in the wind. The surrounding Devourers screeched in fury.

The gnomes cheered triumphantly, their faces beaming with pride for their success. Mikey felt a surge of hope wash over him as he witnessed the power of unity and ingenuity in combatting the monstrous threat.

"How many of those do you have?" he asked the grey-haired gnome.

"Onlythree. Wellnowtwo," they responded.

The gnome's words sunk in as Mikey scanned the battlefield.

Not enough.

There were still countless Devourers wreaking havoc, their dark forms seemingly endless. A heart-wrenching cry came from the sky to his right as a swinging tendril clipped a large green dragon. Its wing turned black, and the beautiful fae plummeted to the ground. It suddenly froze in midair just before hitting the ground.

Izildora, he realized, exhaling in relief.

The gnomes were reloading the makeshift Source cannon, their movements frantic yet precise.

As he scanned the chaos around him, his eyes locked onto a group of Shielders who were struggling to maintain their barriers against the relentless assault of the creatures.

Mikey was torn; they'd managed to kill a few, but he knew they needed more than a temporary solution. The Devourers were overwhelming them, and if they didn't find a way to stop the creatures permanently, all would be lost.

Most of the ones that had been eliminated were taken down by Nevra and Orsa. The younger but much larger Gwyllion used her ability to manipulate time to freeze the creatures, while Orsa's mysterious power allowed her to destroy the Source crystals within them.

Still, they would eventually run out of Source. Even now, he was beginning to run low on reserves.

Crap, crap, crap. What do I do? And where is Laken?

Too many areas needed help, and he was just one person.

Panic started to creep into his gut, threatening to freeze him with doubt, but Mikey pushed it away.

I'll have to use it.

He couldn't be everywhere at once, but he also couldn't stand by and watch his friends and allies fall one by one. He made a split-second decision and flew toward the Shielders, who were buckling under the weight of the Devourers' assault.

Kill that Devourer! Drain its Source, he commanded, opening the void in his left hand.

"*Yesssssss!*" The Edax inside him hissed in satisfaction—black tendrils of void burst from his palm to burrow into the nearest Devourer like hungry serpents.

The creature let out a blood-curdling screech, swatting at Mikey with a tentacle as big as a house. He flew upward, dodging the attack, his focus unwavering as he continued to channel the void energy into the Devourer. The Edax's tendrils found the heart of the Devourer and wrapped around it, draining the creature of Source. The Devourer convulsed violently, its dark form shrinking and withering until it collapsed into a heap of lifeless dust. Mikey could feel the rush of power as the Source coursed through him, making every cell in his body ache in ecstasy. There was so much. More than he'd ever taken in before.

"More!" The Edax demanded.

Mikey's vision blurred at the edges as he struggled to maintain control.

The Devourer inside him reveled in the feast, urging him to take it all, to drain everything in sight. But as the tendrils of void extended from his hand, they moved on to the next prey, and another of Greel's minions fell.

The ever-present hunger grew stronger, gnawing at his insides and twisting his thoughts and desires into a tangled web. It was an unquenchable thirst for more, a bottomless pit that could never be filled. Every fiber of his being ached for more, like a starving wolf in the dead of winter. But no matter how much Mikey consumed, it was never enough. The constant craving only intensified with each passing moment until all he could think about was satiating this insatiable urge.

More...

He needed more to satisfy the endless void within him.

There was a whisper from somewhere below.

No, not a whisper Mikey realized, it sounded like—shouting. He opened his eyes, unsure of when they'd been closed.

"Mikey! Stop! Don't let it take control of you!"

That was Viki's voice.

The world rushed back as if he was violently woken from a dream.

Mikey blinked, sweat trickling down his brow as he fought against the insidious whispers of the Devourer inside him. Viki's voice pierced through the fog of his mind, grounding him in reality once more. His eyes widened in horror upon seeing that some of his void had branched off and was attacking his allies. His hand trembled as he used the relic glove to grab the darkness and force it back within.

The Edax shrieked in protest, this time fighting him.

Mikey gritted his teeth, his willpower battling against the dark part of himself. Except it wasn't only the Edax; it was the shame of losing control again and again—the frustration of never being strong enough. The weight of every life lost, every mistake made, bore down on him like a collapsing mountain.

But he couldn't give in. This was it. If he lost, there would be no more battles. His family, his friends, and everyone Mikey swore to protect would be gone forever.

With a final surge of determination, Mikey resisted the Devourer's influence, forcing it into the depths of his being. With a furious roar, the void tendrils retracted, disappearing as quickly as they had emerged. He gasped for breath, his heart pounding in his chest.

Mikey flew down and collapsed to his knees, panting heavily as the battle raged. The cacophony of sounds and chaos felt like a storm brewing in his head, but he made a conscious effort to stay focused on Viki's voice. Her words were like a beacon of hope amidst the darkness.

"Hey, are you okay?" Viki asked, her concern evident.

Mikey nodded, getting to his feet. He'd never felt more powerful yet weak at the same time.

"Thanks," he said, giving her hand a squeeze.

"I've always got my eye on you," she said, trying to keep her tone playful, but Mikey heard the truth behind her tone. Things weren't looking good.

Another dragon fell, its roar cut short as it turned to dust.

Mikey's heart ached at the gut-wrenching sound.

"I've got to go help the east flank; keep your head on, alright," Viki said, kissing him on the cheek. Just before she took off, she added, "You're stronger than you know, Wonderboy."

Oh, Avalon, what can we do?

Izildora came beside him. "I thought you had control over your darkness?"

Mikey grimaced. "I don't know if I've ever had control over it."

The fae Queen surveyed the battlefield, her eyes growing distant.

"I'm sorry," she said. "Perhaps if I'd listened..." Izildora's normally regal demeanor seemed to deflate, and her shoulders sagged. "No. I knew you were telling the truth about how many were sealed inside the mountain. Which is why I knew this was a battle we cannot win. There are too many, even with the numbers we have slain. My Source is not limitless."

Up ahead, Mikey saw Orsa slay another Devourer with the help of Nevra. The shorter Gwyllion fell to her knees, her radiant glow of Source dimming to dangerous levels.

Izildora followed his gaze. "Nor are theirs or Helena's. And without your full power—"

Mikey didn't hear the end of her statement. He took to the air, gathering the energy he'd consumed, and headed toward Nevra. The others may not have endless Source, but he wasn't like them. And there was plenty inside the enemy.

The air grew cold as a thick dome of ice formed around him and the nearby fighters.

"Are you all right?" Mikey asked the gnomish Gwyllion.

"Just tired, boy," Orsa grumbled as he helped her to her feet. "It seems nine is my limit. I'm out of Source, save for the little keeping me upright. The last Devouring had far fewer in number. And we had my mother and several more Daughters. Send me to my swamp. Maybe I can recover enough to take out another before they get to the shard. I'd rather my life end at home, doing my duty."

"Getting old, are we sister?" Nevra grunted as she created some space distortion that tore apart a large Devourer tendril swiping toward her head.

"Tchh," Orsa scoffed. "You forget the one I destroyed yesterday—without your help, I might add. Manipulating the Source in one of those things while they're moving isn't easy, sister. It's something your bullish power could never do."

"Bullish?" Nevra said, her old, gravelly voice sounded surprised. "My craft is elegant and beautiful." The two ancient fae locked eyes, before Orsa bit her lip and nodded. Nevra returned the gesture, opening a portal near her sister and saying, "If we fail, you know what you must do."

"As long as a piece of the goddess exists, there is hope," Orsa replied as if saying a mantra. Then, the tiny woman was gone.

Nevra muttered something, shaking her head. It was hard to make out through the muffled chaos outside the icy dome, but Mikey heard, "Fool of a sister. You could have killed yourself with that last attack. Avalon, help us."

A massive black tendril burst through the top of the barrier, barely missing a group of Jaecar catching their breath. Nevra threw her hand up, and the space around the appendage warped and it disappeared.

"No time for rest, boy. I've got a few Temporal Stases left if you can get to their hearts," she said.

Mikey nodded, looking across their dwindling force for the area that needed their help the most. Helena was in the air to his right. The fae Queen commanded giant roots, using them as extra arms that rose from the earth to bat away the enemy. Her golden wings rippled, and a crack, like a lightning strike, rumbled from them. Chunks of the void were torn away, exposing cores that the queen and those in her section tried to destroy.

Was that sound?

Mikey reached out and felt her Source and how it was being manipulated.

Yes. Helena was definitely manipulating sound. He had to put analyzing it on hold as cries of pain came from his left.

Izildora and three Coercitors were desperately holding off a large group of Devourers. The pale fae monarch was smashing the titanous Devourers to the ground with gravity manipulation while the Jaecar bombarded them with attacks. Two of the nightmarish creatures had broken through, managing to take out a contingent of fighters. Mikey's heart ached as he took in the sight of those who survived. They bore shriveled limbs, their eyes conveying wounds that couldn't be seen but were no less damaging than missing an arm or leg. Several Healers tended to them, and Mikey saw Luke among them.

He let out a breath, thankful his friend was still alive.

But how was everyone else? Viki, his father, Sabrina. There was too much going on, and if something happened to them—a panic gripped his throat, along with the sudden urge to make sure they were okay.

"We must help them," Nevra shouted, starting toward Izildora. Her words snapped Mikey out of his anxiety spiral.

He followed, reminding himself that those before him needed help now, and whatever happened, he had to trust that the others could hold their own. As they reached Izildora's group, Mikey began gathering energy, an idea forming in his mind after encountering Orsa and Helena's powers.

Glowing blue threads formed at the fingertips of his right hand, growing until they reached the floor and further still.

"Do it now!" he said to Nevra. The Gwyllion wasted no time, unleashing her power to freeze the closest Devourer in place. Mikey knew it would only last a few moments as the Source charging the ability would be drained quickly.

The threads rose from the ground before burrowing into the void monster. He commanded them to go deeper, searching for the Source he had grown exponentially better at sensing.

Come on, come on! He had to keep infusing the threads with more Source to prevent them from disappearing. Finally, he felt it, a dense mass of energy.

He willed the filaments to wrap tightly around the core. The creature released a deafening wail and began to fight Nevra's bonds.

"Hurry," the large woman urged. "I can't hold much longer."

Mikey focused all his energy on constricting the threads further, crushing the core of the Devourer until it shattered. The creature shuddered, and the void began to dissipate.

Yes!

But his celebration was abruptly cut off, as Mikey felt something inside it try and bring the pieces together, reabsorbing the energy.

He cursed, shaking his head. "Oh no, you don't!"

Mikey opened the doors to his void just enough to drain Source but not let out the tendrils. No one was within a hundred feet, so it was safe to use it this way. The delicious energy flowed into him. Mikey's teeth ground together as he fought to maintain control as his body came alive. Oddly enough, it was easier to overcome when he had the least control. Using the tendrils allowed him to drain the Source from specific things, but the Edax fought him much harder. Though he knew the relic played a large part in that regard.

With a surge of power, Mikey channeled the energy he had absorbed into reinforcing the threads constricting the Devourer's core. The void creature gurgled a final, desperate cry as it crumbled to dust.

Mikey staggered back, the rush of draining the Source still tingling under his skin. He took a deep breath, trying to steady himself. Their attack had bought them some time, but the bright glow of life from those around him was starting to dwindle.

"Again!" Nevra shouted, her voice barely audible over the chaos surrounding them. Mikey saw that she, too, was dimming. But he was renewed with the knowledge that he didn't need to unleash the Edax to kill these things.

As Mikey rose in the air to attack, something grabbed his leg.

He looked down at Luke. Tears streamed down the Healer's face, and he was shaking. "I-I'm sorry, Mikey. I...can't fix it. Whatever those things did, I can't fix it. Arthur he—"

Mikey's eyes wandered past Luke to a man lying on the ground, his chest barely rising.

No. He shook his head, blinking rapidly as his mind refused to believe what it saw. *No. No.*

CHAPTER 26

"No, no, no." Mikey repeated the words like a mantra, his heart pounding. Arthur was lying there, the entire left side of his body shriveled and blackened.

Someone cried out for help behind him. Luke gave Mikey a quick embrace, wiped at his face, and apologized again before saying he was needed elsewhere. But Mikey barely heard him.

The battle faded, and time seemed to stop. This was the man who had saved his life. Who had taken him in, given him a family when his own had been taken away.

"Child, you have to help us," Nevra called out, her voice cracking with urgency. But he couldn't move, couldn't tear his eyes away from Arthur.

"No, no, no," Mikey muttered, the mantra becoming louder. But the Shielder's Source was almost gone.

He reached down, gently touching the man's face with trembling hands.

His eyes fluttered open.

"Mikey," Arthur whispered, barely above a hoarse rasp. "Son. They-they got me good. I don't have much time left, so—"

"No." Mikey didn't want to hear it. He refused to believe. "You're gonna be fine." Mikey jerked up, desperately searching for someone to help. "Maybe one of the queens, maybe—"

Arthur grabbed the back of Mikey's head with a firm grip.

"Listen to me, son. This is not your fault. Don't you spend another second thinking otherwise! I'm dying, and there's no other way about it. I just... I just...." Arthur's gaze took on a far-off look before he winced in pain and refocused on Mikey. "Thank you for giving an old man a second chance at life. I love you, and I'm so proud. Now you go and save the world. I know you can. You're stronger than all of us."

"I—" Mikey's heart shattered to a million pieces as he felt the finality of Arthur's words.

This man who had become a father to him, who had shown him kindness and love in a world of crippling loneliness, was slipping away. Tears streamed down Mikey's face uncontrollably as he tried to speak, but the words caught in his throat.

Arthur's hand dropped from his head, falling limply to the ground. Mikey knelt beside him, feeling the life ebbing away from the man who had meant so much to him. At that moment, all the power he wielded, all he'd been through, paled in comparison to the grief that threatened to consume him.

Arthur's eyes grew distant, his breaths becoming shallower until they ceased altogether. Mikey couldn't breathe, couldn't think. A sob tore through his chest as he cradled Arthur's lifeless body, "I love you, too," he choked. "I love you, too."

"I'm sorry," a Jaecar to his right said. The dark-haired man was missing a hand and part of his leg. "He saved us...I've never seen a shield so strong. But the darkness was..." The man's face twisted into a grimace, his gaze glazed over as if reliving the horror.

Mikey looked up at the Jaecar, eyes red and swollen from tears. He nodded, still unable to speak as he held Arthur.

"Mikey!" a voice called out.

Somewhere in his mind, he registered its owner.

Sabrina appeared beside him, breathing heavily.

"Oh, no," she gasped, putting her hand to her mouth. "Arthur..."

She swallowed, then blinked rapidly with a shake of her head.

"I'm so sorry, but Thomas is hurt, bad. We're barely holding on, we need you—"

Mikey stood slowly, his eyes fixed on Arthur's peaceful face.

He looked up at the battlefield.

Mikey's heart felt like it had turned to stone as he surveyed the chaos unfolding before him. The field was now a wasteland of destruction. His comrades fought valiantly, but the enemy was relentless, their numbers seemingly endless.

As he looked out, Mikey realized the devastating truth—more than half their number was gone. But there were almost no bodies left behind, for the Devourers had drained them to dust. The ground beneath his feet was littered with black particles, a grim testament to the horrors that had transpired.

A sense of hopelessness threatened to overwhelm him as he watched the strongest of Otherside fall one by one, their cries of pain and defiance echoing in his ears. The realization dawned on him that they were losing this battle and, with it, everything else.

What had he been thinking? That a teenage boy would be able to save the world against the minions of a god? Deep down, Mikey knew they'd never stood a chance, not after facing the Devouring in the mountain. He was no savior.

I couldn't even protect my family...

Mikey's chest heaved with emotions he couldn't name as he watched the destruction unfolding before him. The weight of loss pressed down on his shoulders, threatening to crush him under its unbearable burden.

Another section of the army fell, and humans and fae alike disintegrated as several Devourers broke through their dwindling forces. Was his father among them? Marcus or Chase? Mogrin?

He felt hollow.

Viki came beside Sabrina, her face grim as she surveyed the scene before them.

"Oh, Mikey," Viki whispered, her voice heavy with sorrow. She wrapped her arms around him. "What can I do?"

"Nothing," Mikey muttered. "There's nothing you can do."

At the rate they were going, everyone was going to die. Nevra and Izildora had killed another of the creatures, but five more took its place.

Better for them to only face one.

The cold reality of what needed to be done hit Mikey like a ton of bricks, and the prophecy replayed in his mind.

"When darkness and man merge,
a child of life and death will rise.
Only with each in hand
will the Devouring fall.
But it must be resisted,
Death's call."

It was me. Always me. The words never said anything about Otherside, humans, or the fae. There was only one person who could have ever stopped this. And even though Mikey was sure he'd fail on the last part of the prophecy—as he had so many times before—the Devouring *would* fall.

He'd make sure of it.

Turning to them, he said, "Run. Spread the word. Get everyone and get a mile or two away from here. After the Devourers are gone, you'll only have me to kill."

His voice was barely above a whisper as he said the last words, his eyes reflecting the weight of the world upon his shoulders.

"What? What are you talking about?! No. I won't leave you," Viki stated firmly, her jaw set with unwavering resolve. "We're in this together."

Sabrina nodded in agreement, her expression mirroring Viki's steadfast stance. "We haven't lost. We can still fight," she affirmed, her voice unwavering.

"You'll die, and I'll lose myself anyway. This way, you'll have a chance, and I don't have to watch everyone I love sacrifice themselves for nothing."

Mikey's voice cracked with emotion, his eyes pleading with Viki and Sabrina to understand the weight of his decision. He couldn't bear the thought of losing more family, of seeing them fall one by one to the relentless onslaught of the Devourers.

Viki's gaze softened as she reached out to cup Mikey's face in her hands, her eyes searching his.

"Please," he choked, voice trembling. "For me. I'll distract them while everyone retreats." His eyes unconsciously went to Arthur, and his body tensed, fists clenched. "And then I'll kill them."

Viki hesitated for a moment, her palms hot on Mikey's cheeks. She closed her eyes as tears welled in them, then nodded.

"All right," she whispered, her voice cracking. "We'll go. But don't you dare give in. You fight the Edax with everything you have."

Mikey nodded, then his eyes shot open as Viki pulled him in for a kiss. It was a fierce, passionate kiss that lasted only a moment but held the weight of a thousand words.

He turned to Sabrina. "Get Thomas and the rest of our Omada to safety. Try to paint me in a good light when you record this day in history."

She laughed forcefully before punching him in the arm. "You'll be here to give me a first-hand account. Besides, you need to do the illustrations for me, remember?"

"Right." Mikey nodded, meeting her eyes.

Sabrina hugged him tightly and whispered, "This world needs you. Come back to us."

With a last squeeze of Viki's hand, Mikey rose into the sky toward the swarm of darkness, gathering Source into his right hand.

Look at me, you bastards. I've got dinner.

CHAPTER 27

Mikey radiated with a luminous blue aura as he channeled cosmic energy into his hand. "More!" he demanded, refusing to stop even when half of his Source was depleted.

The Devourers bore no faces, but their dark forms twisted toward him.

"That's right. I'm right here."

Mikey deftly dodged the mass of wraith-like limbs that shot outward as he headed away from the living and up toward the mountain.

He spared a glance behind him and was glad to see the armies retreating.

Mikey grunted as a black appendage hit him on the side, sending him flying toward a river of magma running down the mountain.

He didn't have the control to stop the momentum but was able to adjust the trajectory, slamming into a rockface instead.

The impact reverberated through Mikey's body, but he gritted his teeth and pushed himself off the rock, refusing to let the pain slow him down. With a surge of determination, he propelled himself back into the air, ready to face the Devourers head-on. As he ascended higher, his aura blazed brighter, illuminating the darkened sky with a flickering blue light.

The twisted mass closed in on him, moving like a school of fish made of black ichor. Their eerie screeches pierced the air as they sought the energy.

Mikey condensed the huge concentration of his Source, giving it no direction or form. A deep hunger tore through him, but he gritted his teeth and bore with it.

A bit closer.

Mikey looked up at the tsunami of black towering over him.

As the Devourers loomed closer, their malevolent presence sending shivers down Mikey's spine, he made his move. With a primal roar, he unleashed the condensed energy in his hand, a blinding wave of brilliant blue light that surged forth like a tidal wave crashing against the darkness.

Mikey didn't give them a chance to recover.

Drain them all! he ordered, before completely opening the meridians of his left hand.

Void erupted from it like a thousand black eels, piercing through the Devourers in search of their pulsing hearts.

The countless tendrils wriggled and tore through their forms with ease. They found one, then another, as Mikey's body burned in a bliss hotter than the lava beside him.

The wails of the Devouring reverberated through the desolate forest. Suddenly, one of the monstrous creatures lashed out with a tentacle and grabbed hold of him, squeezing tightly. Mikey cried out in excruciating pain as his flesh shriveled and his very essence was drained away.

"No! Mine!" the Edax, hissed. It found the core, and the Devourer turned to dust. Mikey's skin reknitted, and the euphoria returned.

A surge of satisfaction coursed through Mikey as he continued to drain them, their forms crumbling to dust as the darkness within him grew stronger from each heart he claimed.

As the Devourers crumbled to nothingness, Mikey's aura blazed insanely bright, illuminating the entire mountain range. The intensity of the cacophony within him was almost unbearable, but he reveled in it. Each heart he claimed strengthened the whispers of the Edax inside him, and he felt a deep, primal connection to the void coursing within.

He felt invincible as he destroyed more and more of the Devourers, each one releasing a torrent of energy that brought him closer to the darkness.

"*More. All of it!*" the Edax cooed. "*Let me in. I'll take it all.*"

Yesss, Mikey thought, the world faded away, leaving only—paradise. All the pain, all the worries, all the sorrows, gone in an instant. He could feel the endless void consuming him, and he welcomed it. The loss of Arthur, Elder Neema, and his mother, the ten years his dad was imprisoned, his hatred for Magnus, and his love for Viki—it all burned away in the darkness.

The Devourers howled in agony as Mikey continued to drain their hearts, feeding the beast within him. It craved more, always more, and he gave it everything, surrendering himself to the dark energy, losing all sense of time and space.

As the last of the Devourers succumbed to Mikey's wrath, the world around him began to warp and twist. Shadows danced across his vision, and the air grew thick with the stench of decay and hunger. The void inside Mikey grew immeasurably powerful, and the split between him and the Edax began to blur.

With one final roar, Mikey opened himself completely to the darkness, and the Edax surged forward, consuming his very essence. His bones cracked, his muscles bulged, and his skin turned a sickly black.

Through the bliss, Mikey felt the very fabric of reality begin to fray as the darkness overwhelmed him. His sense of self began slipping away, and with it, his control.

But he never wanted this feeling to end. *More.* He needed *more!*

Then the world around him stopped. Something felt very wrong.

Mikey opened his eyes and froze, his mouth aghast. He couldn't breathe.

Oh God, what have I done?

CHAPTER 28

Viki smiled as she caressed Mikey's cheek, blood filling her mouth.

"Good, you're back," she said, smiling before turning her head to hide the wince of pain.

The Edax's tendrils had pierced her stomach, which was shriveling, along with her arm and leg.

Mikey stared at her in disbelief, horror washing over him. His eyes widened as he took in the sight of her disintegrating limbs.

"Wha—why are you here? Viki, no..."

She squeezed Mikey's hand. "You did it. You stopped them," Viki whispered, her voice trembling. "And you came back to me."

No! He cried out, pushing with all his might against the Edax.
Let her go! LET HER GO!

But the darkness within him was too powerful, and Mikey could feel the void's grip on him tightening.

"*You are mine! Morrrrree,*" it hissed.

He tried to move his body, tried to do anything to stop this. It wouldn't respond; the black meridians had spread everywhere, and they weren't his to command.

"It's okay, I'm here," Viki said softly. "I couldn't leave you in the darkness all alone. I'm here."

She coughed, and blood splattered the ground beside them.

Mikey watched in shock as the woman he loved slowly faded away.

He screamed her name, a primal howl of anguish, but it was lost in the howling winds that had picked up around them.

Mikey desperately yelled, "Someone help, PLEASE! KILL ME!"

Viki lifted a weak hand and made a gentle circular motion on the side of his head. "Sssh. Just stay with me til the end. It's okay. We're together. We're not alone."

Mikey shook his head, refusing to accept what was happening. "No."

None of it was okay.

Viki's eyes began to fade, slowly losing their light as the darkness within Mikey consumed her.

"I won't let you die," Mikey whispered, his voice trembling.

With a fierce determination, he delved into the depths of his being, desperate for a way to save her.

Mikey found himself surrounded by darkness. He reached out, touching it. The void was soft, like a cold black silk that ran through his fingers like fine sand. He pushed through it and found only the same. The void's embrace was all-consuming. A flicker of light caught the corner of Mikey's eye, and he waded through the dark toward it.

My core!

In the center of a maelstrom of void, there was a radiant, pulsating orb of light. It called to him, a beacon of hope in this sea of nothingness.

He reached for it, and a black tendril slapped his hand away.

"Mine!" a voice Mikey knew all too well said from the darkness.

"No...Not yours," he growled through gritted teeth. His heart raced as he faced the creature that'd been a part of him since the beginning. The Edax loomed before him. Its shapeless form shifted and twisted in the darkness of his mind, a mass of shadow and hunger.

The creature huffed, almost as if laughing, a menacing sound that sent a shiver down Mikey's spine.

Was this really a Devourer? Or was it just some twisted part of himself?

It seemed to grow larger, its form solidifying from the darkness as threads of black ichor lashed toward him.

"Let go," it cooed.

Mikey shook his head.

Never. Not while Viki's life was hanging by a moment.

He dove to the side, evading the tendrils. But more sprouted from the ground at his feet.

The dark was everywhere.

Mikey ripped free as several vines coiled around his legs.

He looked around, frantic. There was nowhere to go.

The Edax let out another laugh before the walls around him began to bleed black ichor, coalescing into a monstrous beast of shadow.

"It is all *mine*," it declared.

The creature loomed over Mikey, a grotesque fusion of darkness and hunger. Its features were indistinct, molding, and melting like the black oil that dripped from its body. The upper portion of the Edax started to shift, changing into the outline of a face with black hollow pits for eyes and an open mouth that led to the end of all things. It stretched toward him, and Mikey, despite shaking legs, stood tall, staring at it defiantly.

A small coil of void broke from the face and caressed his cheek almost lovingly.

Mikey recoiled from the touch that seemed to seep its cold into his soul.

And then, in a split second, he saw a glimmer of hope—a glow of Source to his left. In gathering itself, the Edax had briefly exposed his core. He lunged toward it, managing to absorb a tiny fraction of the energy before the Edax viciously pushed him away.

The power ignited the decaying meridians of light, and tiny claws erupted from the fingertips in his right hand. Not wasting a moment of control, Mikey cut the tendrils holding Viki, and she fell limply to the ground. The yellow of her Source had faded to nothing; only a tiny flicker remained.

The Edax growled in his mind and sent out threads of death toward the unconscious vampire.

"Goodbye," Mikey exhaled, looking at Viki and praying she lived. He closed his eyes and plunged the Source blades into his chest, shattering the core inside him.

CHAPTER 29

A searing pain exploded from his chest like his soul was broken into countless pieces. Mikey gasped and choked on his blood as he stared at the red puddle spreading beneath his shirt. The Edax roared in fury.

He felt the void wrap around the pieces and attempt to mend them together.

"No...nonononono..." Mikey whispered, the pain radiating through him like a thousand needles as each sliver of his being was stitched together by the darkness.

He fell to his knees, clutching his chest; the suffering of reassembly surged like a torrent of ice and fire, tearing through him.

His body spasmed as the Edax spread, unfurling its tendrils through his veins. He screamed, a primal agony echoing through the swirling eddies of lucidity.

"You are mine," it croaked, except this time, Mikey's lips said the words.

He gasped for air, but the void closed in on him like a vice, squeezing his lungs and constricting his throat. His body contorted into a monstrous form, unrecognizable to himself. The pain was an inferno raging through his entire being, ripping him apart from the inside out. It was a level of agony he had never known, tormenting every nerve and fiber of his being until he could barely think or move.

Despite his best efforts, Mikey could only watch as lashings of void sprang from his body, their dark tendrils slithering toward Viki's weakened form. It was like a cruel curse, this lingering fraction of himself that remained, unable to save the woman he loved—a woman who had refused to let him face the Devouring alone, who had accepted him wholly and truly, darkness and all.

As Mikey watched in horror, the tendrils reached Viki, their black tips piercing her skin.

He wanted to scream, to rip his own eyes out, anything except watch this. But Mikey was trapped, an observer in his own body, consumed by the Edax's ever-growing void.

Please! Anybody! Thomas, you've always wanted to kill me. Now's your chance.

Mikey's pleas fell on deaf ears. The pain of helplessness was overwhelming. The darkness within him was now a living, breathing entity. He could feel its hunger growing, consuming him from the inside out.

The Edax spoke directly to him, a sickening blend of hunger and desire.

"We will take it all. Do not fight. And the pain will end."

Despite the creature's wishes, Mikey did fight. He tried to call upon the Source that had saved him so many times before. But the Edax crushed his will, smothering his very soul.

He could see Viki's body lying beside him.

Avalon, if you can hear me, please, please do something. Help me, kill me, ANYTHING!

But no one was coming—the same dark thing trapped the goddess.

Mikey's vision began to blur, whether from tears he couldn't feel or from losing himself to the darkness. Either way, he felt it was a blessing.

At least I don't have to watch her die.

As the darkness consumed him, Mikey felt himself losing control, his sense of self slipping away. He prayed that Viki's Source would hold out, prayed for her to be saved, for a miracle. Unfortunately, that wasn't how the world worked. People, wonderful people like his mother, lived and died, and the world continued on, oblivious to its great losses.

The pain that once filled Mikey began to ebb, replaced by a pleasant numbness.

As the feeling took over, he could hear the Edax's voice in his mind, whispering sweet nothings that only served to lull him deeper into its grip. He felt as though he were falling into a dreamless sleep.

A sudden, stabbing pain erupted from his chest, and Mikey heard the Edax shriek. The unnerving event brought him back, and Mikey opened his eyes to see Sabrina, tears flowing down her eyes as she launched a barrage of Source kicks at him. His Omada and a few other fast fae and Jaecar surrounded Sabrina. The armies were slowly coming behind them.

"S-save her," Mikey choked out. "Then kill me. I-I can't stop it—" He forced the words through his ragged throat before the Edax overpowered him.

Magnus appeared, sword deflecting the threads of void that reached again for Viki. Sabrina dashed in and grabbed the vampire, using her relic to step into the air, deftly avoiding the Edax's attacks.

One of the tendrils got around Magnus, heading fast toward Sabrina.

No, run! Mikey wailed, a prisoner in his own body.

Marcus's green barrier appeared just in time to stop the wraith-like appendage, and Magnus plunged his sword into it with a roar. The tendril shattered, but the Edax was not deterred. It sent out more, hundreds more. One of them grabbed a Jaecar who'd just arrived. The man's scream was cut off as he crumbled to dust.

Sabrina's eyes widened in horror as she stared at the pile of black sand.

A war brewed inside Mikey, between the pleasure of Source coursing within and the utter agony of feeling powerless, watching as his friends and allies fought against their greatest foe: Mikey Black.

"The darkness has consumed him. The boy said so himself," Magnus stated, his voice grave. "The queens have used up their Source. Our army is exhausted. We must act quickly before it's too late." The Verdaat Lord lunged for Mikey, but the twisting mass of void surrounding him kept the ancient vampire at bay.

"That's my friend!" Marcus spat.

"Not anymore," Magnus replied.

Yes. Kill me.

He could feel the Edax grow stronger as it fed on their attacks, though Mikey sensed they were all holding back. But their hesitation would lead to everyone's doom.

A dark-haired man emerged from the smoke and ash, and Mikey recoiled.

Jacob Black, his father, stepped forward, wearing a determined expression.

"Fight this, son."

I can't...

"You're stronger than it."

I'm not.

Jake took another step toward him, hands up in a gesture of peace.He jerked as a spear of void pierced his shoulder.

No, stop! Get away!

His father took another step. "Fight it, Mikey. Come back to us."

A tendril stabbed through Jake's side. He stumbled, faltering momentarily before pushing himself forward with gritted teeth.

Magnus came to the man's side, cutting the void with his glowing sword. "Yakub, that is not your son. Do not throw your life away."

Jake shook his head, waving Magnus aside. "He's still in there. I won't lose him again!"

Mikey's heart felt like it was being ripped to pieces by his father's faith in him. The gruesome sight of Jake's necrosed arm and side caused a wave of guilt that washed over him like a tsunami. He felt sickened at how good draining his father's Source had felt.

The Edax's voice echoed in his mind, a malicious taunt that drove its poison deeper. *"We will take it all. Let go."*

Jake continued as more tendrils reached out, stabbing into him.

Magnus and Mikey's Omada desperately tried to shield Jake from the worst of the attacks, but it was clear that the vampire lord's words held true—the Edax was growing stronger with each passing moment.

Finally, Mikey felt an arm wrap around him, the only good one his father had left. A dozen more threads of void lunged at him, but Jacob Black didn't flinch. He clung to Mikey with a fierce determination, a silent plea burning in his eyes.

"I love you, son. No matter what, know that I'm proud of you. And I'm so sorry I couldn't protect you."

Tears welled up in Jake's eyes, and he squeezed Mikey one last time before dropping to his knees, legs shriveling as they were drained of Source.

A searing agony tore through Mikey like a lightning bolt, filling his soul with deep, abyssal sorrow.

The Edax continued its relentless attack, consuming the life that remained in Mikey's father. The twisting tendrils of void seemed to dance around him like in a macabre ballet. Yet, all Mikey could see was the image of his father, weakening under the onslaught, desperately trying to save his child from a fate more terrible than death.

With a defiant roar, he pushed against the suffocating darkness with all his might.

You. Will. Obey. Me!

Mikey latched onto the relic still on his left hand and willed the void to retreat.

A bloodcurdling screech erupted from his lips as the tendrils recoiled from the sudden burst of defiance.

Sabrina, her face etched with grief and determination, stepped forward. "Mikey, we're not giving up on you! You can fight it. We know you can!"

"Yeah, I don't actually want to kill you now," Thomas added.

Luke and Marcus joined in, each voice echoing through Mikey's mind, a symphony of hope and support that gave him strength.

But the dark thing inside him was not so easily defeated. It began to push back against Mikey's will. The Edax's power was like an endless abyss, pulling him deeper into its grasp with each passing moment. He'd given it too much energy.

His body trembled, every muscle, every fiber of his being aching from the effort.

The Edax fought with a vengeance, causing his mind to scream in agony as the void began to close back in on him.

The darkness swallowed him whole, its tendrils reaching out to seize his essence. Mikey struggled with every ounce of strength, but the Edax was relentless. It seemed to devour his very willpower.

As he battled for control, he could see the husk of his father, who had selflessly tried to bring him back. He heard his friends' voices in his mind, urging him to resist and keep fighting. He focused on their words, imagining their faces, and drew strength from the love and support they had for him.

But as the darkness kept encroaching, Mikey was losing himself again. His vision began to blur, and his thoughts spiraled into a mixture of despair and bliss.

This was the real world where grit and effort could only take one so far. In the end, he wasn't strong enough. The void engulfed his consciousness, pulling him down into its endless depths.

As Mikey slipped away, he felt the cold touch of void slide over him like a second skin, their inky substance sinking into every pore.

He was so tired. Tired of fighting, tired of the pain.

"*Yes. Let go,*" the darkness muttered.

As the Edax engulfed him, Mikey feebly struggled, giving it a last-ditch effort. Then the void completed its conquest, and Mikey Black was no more. He had failed his friends, his family, and himself. The images of Viki and his father, of Arthur, and all the others he'd let down flooded his mind as he was consumed.

I'm sorry.

All he had left was the hope that the ones left would be able to stop him.

"*My dear boy, you've nothing to be sorry for. I'm so proud of you. Mikey, you did so well,*" an ethereal, feminine voice appeared in his head. The angelic tone surrounded and warmed him. He opened his eyes but had to slam them shut from the bright light that bathed him.

Something grabbed his arm, and Mikey squinted one eye open to see a glowing hand reaching out. It pulled him from the black depths of the abyss.

Mom?

But the voice didn't sound familiar.

"No. Though now that I'm not bound, I can finally tell you how sorry I am for what happened to her. I... I wasn't allowed to interfere. There are rules to creation."

The light dimmed enough that Mikey was able to open his eyes fully. Hovering beside him was an angel. Laken, now regular-sized and surging with Source, pushed back the void. Her wings shimmered like millions of tiny stars.

But more amazingly, she was *talking*.

"I have so many sorries for you, but to save some time, I'll jump to the last one. I'm sorry to leave you alone so long. Once I saw the darkness in the mountain, I realized what had to be done. But manipulating a part of Mother isn't easy and takes time. I had to warn you once I felt the barrier weakening, but needed to go back."

Mikey stared at Laken in disbelief, trying to process the conflicting emotions that surged through him.

Then he hugged her, tears streaming down his face, and said, "I'm so glad you're here."

"There, there," she said fondly, patting him on the head.

"It's nice to hear you talk," he added.

She raised a hand to her chin, tilting her head. "Hmm, it's nice to hear me talk, too. I mean, I do in my head all the time, but I've never actually *heard* my voice. "

Then, she sighed. "Sadly, there is still much to do and little time. He will notice you after this. Once I give you the knowledge boosted with Mother's power, the piece of him within you will be quieted."

Mikey broke away from the embrace, shaking his head in confusion. "The piece within me?"

She flinched at the question.

"You'll know everything soon enough."

Laken's expression turned somber. Then she cupped Mikey's cheek and smiled. "After waiting so long, you are everything I could have ever hoped for. I wish we could have had more time together like this..."

Her eyes darkened, and she bit her lip, looking down. "Please don't hate me—once you know the truth. It was for your protection. And please save my mother and restore the balance. I believe in you. They all do. "

The air in front of him shifted, and Mikey could see his friends and family, joined by the remnants of the armies, trying to keep the void at bay while a blinding light surrounded his body.

Something about the finality in her tone made Mikey's insides twist with panic. "Wha—what do you mean?"

She didn't respond but patted him on the top of his head. Her body began to glow with the same blinding brightness.

"Laken!" he gasped as her hair turned to shimmering dust and broke away, sucked into the void.

The rest of her began doing the same.

"No, wait—whatever it is, I forgive you. You don't have to—we can..." He searched for the words, knowing none would stop what was happening. "Don't leave me."

She pressed a hand to his heart.

"I won't. You'll see. This was my part to play all along."

Mikey couldn't believe what he was witnessing. The light, darkness, void, gods, and angels—it was too much.

As Laken's body split apart into particles of Source, the warmth inside him grew.

"Wait!" he cried, reaching out.

His outstretched hand passed through her light, and he felt Laken's essence seep into him.

Her voice echoed in his mind. *"My knowledge is yours. Restore the Balance. It is your power. I'm with you."*

Suddenly, his entire body burst with Laken's light, consuming everything around them. A nightmarish shriek rattled his psyche as the brilliant sea of cosmic energy washed away the Edax.

The power coursing through Mikey was immense, intense, and overwhelming. It was as if the universe was trying to communicate with him, pouring its wisdom, knowledge, and secrets into his very being.

Mind-bending information flooded his consciousness, making it difficult to process everything simultaneously. Mikey's vision blurred, surrounded by swirling vortices of color and light. He saw galaxies spiraling through space, planets orbiting their stars, and life forms he couldn't even begin to understand.

His head pulsed with the rhythm of the cosmos as he felt the interconnectedness of all things. Each memory and feeling was a particle of light merging with his.

He was everywhere and nowhere all at once.

Scenes played before him like a flip book entailing all of existence.

He saw the universe's formation and life's birth from the shards of Avalon scattered throughout space and time. Civilizations rose and fell, while wars and love stories endured through generations. He looked upon Earth's history, its people, and their journey from the dawn of time to the present day.

His mind stretched beyond the confines of space and time, exploring the mysteries of the universe. He understood the laws of physics, the intricacies of quantum mechanics, and the nature of gravity. He delved into the depths of biology and chemistry and the wonders of the cosmos.

As the knowledge flooded his mind, a profound realization washed over Mikey. This was not just about understanding existence; it was about shaping it. He was not just a passenger on this journey; he was the architect. His power exceeded anything he could have imagined, for it was the knowledge of creation herself.

I am a god!

The words echoed in his mind, the weight of their meaning sending tremors throughout reality. And then, as the swirling vortices subsided, Mikey opened his eyes.

CHAPTER 30

The world that greeted Mikey was now an entirely different place. Every object, every creature, every particle of matter was suffused with a vibrant energy. The sky was no longer blue but a kaleidoscope of colors, swirling and shifting with every breath he took. Nearby were also places of darkness—black stains amongst the colors where the Devouring had consumed all.

We knew nothing.

He could hear the whispers of the universe itself, the quiet rustling of creation's fabric. The air around him buzzed with life, like the hum of a thousand hives.

"Mikey?" a voice called behind him.

Sabrina.

Mikey turned around, still reeling from the intense experience, and saw Sabrina standing there. Her eyes were wide with fear and wonder.

He smiled.

Through her bright red Source, Mikey could *see* her. Past, present, and possible futures, depending on her choices. There were so many, a tree with infinite branches spiraling outward from her core.

But he knew her and saw the path that lay ahead.

"Are-are you with us?" she asked.

His smile grew wider, and he nodded. Every cell, every fiber within him felt energized. Mikey was bursting with power, with the need to create and just... *do*.

What was left of the two remaining armies stared at him in awe. Izildora's mouth hung open, and she swallowed nervously.

Ah, he saw now her pain, the loss of her sister at Magnus' hands.

The Verdaat Lord's past was even more tragic, a story that troubled him to watch.

He could see them all—their dreams, hopes, and darkest depths. He could also see the future, the countless possibilities that lay ahead. And yet, unlike the rest of reality around him, Mikey knew instinctively that he could not manipulate their wills.

Freeze time? Sure. Create a new planet, filling it with life? Definitely.

But force a mind under his control? Never.

It was a strange feeling to be all-knowing but not all-powerful.

The rules were etched into the very fabric of existence, a natural, unbreakable, and divine law.

His attention was drawn to a flicker of yellow Source.

Mikey appeared beside Viki the next moment, kneeling down and pressing a hand to her chest. Source flowed into her, mending flesh and bone in an instant.

The young vampire gasped for air, taking several deep breaths before sitting up. Her eyes widened as she processed the scene around her.

"Mikey?" she questioned, still disoriented.

"It's okay," he told her gently, wrapping her in a comforting hug. "I'm here."

She kissed him deeply, her relief and gratitude pouring into the embrace. Her head settled into the crook of his arm, and she whispered. "You did it. I knew you would. You just needed some motivation, Wonderboy."

Despite obtaining a deity's omnipotent knowledge and infinite power, Mikey's laughter echoed through the heavens.

True to her nature, Viki had decided to risk her life, betting that once he saw her being consumed, Mikey would be able to push through and defeat the darkness within himself.

You crazy woman.

He raised his arm, and Source flowed over the rest of the injured like a healing balm, mending wounds and reinvigorating life. Thankfully, Jacob Black was one of them.

There was a tap on his arm. "Mikey, can you..." Luke asked, motioning toward the battlefield where thousands had died.

Mikey shook his head slowly.

He could not bring back those whose Source had completely gone out. Death was the domain of Greel, and the dark god was coming.

With a single, focused thought, Mikey halted the passage of time. The world stood still, suspended in a moment he could manipulate and control. Everything was frozen - leaves mid-fall, birds mid-flight, people mid-step.

The real battle was about to begin, and he needed a moment to think.

An oddly familiar pulse pounded in his chest. With it came warmth and a feeling of—warning.

Laken?

It came again in response.

He sensed a bright and kind consciousness within, opposite the Edax. She had become a part of his core.

Her last words replayed in his mind. *"I'm with you."*

A tear streamed down his face at Laken's sacrifice. Thank goodness she wasn't gone.

Are you sure this is what you want?

The Daughter of Avalon had fused with his very being, leaving her trapped with him as long as he lived. But Mikey sensed the action wasn't complete yet, and if she wished, he could free her energy here and now. Though without a physical body, he wasn't sure what would happen with that choice.

Laken sent a pulse, and he grinned.

Okay.

She didn't communicate in words, exactly. It was more of a feeling or emotion. The one he just got said something like, *"Of course, dummy."*

It was followed up with another vibration of warning.

Yeah, I can feel him, too.

Staying here would put this section of reality in jeopardy. Greel was death incarnate, not only of life but of matter itself. Galaxies near the God would rip apart, forever lost in the void.

He sensed Laken's hesitation and possibly regret. Accurately deciphering her emotions would take some time.

What is it?

Something shifted within him, and an image began to form in his mind. Mikey was hovering above a young crying child walking through the woods alone in the dark.

Is that...

He flew down toward the child version of himself, and the memories of that night flooded back like a tidal wave.

Mikey awoke from his nightmare, lying in the dirt. He looked behind him at the wreckage of their burning car in the parking lot and the black sand that littered the ground in piles.

"Mommy! Daddy!" he sniffled, then got to his feet and started for the lot.

A beautiful, glowing fairy flittered down from the sky.

"Are-are you here to help me?"

She hovered before him, wearing a solemn expression, then nodded.

The fairy patted him on the arm and waved him deeper into the woods.

"But Mommy. She—"

The tiny woman shook her head and pointed away from the lot before flying in that direction.

Mikey looked back, torn. He couldn't see his mother or father anywhere. Maybe the fairy was leading him to them? Maybe they were okay, and it was all just a nightmare. So Mikey followed.

After he'd been walking for what seemed like forever, she stopped.

"Where are we?"

They were surrounded by dense forest.

She came to his side, and lifted her hand, palm up.

Mikey squinted as a blinding rainbow of light erupted from it. The colors swirled around and around like a tornado of shimmering glitter. Something black started to form in the center, and Mikey shivered. That part felt...cold and scary. The bright light condensed into a mass the size of a tennis ball.

Mikey watched with a mix of awe and horror at the writhing dark thing that seemed to be trapped by the light.

The fairy looked into his eyes, and the sadness in them made his heart hurt—the same sadness he felt. But she tapped at his left hand before Mikey could say anything to comfort her. Confused, he lifted it, and the tiny woman touched his palm with the light.

Mikey screamed.

Cold black ichor burst from the light's center like death itself hatched from a cocoon.

Dark tendrils like worms coated in shadow burrowed into the skin of his hand. His face twisted in horror as Mikey felt something take hold within him. Something hungry. Something...wrong.

The dark force whispered in his mind, a voice like nails on a chalkboard, but he couldn't understand what it said.

Mikey blinked, and the torrent of memories that had flooded him receded as if ebbing tide.

Shortly after, he'd been woken up by hunters. Not Jaecar, but Saps.

I remember now—you put that thing inside me?

Her words from before made more sense. The plea to not hate her.

Laken pulsed, the feeling apologetic but a definite yes.

I assume it was for a good reason?

Another yes.

Then, of course, I forgive you. You didn't need to show me this before the fight.

He sensed an immense relief.

Laken continued sending pulses, and Mikey could feel her appreciation. She was an angel, the last of her kind on earth and one of the few who'd understood the weight of his burdens. Most of all, she was one of his dearest friends. And now, he guessed, feeling her pulses within him, Laken was even more.

I wonder how Viki will feel having another woman in her life.

Literally, she was forever part of his soul.

At least they were separate enough that Mikey could have his own thoughts but could easily open them up to Laken.

"Well," he sighed as Greel's oppressive will grew nearer, "let's go and fight the scariest thing I've ever seen. And free Avalon."

His new permanent companion sent a thrum of agreement.

Though I've got no idea how...

Mikey vanished from the realm.

CHAPTER 31

There were some benefits of living in the realm of creation, especially when one had knowledge of its creator. One such benefit was the ability to travel instantly to the beginning—to the Big Bang, as many called it on Earth—where reality itself started.

Greel couldn't create. So the God had to move through Avalon's domain sluggishly, consuming all as he went. Unfortunately, Greel had already taken in a lot.

When Mikey appeared, there was nothing but void, stretching on endlessly toward the expanding universe which hadn't been consumed yet.

The cold void surrounded him like an endless black hole. The only thing he could see was a faint glow of the distant universe. Mikey felt Laken's comforting presence within him, but honestly, he'd never been more terrified in his life.

How do you defeat something like Greel?

From the Treasurer's knowledge, he knew Avalon was held nearby in a prison of void. Mikey reached out with his darkness and tried penetrating the thick, dark emptiness. He felt immense resistance as if moving through dense sludge.

There was no Source to be found. Mikey was shocked to find that Greel had consumed more than half the expanding universe. And at the rate the god was going, there would soon be nothing left. Even if the Devouring hadn't been defeated, another few hundred years and the Milky Way would have been destroyed.

I can't fight him here.

Even though draining the Devourers had given him more energy than he'd ever thought possible, Mikey felt like fighting in an area surrounded by void wouldn't be to his advantage.

He'd also technically absorbed Laken as well, but that wasn't something he wanted to think about.

Being able to feel everyone and everything, everywhere, was overwhelming and the most difficult thing to get used to.

How did you deal with this for...how old are you again?

Laken pulsed with laughter.

She was as old as the universe itself.

Mikey frowned, trying to process the endless information and sensations flooding him. He couldn't imagine how Laken had managed to cope with it all for so long.

He closed his eyes and took a deep breath, trying to center himself and focus on the task at hand, blocking out all unnecessary stimuli. With Greel so close, there was no time to waste.

There, Mikey decided—a galaxy group containing only basic organisms.

The galaxies before him were mostly made up of nebulae and star clusters, with no advanced life forms in sight. Size was irrelevant. The power of something had little to do with how big it was. Mikey could stretch himself to infinity, but against Greel, that would do little.

Can my void even do anything?

It sort of felt like fighting lava with fire. He hoped Greel had a core somewhere like the Devourers. The piece of the God inside him had been overwhelmed and gone dormant, so he wasn't worried about losing control again. That in itself was a relief Mikey had never known. Controlling the darkness within had always been his biggest struggle. And now, with everything that had happened, his creation side was stronger than ever.

For whatever good that will do.

Any attack with Source would just make Greel stronger.

Laken pulsed with uncertainty, and Mikey could feel the worry in her reverberations. It was unprecedented territory, and neither of them knew for sure.

"Balance" seemed to be her only advice.

Mikey stood at the edge of the void, looking out at the distant galaxies. The power he felt within him was immense, but it was still unclear how it would manifest against Greel. The idea that he had to find Greel's core was daunting, but if he could do it, it might be the key to defeating the god.

A pervasive feeling of emptiness began filling him.

The guest of honor had arrived.

Darkness, so black that not even a flicker of light could escape it, came toward Mikey like a storm wall made of shadow.

Mikey's heart raced as the darkness approached, and he could feel Laken's anxiety pulsing within him.

What the hell am I doing?

Divinity or not, he was just a seventeen-year-old kid. Sure, he could mold reality with a thought, but he had no idea how to fight a god.

Laken sent a vibration of calm, stopping the panic attack before it could take root.

Mikey took a deep breath, though breathing was unnecessary where he was, and reached out to meet the advancing void with his own darkness. The two powers collided, and Mikey could sense the immense force of the encounter. As he expected, Greel overpowered his void with ease.

The Edax within him stirred as if sensing a kindred spirit, but Mikey clamped down on it with a will of iron.

The darkness of Greel was a relentless tide, a black ocean that threatened to engulf him entirely. Mikey moved back as the galaxy cluster was consumed. Suns, planets, and moons broke apart, lost to the all-consuming tide of death. The sight was as beautiful as it was terrifying to behold.

And still, it pressed on.

Mikey wracked his brain for a way to stop the God. They weren't too far away from Earth, and at this rate—

No, focus.

A figure appeared from the twisting, swirling void. It held the outline of a man, made entirely of shadow.

*Greel...*the embodiment of darkness itself. A primal hunger emanated from the god as he looked at Mikey with lifeless, hollow eyes. His voice echoed like the rattle of chains throughout the cosmos.

"It is mine," he stated.

Not one for words, just like the Edax.

As if sensing his thoughts, Greel added, "You cannot fight me, child. I am death, the end of all things. Our balance *will* be restored."

Mikey's heart pounded in his chest as he stared at the God, feeling the weight of his words. A balance of darkness and light... but he knew that wasn't the truth. Greel only wanted to consume everything, to end the universe.

"This isn't balance," Mikey said, motioning to the crumbling galaxies. "It's chaos."

"Chaos is what the Creator wrought when she broke our harmony," Greel replied. "You know nothing of our bond. It was timeless, binding, eternal. I will restore it and return us to before. Her knowledge will not help you."

Mikey studied the shifting shadows of Greel's form, his mind racing. "What if the Creator never intended for that bond to be broken?" he challenged. "What if the universe needed that disruption to evolve, grow, and change?"

"We are not meant to change," Greel sneered, his voice shaking the fabric of reality around them.

"Change is the essence of life," Mikey countered, feeling Laken's reassuring pulse. "We have evolved, grown, adapted, and survived because of change. Avalon designed the universe with that in mind. You're focused on the past while the rest of us move onward."

Greel's shadows shuddered as if trying to contain an unspoken fury.

"Death does not change. *I* do not change!" he bellowed.

A tidal wave of darkness was unleashed from Greel's silhouette, threatening to drown Mikey in its infinite shadow.

"Good talk," Mikey muttered, meeting the void with his own. The two forces collided, and again, he was rebuffed. As the darkness surged around them, Mikey found himself losing ground.

With no other ideas coming to mind, he tried throwing Source against the god, hoping to at least slow his advance. It was a desperate attempt, but he didn't have many options left.

The Knowledge Laken had bestowed on him, along with the incredible reserve of Source, had given Mikey a false sense of security. Greel laughed as the energies met and clashed in a cacophony of interstellar destruction. The void won out, taking in the Source like roots hungrily draining precious water.

Greel's voice erupted around him with a deafening clarity, "Yes, give me more. It should have all been mine. Fighting me only serves to hasten the end."

Mikey cursed.

The tide of void was moving faster than before.

I just gave him a freaking power-up.

The Local Group, a galaxy cluster of twenty galaxies, of which the Milky Way belonged, was much closer than Mikey was comfortable with. He needed to stop Greel, and quickly. Time was not constant. It had a presence, like space, but it was malleable, bending and slowing based on the forces enacted upon it. The gravity emitted by the void was so strong, nothing could escape it. Not even time. It might have seemed a couple hundred years from Earth. But from Mikey's divine perspective, Greel would reach Earth in a matter of minutes.

I need to stop him! But how? Source is out...

Greel's presence loomed over him, the darkness swirling around them in a whirlwind of malevolent energy. Mikey looked out at the distant galaxies.

"*Balance,*" Laken pulsed again.

I don't know what that means... Mikey said, panic rising within him. *His void is stronger than mine, and if I use Source, it just makes him more powerful.* It was like facing the Devouring times a bazillion. Whatever he created would just get sucked in, crushed to an infinite density.

And made into a core—

An idea began forming. Greel had been consuming Source for eons, since before time and space were created. His core would be massive, maybe not in size, but in energy. And Source was the essence of Avalon, of creation itself.

Maybe...

Just like that, Mikey focused, searching for the energy. The connection was tenuous at first, but as Mikey focused, it strengthened. He could feel the core, the heart of Greel, pulsating with untold energies and boundless potential.

He visualized it and felt it pulsating within the darkness. It was back at The Beginning, shrouded in the center of a black hole so big that trillions of suns would barely give it sustenance.

I need to destroy it, somehow.

Laken responded, sending him what felt like the number two.

Two?

"Yes."

He felt a thrum move down both his arms.

Then Mikey understood. It was the one thing he had over Greel *and* Avalon. He was both light and dark in one.

I hope this works.

With a thought, he bent time and space, warping it around him to a single point. To the core, to Avalon's prison, to defeat the God of Death, to save the universe. And he needed to do it before everything and everyone he loved was destroyed forever.

CHAPTER 32

Mikey's glow of energy was like a beacon among the darkness surrounding him. Within the swirling vortex of nothingness held the heart of a god. He hoped that as soon as Greel sensed what he was doing, the deity of death would try to stop him—better Mikey as a distraction than the Milky Way and the other galaxies teaming with life.

He took a deep breath. With the Knowledge and power given to him, a physical body wasn't necessary. But the form felt right.

Mikey braced himself and gathered all his void, pushing it into a single point at the massive black hole. As the two similar energies collided, they created a ripple across the universe. A resonance erupted from the collision, a wave so powerful that it threatened to tear apart the fabric of reality. Still, he was rebuffed.

Here goes nothing.

Glowing Source burst from him, swirling around his void like a vine wrapping around a tree. The cosmic energy of creation fed the darkness, strengthening it.

It's working!

He pushed the resonating darkness further, and it began breaking through. Mikey's energies dove deeper like a drill into wood, his void heading for the immense power within. His hunger for more Source was still present as a being of both sides. Mikey didn't know how much of that was due to the Edax. Thankfully, the piece of Greel remained dormant, partly due to his vigilance in keeping it at bay.

Mikey felt a shift in the void and surrounded himself in energy just as a giant hand burst from it to crush him in its grip.

"Like everything else, you will die here and become a part of me for eons to come," Greel boomed, his voice echoing through the darkness.

Mikey pushed back, feeding his dark energy with Source. The extra boost allowed him to break free.

Dammit!

He had been so close to getting the core.

Greel's shadowy figure formed before him, casting an ominous silhouette against the endless nihility. Mikey could see the hunger in his eyes, like a predator about to pounce on its prey.

Almost quizzically, the god tilted his head and said, "Ah, I see now. You already carry a piece of me within you." Greel looked toward a particular section of the thick, dark void. "Clever, bright one, clever. Hiding this..."

It was hard to tell due to not having eyes, but Mikey got the impression Greel was studying him before he finally said, "You are not like any living I have ever consumed."

"Yeah, well, apparently, I'm the *'living'* who will defeat you. All because of dumb chance," Mikey replied.

Greel chuckled darkly, the sound echoing through the void.

"I cannot be defeated. Death cannot die. Had you pierced my core, I would only piece it back together. Come, meet your end."

Unfortunately, Mikey could sense that Greel hadn't stopped the tide of destruction toward Earth. This being was truly a god in all ways imaginable. There hadn't been a lie in a single thing Greel had said.

It will take everything I have to pierce his core. And if he can reabsorb and form it again...

Mikey gritted his teeth, his determination unwavering. He couldn't let Greel win. He had to find a way to defeat him.

Laken pulsed down both of his arms again.

Right. I have to try.

Instead of one, multiple giant hands burst from the void, each encased in a shimmering, pulsating shell of dark energy. Their fingers twisted around his body, threatening to crush him. Mikey surrounded himself in his own darkness, feeding it with Source.

The hands tightened around Mikey, squeezing him. He could feel the pressure from the immense power of the deity's grasp as the hands closed in. With a sudden surge of energy, he pushed back against the grip, his void and Source slowly rebuffing Greel's attack.

The god's voice, deep and menacing like the crashing of thunder, echoed around him. "I told you, it all belongs to me." Greel's void began draining the Source, stealing it.

Desperation surged as Mikey felt himself losing the battle against Greel. The Source he had mustered was being absorbed by the god's void at an alarming rate. Not only that, Mikey's home was minutes away from being consumed.

He'd already used a tremendous amount of Source, and there was none around to replenish his reserves. Mikey's void was getting just enough boost to keep him from being crushed into oblivion. But everything would be lost if he let up for even a moment.

As Greel tightened around him, Mikey's emotions were torn between anger and frustration. He had come so far, sacrificed so much, even gaining the knowledge of one god and the power of two. Yet here he was, failing once again. This wasn't how it was supposed to go.

Doubt gnawed at him as he questioned if all of his sacrifices had been for nothing. What was the point? His entire life had been geared for this moment. The loss of his parents. Then, growing up so alone that sometimes he'd wish to have never been born at all. Meeting Arthur, a man who had taken him in and gave him a family. That act led Mikey to make the dearest friends and find a woman who loved him enough to fall on the sword for him, literally and figuratively.

Then, there was Laken, an angel who had given up her body and soul because she was desperate for someone to save her mother, a sentiment Mikey could understand all too well.

I'm sorry.

His Source would run out soon. His planet would be consumed, and he'd again let down those he loved.

But at least no one can say I didn't try…If only that were good enough.

Laken thrummed in his chest, and a feeling of harmony resonated within. She sent him the image of a moving symbol. It consisted of two teardrops, one black and the other white, swirling around each other in perfect symmetry. Within each drop was a piece of the other represented as a small dot. It was one he'd seen his whole life. In Chinese philosophy, it was called Taijitu, or the diagram of the Supreme Ultimate, more commonly known as the yin and yang symbol. The emblem represented two complementary forces that made up all aspects and phenomena of life. It embodied the idea that all things in the universe were connected and that balance and harmony were crucial to the natural order.

Mikey was going to tell Laken he still didn't understand what she meant, but then he felt the pulse down his arms again, and it all clicked into place. Whether it was the Knowledge of Avalon, his connection to Laken, or sheer dumb luck, Mikey finally knew what to do. Whenever he heard the phrase "Child of Balance," he thought it meant his destiny was to restore balance to the cosmos. But he'd been wrong. He *was* balance. His body was a duality unto itself.

Mikey suddenly understood it all. If both sides of his being were united within him, then he would be something...more.

With renewed determination, Mikey embraced the duality within him, using his relics to feed the void of his left side with Source in his right, this time with perfect equilibrium. The energy was brought back in, and he pushed it out again, creating a circuit of balance. As his body became the epitome of yin and yang, a new power surged between his hands, unlike anything Mikey had ever experienced. Against it, Greel's void began to crack and crumble like shattering glass.

The contrast of light and dark, the meeting of life and death, flowed seamlessly within him, creating a harmony that transcended gods and men. It was as if the universe had aligned just for this moment, and he basked in its serenity.

The cracks in Greel's void widened until it broke.

A look of shock and disbelief washed over Greel's shadowy face, and he let out a guttural roar that rippled through the void.

"What are you?!"

Mikey didn't answer the god's question. There wasn't time. Greel's encroaching darkness was only seconds away from reaching Earth. With a thought, he appeared at the expanding void's edge. Panic rose within him, threatening to disrupt his delicate circulation of energies. He didn't know what he'd do if his home were lost. But Laken pulsed a calm feeling of strength and resolve, grounding him in the moment.

The new energy, a force of harmony, bent and folded within his palms like molten metal, ready to be forged. Mikey shaped it with his will, forming an opalescent blade that shimmered with the essence of balance itself. It glowed with a brilliant light that contained both the brightest day and the darkest night within its core.

Divine Mikey was too mature to note how incredibly awesome the energy weapon was. At least, that's what he told himself to keep from gawking at it gleefully.

With a swift and determined movement, he raised the blade and cut the encroaching darkness. It pierced the void like a hot knife through wax, and it began breaking away. Greel appeared a moment later, his mouth agape as his domain collapsed around him.

The god tried to regain control, sending waves of dark energy at Mikey. He easily batted each attack away, every movement of the opalescent blade slicing through the darkness.

Mikey could sense fear and anger emanating from Greel, a being who had never before faced someone who could challenge his power.

The god of death's attacks grew more desperate and erratic. Void came at Mikey from all directions like dozens of tsunamis.

But Mikey stood strong, his newfound power of balance resonating within him. With each strike of the opalescent blade, he carved through the onslaught of darkness, dispelling it with an elegant ferocity. The harmony within him guided his movements, allowing him to anticipate Greel's attacks before they even materialized.

"This...this cannot be! I *am* death. I *am* eternal," Greel roared.

"And I am balance," Mikey replied, his voice steady and strong as the duality within him hummed. "And it must be restored."

The void around him trembled at his words as if the very fabric of reality recognized the truth in his declaration. Mikey pinpointed the location of Greel's core and then lifted his blade.

He hesitated momentarily as a feeling of sadness crept into his soul. This was a being older than time itself. But Mikey knew what needed to be done. The god of death had taken countless lives before their time, and he needed to be stopped.

With a heavy heart, he brought the blade down. It cut through reality, space, and time to strike at Greel's core. The iridescent blade pierced through the massive black hole, and for a moment, everything stood still.

A blinding light erupted from the point of impact, spreading out like a shockwave through the cosmos. An otherworldly scream echoed as Greel's form began to disintegrate, fading to dust by the intense, harmonious energy.

Mikey felt a wave of sorrow wash over him as he watched the god of death fade away. Behind him, where trillions of galaxies teaming with life once stood, now lay a pervasive sense of emptiness. True, he'd saved his home and many other lives further out into the expanse of space, but something felt—wrong.

I killed death.

The energy of his blade fizzled out, and Mikey looked at his hands, dumbfounded. The harmony he'd felt was gone, his void barely a whisper of what it was.

If he were on solid ground, Mikey would have sank to his knees from the weight of his actions. Without Greel, there was no balance. How could there be life without death?

"What have I done?"

"You've freed me and stopped the end of all I've created," a woman's voice rang out around him.

Mikey spun around toward the blinding flash on his left. Hovering before him was a feminine silhouette cloaked in shimmering light, her eyes like pools of wisdom and compassion.

"Avalon."

She smiled motherly, her presence radiating warmth and understanding. "You have done what needed to be done. I truly apologize for all you've endured because of my mistake."

"You..." Mikey started, his voice filled with a mix of reverence and accusation. "You broke the balance with Greel by creating all this." He motioned ahead to the galaxies, planets, and stars.

Avalon's expression softened, her eyes full of regret. "Yes, I did," she admitted, her voice tinged with sorrow. "I gave in to my nature selfishly without thinking of the consequences and without taking his nature into account. This universe is based on the balance between life and death, creation and destruction. It is essential."

As he gazed at Avalon, a mix of emotions churned within him. Anger at the gods who were supposed to be above "mistakes" and petty emotions. Frustration at their arrogance and indifference to the lives they toyed with. He wanted to hate her, to hate Greel. Then Mikey thought about all the lore about gods he'd ever read. In all of it, they were flawed beings, prone to mistakes and fits of rage, causing undo suffering to mortals—especially the Greek gods.

If only those authors knew how close to the truth they really were.

A sense of understanding began to bloom, and Mikey realized that even beings as powerful as Avalon were not infallible, that they, too, were bound by their own natures and desires.

They were living beings, weren't they? That meant opportunities for screw-ups.

Except when I mess up, the universe doesn't get destroyed.

However, Mikey was unsure if that was true in his current state.

Avalon regarded him, her ethereal form pulsing with an inner light that seemed to radiate wisdom beyond comprehension. "It is not often that a being such as yourself emerges from the tapestry of existence, Mikey. I had hoped, with the help of my daughters, that it would come to be so, though the loss of so many of my children hurts deeply."

The deity leaned forward as if inspecting him. Then Avalon gave a contented smile. "I'm glad to see one of them is with you. You have done well, Laken. "

The goddess extended a hand, and Source flowed from his chest to coalesce into a tiny fairy in her palm.

"Laken!" he cheered, beaming.

Avalon patted the angel endearingly. Laken flitted her glittering wings and then came over to give him a hug. She yawned, stretching out like a lazy cat before turning to Source and zipping back into his chest.

A wave of warmth pulsed inside him.

"I have given back her physical form, but she has fused to your soul and will never be able to go far from you. Obtaining a body is exhaustive; she will need to rest. Please keep her safe."

Mikey's head spun with a whirlwind of revelations and emotions. He struggled to digest the implications of what had just transpired—Greel's death, Laken getting a body again, and, from what he could sense, the disruption of the fundamental balance between life and death in the universe.

"Of course I will. And thank you for helping her. But something feels off. I can't form the harmony anymore," Mikey said, uncertainty in his voice.

"The balance has been shattered. With Greel's demise, a void has been left in the fabric of existence that cannot easily be repaired. The cosmic scales have been tipped to creation. And unless that balance is restored, the consequences will be catastrophic," Avalon continued, her voice grave. "Without death to counteract life, the universe will spiral into chaos. Life will propagate endlessly, consuming all resources until nothing is left but barren desolation."

Mikey felt a weight settle in the pit of his stomach. The magnitude of his actions crashed down on him like a tidal wave. "What can I do?" he asked, desperation lacing his words.

Avalon's luminous gaze bore into him with intensity. "You have done all you needed to do, Mikey. And more." She waved her hand, and the space around them blurred.

Mikey was stunned to find himself transported back to the beginning of creation. He stood in the midst of a massive vortex of pure Source energy, pulsating and swirling around him in an awe-inspiring display. The colors and shapes were indescribable, constantly shifting and morphing into something new. Mikey could feel the power emanating from this primal force—the remnants of Greel's core.

Avalon reached out a glowing hand, and Mikey felt something pull at him.

There was a hiss inside his mind as the Edax stirred. Avalon's power grabbed the creature, and Mikey felt tendrils burrow into him as if it were digging in its heels.

"No, mine! He is mine!" it spat. The goddess gingerly wrapped the sliver of Greel in Source, feeding it.

Mikey felt the Edax finally let go, and a twisting, swirling mass of void was extracted from the left side of his body. The sensation was extremely unpleasant as if hundreds of porcupine barbs had been plucked from his skin simultaneously. Then, it ended with a final, wonderful burst of relief.

For the first time in his life, Mikey felt *whole*. Like a weight, a tumor—one that constantly tried to take over his body and kill those he loved—had been excised. The feeling was indescribable, the absence of the Edax leaving him feeling light and finally in control.

He looked over to Avalon, who was feeding the shard with her energy.

"Laken put that in me?"

"Yes," Avalon replied. "I knew that Greel wouldn't take kindly to my actions, though I did not foresee the anger that overtook him. In our brief conflict when he imprisoned me, I stole a sliver of his essence, giving it to my daughter in hopes of hiding the one who could free me."

"You put a piece of the god of death into a five-year-old kid! It tried to kill everyone I ever loved! Repeatedly."

The goddess winced. "I know," she whispered. "But it was the only way to protect you, keep you unseen. With this piece, you remained hidden from him, just another of his minions. We hoped you could fight it and remain in control to develop your powers."

Mikey's mind reeled. The realization that a sliver of Greel's soul had been within him all along, manipulating his actions and endangering those he cared for, left him feeling a mix of anger and gratitude—gratitude for Avalon's foresight in protecting him and anger at the manipulation he had unknowingly endured.

Before he could respond, Mikey sensed a transformation taking place as Avalon continued to infuse the sliver of Greel with energy, now from the vast remnants of the core. The void shard was rapidly growing larger.

"What are you doing?" he asked.

"What must be done," she answered, lifting her hand. The surrounding Source shifted above her arm, creating a whirlpool of vibrant colors and pulsating energy. Avalon poured Source into the shard. The fragment of Greel expanded, swirling with dark tendrils that reached out hungrily for more.

"Yes, you must be starving," she said to it. "I'm sorry for what I've done to us, dark one. Only recently have I begun to know your pain, your hunger."

As the aspect of death grew, Mikey couldn't help but wonder if there was another reason Avalon had placed the sliver within him.

"Wanting to hide me from him was only a half-truth, right? You wanted to preserve Greel, just in case I succeeded in stopping him, didn't you?"

Mikey's accusation hung in the air, and Avalon hesitated before her luminous eyes met his. "Yes," she admitted. "In inserting that sliver of Greel into you, not only did it protect you, but it ensured his essence would live if you succeeded and managed to overcome him. The cosmos would inevitably be thrust into chaos if were completely eradicated. There must be a balance. Life and death, dark and light."

Avalon had used him as a pawn, not just to protect him but also to ensure the survival of Greel's essence in case he defeated the god of death.

"So...you wanted me to win...but also didn't want me to win?"

"In a way, yes," Avalon replied, her voice heavy with regret. "Only recently have I begun to understand the duality of our natures." She looked endearingly toward the rapidly growing mass of darkness. "As my essence wanes...there is an emptiness forming within me. A hunger."

Mikey couldn't help but feel conflicted. He was grateful for the protection Avalon had provided but resentful of the manipulation. Despite these feelings, he couldn't deny the truth in her words. A balance needed to be struck, and without Greel, the universe would surely collapse.

"What's going to happen to the sliver?" Mikey asked, his voice laced with tension. "What will it do now that it's growing so large? Won't Greel just start all over again?"

Avalon smiled softly.

Wait, are her eyes changing?

The once luminous gaze of Avalon now seemed sunken and hollow, a darkness lurking within that had not been there before.

Mikey's unease grew as he watched the transformation taking place before him. The sliver of Greel, now infused with an immense amount of energy from Avalon, pulsed with a cold, dark aura that sent shivers down his spine.

As the darkness within Avalon continued to spread, tendrils of shadow crept along her arms like sinister vines. Mikey took a cautious step back, his instincts warning him of the danger that now stood before him.

Once soothing and wise, Avalon's voice now hinted at something darker. "We are the gods of balance," she intoned, her eyes fixed on the swirling mass of darkness before her. "Light to dark, life to death, and back again."

As the tendrils of shadow spread up Avalon's arms, they twisted and knotted around her like vines of darkness coiling around a tree. The once-radiant energy that had been her essence now seemed to be sucked from her, drawn into the growing darkness of the sliver.

"What...what is happening?" Mikey asked, his voice quivering.

The rapid transformation of Avalon into this shadowy figure was terrifying and awe-inspiring. Despite his fear, Mikey couldn't help but be drawn to watch.

"Fear not, child. For this is how it was meant to b—"

The goddess's words were cut short as a blinding flash came from the shard of Greel. The shockwave threw Mikey back, and he felt a ripple in his soul.

His vision swam as he struggled to regain his bearings. In the place of the dark god's sliver was the silhouette of a glowing man. Beside the figure was a woman made of shadow.

Their forms wavered as if caught between realms, flickering ethereal beings that seemed to embody the delicate balance between light and dark, life and death. The man's features were sharp and angular, bathed in a soft golden light that seemed to emanate from within him. In contrast, the woman exuded a cold darkness that clung to her like a cloak of void.

What the...

Mikey's mind reeled at the sight before him. The glowing man and the shadowy woman stood in perfect harmony, their presence exuding a sense of balance that both reassured and unsettled him.

As he gazed upon the ethereal beings before him, a sense of recognition tugged at the edges of his mind.

Mikey looked at the shadow woman, tilting his head. "Avalon?"

She nodded. Wisps of Source were pulled into her by the shimmering man at her side.

"So that makes you—"

"Greel," he said, nodding.

"Uh..." Mikey stuttered.

Avalon and Greel hovered, embodying the delicate balance between light and dark, life and death. Realizing that the two gods, one of which he'd just killed, were now standing in front of him in new forms left him speechless.

Now cloaked in shadows, Avalon exuded a sense of mystery and power that sent a chill down Mikey's spine. Her once luminous eyes were now hollow pits, and her presence seemed to draw on the essence of the universe.

Beside her, Greel stood as a being of radiance, his pure form of light pulsating with an inner glow that spoke of immense power and wisdom. Despite his previous association with darkness and death, he emanated a sense of serenity and balance that defied Mikey's preconceptions.

Avalon and Greel regarded Mikey with a piercing gaze. The air crackled with energy as the two beings of opposing forces stood before him in their new forms. Mikey felt a strange sense of calm wash over him as if the presence of these godlike figures brought an inexplicable peace to his tumultuous thoughts.

Indeed, he could feel the harmony force return within.

"You...switched?" he asked.

Avalon and Greel exchanged a knowing glance before Avalon spoke, her voice now a haunting echo of its former self. "Yes. We have always been two sides of the same coin," she said. "We embody light and dark, life and death. Even I did not know this was our destined outcome, though I started having suspicions as my essence waned and I began feeling an emptiness."

Greel nodded in agreement, his radiant form pulsing gently with each word he spoke. "I see now the compulsion you felt, my dear one." The now bright god looked down at his glowing form, flexing his ethereal hands. "I feel so full of life, the urge to create almost unbearable."

Avalon's shadowy form shifted as she turned to face Greel, a flicker of sorrow crossing her features. "And I, the insatiable hunger, the need to consume and destroy," she murmured, her voice tinged with melancholy.

This is awkward.

Looking at the two deities, making up like a couple who'd merely argued, was surreal. Trillions of lives had been wiped out, entire galaxies destroyed, and now they were talking about their new understanding of one another as if they were discussing the weather.

As he stood there, grappling with the enormity of this new reality, Avalon turned her shadowed gaze toward him. "Mikey, there is much we must now set right in the wake of our transformation."

Greel looked out toward the empty expanse of space with a pained expression. "What I have done...is unforgivable."

"That's for sure," he snorted.

But then Mikey felt a surge of empathy for Greel as he observed the anguish etched on the once-dark god's face. Despite the destruction and chaos that had been wrought, a raw vulnerability in his demeanor tugged at Mikey's heartstrings.

Who was he to judge? A few hours ago, he'd almost killed the woman he loved and all of his friends. Granted, having a sliver of death inside him hadn't helped.

"I, too, have much to atone for," Avalon admitted, her voice soft and filled with regret. The weight of their actions, the consequences of their existence, bore down on them like a heavy burden. Mikey could sense the guilt and remorse emanating from both deities. It was a stark reminder of their power and the responsibility that came with it.

Would Mikey have done any better?

The once-mighty beings now stood before him not as gods to be worshipped or feared but as flawed entities grappling with their own natures and mistakes. It was a humbling sight, one that made Mikey realize the true complexity of consciousness.

He sighed and said resolutely, "Unfortunately, I'm a sucker for second chances. I take it neither of you can bring back those who have died?" Mikey still had the knowledge of creation and knew in his heart it wasn't possible, but still, he had to ask.

Avalon shook her head, her shadowy form rippling with a deep sadness. "Once an essence enters the void, it cannot be brought back, only allowed to form anew."

Greel's expression darkened, his glowing form dimming slightly with sorrow. "The souls that have passed beyond cannot be retrieved. They have become part of the infinite tapestry of existence, their energy interwoven with the fabric of the cosmos."

Mikey nodded, knowing that even gods couldn't undo certain things.

Unsure of what to do next, he turned to Avalon and Greel. "So what now?"

It was jarring to go from fighting for the fate of the universe moments ago to talking with two gods who were now seeking redemption and understanding.

His life really was just one big ball of crazy.

Avalon and Greel exchanged glances as their actions weighed heavily in the air.

Avalon's voice was filled with a steely resolve as she spoke. "Now, we must try and restore balance to the universe, to mend the fractures our conflict has created."

Greel's luminous form brightened at her words, a spark of determination igniting with him. "Yes, I cannot bring back those that have been lost, but I can foster creation and guide the evolution of new life."

Mikey watched as the two beings of immense power began to pool their energies together, creating a swirling vortex of light and shadow that danced around them in a mesmerizing display. With each passing moment, galaxies began to form, stars ignited, and planets coalesced out of the cosmic void.

As Avalon and Greel worked in unison to restore balance and harmony to the universe, Mikey couldn't help but feel awe at the sheer magnitude of their power and purpose. The once-raging battle that had threatened to tear existence apart was now being transformed into a symphony of creation and renewal.

He watched as nebulae swirled into existence, pulsing with vibrant hues of blue, pink, and gold. The celestial bodies took shape, spinning gracefully in the cosmic dance orchestrated by the two deities.

Avalon's shadowy tendrils reached out, weaving through the fabric of space and time with a delicate touch that belied her dark exterior. Her presence brought a sense of mystery and depth to the burgeoning galaxies, infusing them with a primal energy that spoke of beginnings and endings intertwined.

Beside her, Greel's radiant form shimmered with an inner light that illuminated even the darkest corners of the universe. His ethereal touch brought life to the newly formed planets, seeding them with the potential for growth and evolution. As he moved through the cosmos, stars flared to life at his passing, their brilliance casting a warm glow over the burgeoning worlds.

Mikey watched in wonder as the universe unfolded before his eyes, a tapestry of light and shadow interwoven in a delicate balance. The once-dead expanse now teemed with new possibilities, a testament to the power of redemption and transformation.

As the cosmic symphony continued to play out before him, Mikey felt a sense of peace settle over his soul. Finally, after all he and the others had been through, it was done.

He looked up at Avalon and Greel, their forms now radiant with a newfound purpose and unity. The creation of galaxies and the birth of stars unfolded around them, a testament to the enduring power of life and the resilience of the universe.

Avalon's shadowy visage softened as she turned to Mikey, her eyes reflecting the endless expanse of space that now thrummed with vitality. "You have saved us all, Guardian," she said, her voice filled with gratitude.

"Guardian?" Mikey blinked in surprise. He didn't like the sound of that. Guardian didn't sound like someone who could relax and draw.

Greel's radiant form hummed with a gentle melody as he spoke, his voice resonating with warmth and admiration. "Indeed, Mikey. Your selflessness and courage have guided us back to the path of balance and harmony. You are the Guardian of this new beginning, the protector of the unfolding cosmos."

"Nope." Mikey shook his head. "Haven't I done enough? What else is there to fight? You both seem to have a handle on things now. I just want to go home and be with my girl, my family, and my friends. Live a peaceful life drawing comics."

Avalon and Greel exchanged a knowing look before turning back to Mikey, their expressions filled with understanding. Avalon spoke first, her voice soft but firm. "You have done more than enough, Mikey. The universe owes you a debt of gratitude that can never be fully repaid."

"I feel like there's a 'but' coming," Mikey said.

"But," Avalon said, raising a finger and smirking. "There are other universes with other gods. Though no immediate threat exists, and we will do all in our power to keep peace...we are bound, as are the other celestials, by laws we cannot disobey. You, however, bearing both our powers, are not confined to those laws. There may come a time when our universe is threatened, and you, Mikey, will be called upon once more to protect it."

Greel nodded in agreement, his luminous form casting a warm glow over the vast expanse of space that stretched out before them. "The powers you wield are of the celestials, Mikey. They transcend the boundaries of time and space, allowing you to travel between worlds and dimensions if the need arises. An act we cannot do."

Mikey's heart sank at the realization that his days of peaceful comic-drawing might be far from over. He sighed, nodding, while trying to wrap his head around the thoughts of other gods and other universes. Everything just kept getting bigger and bigger.

Maybe nothing will ever happen? He certainly hoped that would be the case.

"I understand," Mikey said, his voice tinged with resignation. "If something comes, I'll do whatever I can to protect this universe. It's not like I've really got a choice in the matter."

Avalon and Greel smiled softly, their gratitude shining through their ethereal forms.

"Thank you, Guardian," Avalon said, her voice holding a note of respect. "Your sacrifice and bravery will be remembered throughout the cosmos."

Greel's radiant presence enveloped Mikey in a warm embrace of light, "I am truly sorry for all that I have put you through. You have a kind heart and a strong spirit, Mikey. The universe is lucky to have you as its protector."

Mikey felt a surge of warmth at their words, a sense of pride intertwining with the weight of responsibility that now rested on his shoulders. A feeling he wasn't sure he'd ever get used to. Gazing out into the vast expanse of the newly created universe, Mikey knew that his life would never be the same. Becoming "Guardian of the Universe" was never something he imagined.

I'm glad they feel lucky.

Mikey had never been successful in the luck department.

Or maybe he was the luckiest person? Time and time again, when all hope had been lost, when he'd wanted to give up and die or crawl into a corner to forever hide from the world, a glimmer of hope had always come through. His world had been saved, and balance restored.

But deep down, Mikey knew that his journey was far from over. As he looked out at the vast expanse of the cosmos, a sense of foreboding weighed heavy on his heart. The peace that had settled upon the universe felt fragile, as if a storm loomed on the distant horizon, waiting to shatter the tranquility he and the celestial beings had fought so hard to restore.

Stop it. That's just your anxiety talking.

If only the gods had taken that away.

But despite his inner turmoil, Mikey knew that he couldn't ignore the call to duty that now lay before him. While Avalon and Greel continued their celestial dance, creating new worlds and breathing life into the universe, Mikey steeled himself for the challenges that lay ahead.

Though there was no immediate threat at the moment, he still had to return home.

Home...

The word made his heart ache.

For the last three years, Arthur had been his home. Now, the man was gone—so many were gone. Then there was Izildora and her hatred for the Verdaat. Mikey almost wished for a new threat to the universe so he wouldn't have to go back and play peacekeeper among the humans and fae.

But he wasn't alone. Laken was with him, as were Viki, his father, Sabrina, Marcus, and the rest. They were his friends, his family.

Marcus is going to lose his marbles when he hears I killed the god of death—well, sort of.

Mikey's mind raced with thoughts of the past and the uncertainty of the future as he prepared to return to Earth. The last few days felt like a surreal dream.

As he braced himself for his return, a sense of unease settled in the pit of his stomach. The thought of facing his friends and loved ones after everything that had transpired—would they understand or would they, like Sabrina hinted at, see him as a stranger, changed by the powers he now wielded?

While contemplating his coming reunion, Mikey couldn't shake the feeling that he was no longer the same person he was before. The weight of his new destiny as the Guardian of the Universe and the responsibilities it placed upon him loomed over him like a dark cloud.

Maybe I can downplay my power? Or maybe—

He turned to the gods.

"Can either of you take away the Knowledge in my head? Maybe make me less...godly?"

Avalon and Greel exchanged a puzzled look.

"Why would you want this?" Greel asked. "I thought you accepted the title of Guardian."

"No-I mean, yeah, I did, and yeah, I still will be," Mikey stammered, trying to gather his thoughts. "But I also just want to be normal. Well, as normal as I can be."

He was getting better at shutting out all of the extra sensory input the universe was constantly throwing at him, but still, it would be nice to have it gone.

He continued, "Laken gave it to me, so you can take it away, and then if something comes along and you need me, you can just give it back."

"I understand your desire for normalcy, Mikey. You are so young for such a burden," Avalon said gently. "But my Knowledge is a part of who you are now. It was never meant to be removed. You know we cannot alter free will; extracting memories or information constitutes the same thing."

Greel nodded in agreement.

"You cannot separate yourself from the power you hold," he said. "The Knowledge you possess is not a curse but a tool we've given you to protect our universe. It is a bond connecting us all in a way no one can sever. Besides, even if it were possible, depending on the threat, we might not be able to restore your power in time."

Mikey sighed, feeling a pang of disappointment. It was a long shot. *Guess I'm stuck with god powers.*

"That makes sense," he said reluctantly. "I'll have to get used to it."

Avalon and Greel smiled reassuringly at him.

"We know this is a lot to take in, Mikey," Avalon said. "But you are strong and brave, and we believe in you. My daughter will be by your side, and we will help as much as we are allowed."

At her mention, Mikey checked on the extra soul within him. Laken was resting but sent a tiny pulse that felt like a hug.

Thank you.

"All right, it's time I get home," he said, nodding respectfully. "Let's hope no threats ever come, and we can put all this behind us. "

Avalon nodded empathetically. "We hope so too, Mikey, but we trust in your heart and courage. You will do what is right, and that is all that matters."

Greel added, "We will stay alert for any signs of danger. If anything were to befall the universe, you will know."

Mikey gave one last grateful look at the celestial beings before turning to the vast expanse of the newly created universe.

"Let's go home."

With a thought and gathering of Source, he vanished.

CHAPTER 33
Two years later

"That looks great!" Sabrina beamed, looking at Mikey's illustration of a phoenix. "You really captured the nobility in their eyes."

Laken, wings flapping quietly beside his head, nodded enthusiastically.

Mikey smiled, grateful for the praise. "How many more have we got?"

"Hmm," Sabrina looked down at her notes. "About twenty."

"Then the Otherside Almanac is done?" He blinked in disbelief.

For the last six months, he and Sabrina had been working on the book she'd wanted to create all her life—a record of all the different races and creatures of Otherside.

"Yeah, can you believe it?" She looked at the stack of pages scattered across the table with the pride of a mother watching her child take its first steps. "It's been quite the journey, huh?"

Mikey chuckled. "Sure has. But we aren't done yet. What's next?"

"Um, depends. You want to work on some humanoids or stick to beasts?"

Mikey glanced at the clock on the wall. It was ten minutes to seven.

"Humanoids, but it's about time I ordered the pizza. The other *Elders* will be here soon."

"Don't go throwing that word around here; Marcus's head is big enough already," Sabrina quipped. All of his Omada, including Thomas, had become Elders of the Jaecar. Their possession of relics and roles in saving the world had significantly expedited the process.

He dialed their regular place and put in the order, making sure they didn't forget the brownie pizza. Guardians of the Universe needed their ambrosia.

Mikey sensed three familiar auras of Source near the front door as they resumed their work on the Otherside Almanac.

He called out, "Come in, guys."

Marcus came in first, shaking his head. "I don't think I'll ever get used to your godpowers."

Luke and Thomas came in behind him. The latter walked over, giving Sabrina a kiss and a "hey babe," then nodded to Mikey and sat down beside her. Luke plopped down on the couch and mumbled, "Wake me when the food gets here."

Damn, Simon's Healer boot camp must be tougher than I thought.

The oldest Sante brother had created a rigorous course to find and train new Healers, which Haven was sorely lacking. Luke had agreed to be his right-hand man. This was the first time Mikey had seen him in weeks, but Luke always showed up when it mattered.

Marcus continued, patting Mikey on the back, "So, can you like...see people when they're in the shower 'n' stuff? How about x-ray vision?"

Mikey rolled his eyes, smirking. It had been a year of these ridiculous questions after he'd revealed the whole story of what happened with the gods. He'd been too afraid of their reaction at learning he was now "Guardian of the Universe." Of course, they'd accepted him as they'd always had. With Laken's help, Mikey had figured out how to box up most of the Knowledge, tucking it away in the back of his mind.

It was incredibly difficult to carry on day-to-day feeling all life everywhere and seeing the past, present, and future possibilities of everyone around him. And even though he could, Greel and Avalon had stressed that it wasn't his place to interfere in the day to day of mortals. That path led down a slippery slope.

"Sorry to disappoint, but no on both counts," Mikey replied with a chuckle. "Didn't need my powers to know you were there, I could smell your cologne a mile away."

"Ha ha," Marcus fake laughed, slowly clapping. "You're hilarious. This scent is refined and sophisticated. Percy said so himself."

The Jaecar had transferred from SHOP to the Buffalo Sect to be with Marcus, and things were getting serious between the two.

"Your better half is too kind," Mikey said with a grin.

Moments like these made him feel almost normal despite the extraordinary circumstances of his life. He glanced over at Laken, who was watching the exchange with a twinkle in her eye. She had become an integral part of his existence, a constant companion through thick and thin. She sent a pulse of warmth.

"That's true." Marcus nodded. "Speaking of better halves, where's Viki?"

"She's out shopping with my dad," Mikey replied. "Apparently, our house needs a makeover."

Before his death, Arthur made a will, giving him ownership of their house in Buffalo. The blessed man had also left a note that brought Mikey to tears every time he read it. Viki moved in shortly after, and his father had gotten a place a few minutes away despite the invitation to live with them.

"You kids need your privacy," he'd said.

Viki, who'd become inseparable from Mikey after the battle, had accepted his new role without question. He hadn't hidden anything from her and never would. Though now she pretty much called him Wonderboy all the time. He didn't mind.

After Marcus's inquiry, the front door creaked open again, and Viki's voice floated in from the hallway. "I heard my name!" She bustled into the room, her arms full of shopping bags, his father following behind her with an equal number in his hands.

"Hey, everyone!" Viki greeted cheerfully, setting down the bags. She had embraced her freedom from Magnus wholeheartedly. "I may have gone a little overboard with the shopping, but I found some awesome blackout curtains that are super cozy."

Mikey's father waved a hand in dismissal. "If it were up to Mikey, you'd both be sleeping in a bed made of Pop-Tarts."

Marcus leaned in to whisper, "He's kinda got you there, dude. Now, will you materialize the pizza with your superpowers, or is it coming?"

Mikey chuckled at Marcus's comment and stood up, his eyes sparkling mischievously.

"I think I'll materialize it this time," he said, raising his hand with a dramatic flair.

"Whoa, seriously? You can do that?" Marcus said, wide-eyed.

Mikey wiggled his fingers dramatically toward the door just as a knock sounded.

With a grin, he used some Source to open the door with a flourish. The pizza delivery guy stood there, looking slightly confused as to why the door had opened on its own. "Uh, here's your order," he said, handing over the warm pizza boxes.

Mikey chuckled, accepting the food. "Thank you. Keep the change."

As the delivery guy left in a hurry, Mikey closed the door and turned back to his friends, getting a very pronounced eye-roll from Marcus.

"Not cool, man. Just once, I wished you used your powers for good. Like manifesting a gaming computer for your best friend or something, ya know? Like really do some good in the world."

Laughter and banter filled the room as they settled down to eat, and the smell of warm pizza and the sound of good company made Mikey's heart feel full. Marcus, being Marcus, dove straight in, grabbing three slices with gusto. Luke roused from his nap on the couch at the smell, exclaiming, "Finally!" before joining in on the feast.

Viki and his father grabbed a blood pack, and Mikey infused some of the ambient Source into the ruby liquid—a perk of his abilities. For the most part, Mikey rarely used his power, preferring to live as normally as possible. But the infused blood would be more satiating, and he didn't mind indulging occasionally for those he loved.

One major change Mikey had made when returning to Earth was fixing the imbalance within the Verdaat, making it so having children was still rare like it was with the elves, but making the stillbirths even rarer. The act garnered him complete loyalty from Magnus—that, and the fact that Mikey was the most powerful being on the planet.

He didn't like using his authority in that way, but it was needed to bring unity to the fae, Jaecar and Verdaat. The Verdaat would no longer prey on humans, maintaining a peaceful coexistence with the other supernatural beings. It was a delicate balance that Mikey constantly had to uphold, but it was a responsibility he took seriously. Izildora had agreed to a treaty, with the promise of half the spoils inside the dwarven mountain...and a *slight* nudge from Mikey.

The treaty with Izildora had been a hard-won victory, a delicate dance of negotiations and compromises. Maintaining peace among the factions would be an ongoing challenge, but he was determined to uphold his responsibilities as Guardian of the Universe. Thankfully, so far, none of the gods had come knocking, and life had been peaceful.

Mikey raised a glass, and the others joined in, "To Arthur, my mother, and all those who have given their lives in the fight for a better world," he said solemnly. They clinked their cups together, the sound echoing through the room as a somber reminder of the sacrifices made.

As they settled back into conversation and laughter, Mikey's mind drifted to the future. There was still so much to do, so many challenges ahead. But surrounded by his friends and family, he knew he was ready to face whatever may come. The knowledge of the universe may weigh heavily on him at times, but in moments like these, it felt like a gift rarer than being born as a radioactive kid with life and death in both hands.

CHAPTER 34

Mikey sat alone on the couch, clutching a white piece of paper. The others had said their goodbyes, and Viki was in the shower. Three creases lined the letter, marking where Arthur had folded it. His words jumped off the page as Mikey read them for what seemed like the hundredth time.

"I know you may feel unprepared for the challenges that await you, son. But remember, strength does not come from power alone. It comes from the love and bonds you forge along the way. Trust in yourself, trust in your friends, and above all, trust in the goodness of your heart. You are destined for greatness, Mikey, not because of what you can do but because of who you are. No matter what happens tomorrow, you will always have a home here. Thanks for giving an old man one last adventure. I'm proud of you and so glad your dad is okay. Hopefully, we'll all make it out of this and have a nice dinner together. We'll have a pizza party like old times.

-Love, Arthur

TO EVERYONE

Thank you so much for spending your precious time reading one of my stories. I sincerely hope you enjoyed it. This is my first ever completed series, and the fact that you were a part of it means everything to me. If you could, please leave a review on Amazon. Reviews are the lifeblood of authors and they help in so many ways.

All the best and happy reading,

www.ingramcontent.com/pod-product-compliance
Lightning Source LLC
Chambersburg PA
CBHW070331260626
47160CB00003B/1007